EASY DAY
FOR THE
DEAD

EASY DAY
FOR THE
DEAD

A SEAL TEAM SIX OUTCASTS NOVEL

HOWARD E. WASDIN
& STEPHEN TEMPLIN

G

GALLERY BOOKS

New York   London   Toronto   Sydney   New Delhi

G

Gallery Books
A Division of Simon & Schuster, Inc.
1230 Avenue of the Americas
New York, NY 10020

First Gallery Books hardcover edition December 2013

GALLERY BOOKS and colophon are registered trademarks of Simon & Schuster, Inc.

For information about special discounts for bulk purchases, please contact Simon & Schuster Special Sales at 1-866-506-1949 or business@simonandschuster.com.

The Simon & Schuster Speakers Bureau can bring authors to your live event. For more information or to book an event, contact the Simon & Schuster Speakers Bureau at 1-866-248-3049 or visit our website at www.simonspeakers.com.

Manufactured in the United States of America

10 9 8 7 6 5 4 3 2 1

ISBN 978-1-4516-8297-7
ISBN 978-1-4516-8298-4 (ebook)

PART ONE

War does not determine who is right—only who is left.

—BERTRAND RUSSELL, PHILOSOPHER

1

Navy SEAL Alexander Brandenburg rode north in an old Toyota truck, speeding toward Kahar, Iraq. He checked his watch again, reflexively shielding the dial as he pressed the light button—02h14. He looked up from his watch to his tobacco-chewing sniper mentor, Chief Petty Officer Jack "Jabberwocky" Lee. "You're gonna slay 'em, kid," Jabberwocky whispered in Alex's ear, referring to the Shiite terrorists in Kahar. "You know why?"

Alex shook his head and smiled, then realized Jabberwocky couldn't see him in the dark. "No. Why?"

Jabberwocky spit a stream of tobacco juice out the window of the truck before answering. "Because you were taught by the best."

Silence ruled as they entered Kahar. The Toyota rolled quietly through the deserted streets. Inside of a minute they reached the upper-class neighborhood. Alex slung his sniper rifle over his left shoulder before pulling his sound-suppressed SIG Sauer P-226 Navy 9mm pistol out of its holster and clicking the safety off. Nodding at Jabberwocky in the dark, he opened his door. The interior cabin light did not come on, since Jabberwocky had made sure it was switched off before they left. "Details, young Jedi, details."

The truck slowed to five miles per hour. Alex took a breath and slipped out into the night as the truck picked up speed and continued on. He quickly jogged to the edge of the nearest wall, where he slid into the shadows. Had anyone seen him? He waited fifteen minutes, prepared to shoot anything that moved, but Kahar showed no signs of being aware of his arrival. Alex flipped down the night-vision goggles on his helmet and the world took on a greenish hue. He scanned the area. Spotting nothing untoward, he stepped into an alley off the road and followed it as it ran behind the houses. Most of the lights were out and he couldn't make out any talking over the sound of his own breathing. He crouched down in a pile of rubbish, his camouflage clothing and painted skin helping him blend in. He adjusted the sling on his sniper rifle, realizing it was like carrying a death sentence on his back. The enemy hated snipers. If he were captured he would likely face torture, and then execution—*the only good sniper is the one on your side.*

Alex flipped up his night-vision goggles and surveyed the area, staring straight ahead and focusing on his peripheral vision to catch any movement. It wasn't that he didn't trust the goggles, but he knew there could be a time when he wouldn't have them, and even when he did they might not work. A sniper had to be effective with just his eyes and rifle.

He caught the sound of the truck's engine growing fainter as it navigated the deserted streets. Any moment now it would be dropping off Jabberwocky at the north end of town before heading west and out of the village.

Alex remained motionless in the alley for fifteen minutes. Patience wasn't just a virtue for a sniper; it was everything. With no signs of activity, Alex eased himself into a standing position and began stalking through a series of crooked and winding alleys. Thirty minutes later he reached his destination: a wall with a line painted on it—the perimeter wall to a safe house. He was told that the top of the wall was cemented with broken glass to discourage people from climbing over it. He followed the wall around to the front and stopped at the front gate. Reaching into his pocket, he pulled out a set of keys that were tightly connected like the blades of a pocketknife so the keys wouldn't jingle. He unlocked the gate. After closing it behind him, he pulled on the gate and made sure it was locked. He quickly moved across the small courtyard to the front door of the house and waited. He remembered how impatient he had been in training when instructors had drilled caution and patience. He was finally understanding why. Hearing nothing, he unlocked the front door, walked in, and then locked the door behind him—*details*.

He moved away from the door and crouched down, his pistol held ready in the firing position. It was darker inside the house than it was in the alley, but he could see the outline of some furniture and make out walls and doorways. He looked, he listened, and he waited. He was a big cat on an African plain. He would stalk, and he would kill.

Once he was satisfied he was alone, Alex holstered his pistol and laid a claymore mine with an infrared triggering mechanism facing the door he'd just entered. If intruders came through the door, the movement would trigger the mine and welcome them with a hearty *bang*.

Alex drew his SIG back out of the holster and scanned through its contrast sights. He moved through the first floor, closets and all, making sure the house was clear. He inspected a narrow stairway as he climbed up. Then he checked the second floor. Clear. He placed another infrared-triggered claymore facing the top step of the stairs on the second floor.

Here another narrow stairway led to the roof. Alex climbed up and onto the roof, which featured a parapet on all four sides. Clearing the roof, he holstered his pistol and devoted all of his attention to his main weapon.

He crawled toward the front parapet and took up a prone position facing the target house across the street. He stayed back from the edge to make it more difficult to be seen from the outside. Movies too often showed snipers leaning out of windows or bell towers, which was a dead giveaway. You stayed as far back from the edge as you could—at least, you did if you wanted to live.

Alex steadied his customized Remington 700 sniper rifle. Known as the Win Mag, the rifle fired a specially made .300 Winchester Magnum bullet. Alex called his personal rifle Betty, after the Betty Boop cartoon character.

He ran his hands over Betty, checking by feel that everything was tight and in place. Above the Leupold scope he'd mounted a Medium Thermal Weapon Sight (MTWS). Alex pressed his eye against the rubber cup around the MTWS eyepiece, activating the sight's cool-down. He held his eye there for two minutes as the sight's temperature lowered enough for him to see everything cold in black and everything hot in white. There were no colors. His field of vision was 15 degrees, and everything appeared five times larger.

The target for tonight's mission was Raad Nalo, an Iraqi citizen who recruited for Iran, financed and trained terrorists, and targeted Iraqi police, military, and government personnel in order to destabilize the country. Intel was that he didn't talk much and walked with a limp. The SEALs had nicknamed him Verbal, after Roger "Verbal" Kint (aka Keyser Söze) in the movie *The Usual Suspects*.

Alex's SEAL Team Two platoon had recently lost a SEAL sniper pair to an enemy countersniper team. It was a bitter loss, all the more so because the enemy sniper had gotten away. Without time to bring in a new team, Alex and Jabberwocky volunteered to split up and operate solo for this mission. It was breaking rules, but Alex had quickly found out that in a war zone you learned to do what you could within the rules and then what you had to without them.

"Magic Dragon, this is Ambassador. I am in the haystack, over," Alex whispered, radioing the tactical operation center that he was in position.

"Ambassador, this is Magic Dragon. Copy you in the haystack, over."

One minute later, Jabberwocky radioed in on the same frequency that he was in position. Intel was certain, well, as certain as they could ever be, that more of the Shiite fighters were located to the north. If Verbal escaped the kill zone, he'd probably run in that direction to find friends. If he did, Jabberwocky would be the fortunate one to take him out. Alex could see Jabberwocky through his scope, but only because he knew where he would be, and Jabberwocky, like Alex, hadn't created an elaborate hide. This was a quick mission—in and out. Alex went back to scanning the target area, comforted that Jabberwocky was there, even if he was on the other side of the village.

Between the condominium and the street on its west side sat two burned metal drums. Two more metal drums were positioned between the building and the street running along its south side. The burned metal drums clashed with their affluent surroundings, but the drums weren't there for decoration. In the past, the terrorists had learned to set trash in the drums and tires on fire to conceal them in smoke, but Alex had a surprise for them: not only did the thermal sight allow him to see through the night under low light levels, but it also allowed him to see through smoke.

Shortly before dawn, the rest of the SEAL platoon would take down the target building—a two-story condominium that housed Shiites loyal to Iran. Alex heard two Black Hawk helicopters in the distance. He checked his watch—right on schedule. As the helos neared, men armed with AK-47 assault rifles emerged from the target building and moved toward the drums. Alex's personal rules of engagement were simple: kill them all.

Alex trained his scope on one of the metal drums to the south. A man-shaped image in white moved quickly through the black space in his scope toward the drums. Alex centered his sights on the man's head. At seventy-five yards it was an easy shot, but Alex didn't take it for granted. He controlled his breathing, resat the butt of his rifle against his shoulder, gave himself a silent "send" command, and squeezed the trigger. Flecks of white erupted from the figure as it tumbled to the ground five yards short of the drums.

A second man tried to light the same metal drum, actually stepping over the body of the first Shiite fighter to do so. Alex shot him center of mass, just left of the sternum. The man fell directly in front of the first one, creating a long white blob that reminded Alex of a fat night crawler.

A flare of white in his scope meant other terrorists had succeeded in lighting fires in the other drums. Smoke blanketed the area. While it didn't affect Alex's vision through the scope, it did irritate his nose and throat. He kept his sights on the unlit drums and sure enough, a third terrorist moved toward them. The man paused when he came to the two bodies of his comrades. Alex fired, his bullet ripping through the man's rib cage from right to left. The blood spray looked like a burst fire hydrant through his scope.

With no more terrorists moving toward the drums, Alex moved his sight to a window on the first floor of the three-story target building. The shape of a terrorist, hot white head and cold black AK, hung out the window aiming at the sky toward the incoming choppers. Alex aimed for the nasal cavity and fired. The head disappeared back inside the house while the AK-47 tumbled down to the ground below.

The sound of the helos became louder. Alex's left eye wasn't looking through the scope, but it remained half open. He marveled as the Black Hawk blades whipped the smoke into a frenzy.

One Black Hawk hovered above the target building with its skids almost touching the roof. White shapes jumped out onto the roof—SEALs. They quickly blew a hole through the roof and entered the top floor of the building from above. If intel was correct, they'd land in the hallway. If intel was wrong, they could take a flight down the stairwell.

A second Black Hawk landed in the street, kicking up dust and trash, which did obscure Alex's vision. More SEALs hopped off. Four SEALs ran to the four corners outside the building to seal it off while the rest stacked up at the main door. A loud bang and brilliant burst of light marked the detonation of a flash-bang grenade. The SEALs burst through the front door a moment later.

Alex scanned the middle smoky area through his thermal sight—no threats. He panned to the right and up to the top of a building, where he spotted a white silhouette, but instead of holding an AK-47, the terrorist held a much larger, black object.

Damn! It was a rocket-propelled grenade (RPG). Alex's heart jumped. He placed his crosshairs on the terrorist's neck to compensate for the distance and squeezed the trigger. The shot hit the terrorist in the gut, folding him in half like a lawn chair.

In Alex's earphone, he heard the SEALs continue their assault. He scanned back to the target building and saw a figure drop out of a second-story window. The figure stood up and limped away from the building, heading through the smoke toward Alex. *Is he limping from the fall, or is he Verbal? Is he a SEAL?*

"Rover Team, Rover Team, this is Ambassador," Alex said. "One unidentified just jumped from a second-story window, south side. He's moving south across the street and limping, over."

"This is Rover Five, south corner. I don't see him. Is he in the smoke?"

"Affirmative," Alex said. "He's limping through the smoke toward my position."

For several agonizing seconds the radio remained silent.

"He's not one of ours, Ambassador. I repeat, he is not one of ours. You are free to engage, over," the SEAL said.

Alex was tempted to take the shot then and there, but there was no way the other SEAL could be 100 percent sure, could he?

When the limping figure exited the smoke, Alex still couldn't recognize his face through the thermal sight. Alex took his eye off the thermal scope and looked through the Leupold scope. The world and all its color came into view, but he lost the man with the limp.

Alex laid Betty down on the deck, so it wouldn't slow him down. He leaned over on his left side and drew his pistol just as a bullet cracked the sound barrier where his head had been. *Countersniper!* He crawled to the steps and down them. On the second floor, he rushed to the next set of stairs. Without thinking, he almost ran down them, but the sight of the claymore reminded him he needed to disarm the mine. He did.

Boom!

Did the claymore blow up in my face? No, it's still in one piece. Was I shot? I don't feel any pain.

Alex remembered the front door. He walked down the steps and looked at the front door. The claymore there had detonated and the door was shredded. The person who had picked the lock was shredded, too. Blood had splashed all over the ground and into the street. When Alex stepped outside, he slipped on the blood and almost fell. He examined the face and upper row of teeth, but they weren't gold: this wasn't Verbal. *Who was it?*

Alex went back in the house and set up his claymore on the first stair landing before returning to the roof. He carefully retrieved his rifle without exposing himself. Then he descended to the second floor. Staying far back from the window, he scanned the area through his sniper scope, but he couldn't spot the countersniper. He checked Jabberwocky's position—he was gone, too. He'd probably returned to the helo. *I better move my ass, or I'll miss my ride, and I do not want to walk through booger-eater territory in broad daylight.*

Alex disarmed his claymore, grabbed what was left of the mysterious lock picker on the first floor, and dragged him to the helo. Alex looked inside the helo for his sniper mentor, but he wasn't there. "Where's Jabberwocky?" Alex asked.

"You didn't hear?" a SEAL with a bushy beard asked.

"Hear what?" Alex asked.

The SEAL shook his head. Minutes later, two SEALs loaded Jabberwocky's body onto the helo. Blood covered his face, which was swollen from a bullet wound. His trousers were torn and wet like he'd been shot in the crotch several times. The helo lifted up, but Alex felt a part of him had been left on the ground.

Major Gholam Khan stood at the doorway of the American safe house, looking down at the blood-splattered ground. The infidels had taken Abubakar Sawalah's body. Khan knew Abubakar was dead. There was no way he could have survived the blast. The amount of blood and bits of brain matter on the ground made that clear. Khan crouched down, placing himself where he imagined Abubakar had been the moment he was killed.

It was his fault Abubakar was dead. Khan had told him to work his way toward the house across the street where the second American sniper was hiding. The boy, just twenty-one years old, was always eager to please. With a quick mind and sharp eye he was easily Khan's best student. He had all the potential to be a shooter as good as Khan himself, maybe even better. But his youthfulness made him reckless. Khan knew that, but in the middle of the fight there had been no time to caution the young man. Khan stood up. He would have gone through a window, maybe even climbing the wall to the second story. It would have taken time, but it would have been unexpected.

A Shiite fighter ran up to him out of breath. "Sir, I am sorry, but we must leave. American patrols are coming."

Khan waved the man away, but he did turn and follow after him. There was nothing more to see here. He had the satisfaction of killing one of the snipers, of that he was sure, but the other had lived. It was, what was the saying . . . a draw. He spit on the ground.

He didn't play for draws.

2

Major Gholam Khan didn't give much thought to who he was ordered to kill. He'd done the deed many times before, and he thought tonight's assignment would be one of his easier tasks. Now he was in a highly secret and secure Iranian biological weapons lab. As a member of the elite Quds Force within Iran's Army of the Guardians of the Islamic Revolution—the Revolutionary Guard—Major Khan moved about the country with ease. It was widely known, if not spoken about in public, that the Quds' mission was to export Iran's vision of Islam abroad by financing, training, equipping, and organizing foreign revolutionary units. Moreover, the Quds reported directly to the Supreme Leader of Iran, the Ayatollah himself. That made Major Khan all but untouchable, at least in his country. After almost being captured in Iraq several years ago, however, Major Khan had been ordered home. Greeted as a hero, he nonetheless felt cheated. He'd groomed several Shiite countersniper teams in Iraq, many of whom were killed after he left.

Major Khan opened the door to a classroom within the facility and stepped in. A podium with a chair on either side of it stood at the front of the classroom. Behind the podium and chairs a large

Iranian flag covered the whiteboard. In front of the podium were tables and chairs for fifty people. Major Khan had arrived early. It was the sniper in him. To his surprise he saw he wasn't the first. Scientists, assistants, and workers were already filling the seats. It occurred to him that their early arrival had more to do with fear of being late. A few, perhaps, were actually eager to see the star of the show, General Behrouz Tehrani, one of Iran's greatest leaders from the Iran-Iraq War and a celebrated hero. Major Khan took a seat next to the podium and waited for the general's arrival.

Captain Rapviz Shokoufandeh entered the room. Khan and Rapviz had been friends for years, a rare instance of comradeship for Khan. Rapviz nodded at Khan and walked to stand behind the podium. He coughed and then spoke into the microphone: "When General Tehrani enters the room, please stand until he says to be seated."

The crowd stirred.

Five minutes later, General Tehrani entered, putting his black cell phone in his pocket as he did so. It was a subtle but powerful gesture. He was a busy man, an important man. He wore shiny black boots, an olive drab uniform, and four golden stars on his epaulettes. He was a thin man with a white beard that gave him a distinguished appearance.

The crowd stood.

His voice roared, "Take seats."

The scientists and others sat down. Some watched him nervously. Others watched him with anticipation.

General Tehrani stood behind the podium studying them for a moment.

The audience waited for him to speak.

"People, the so-called Arab Spring in Iran is bullshit," General Tehrani began. Those who'd never heard him unedited were clearly shocked by his speaking style, especially the Arab-Iranian scientist sitting near the front. "We are not Arabs. We are Iranians. True

Iranians love their Ayatollah and their government. True Iranians love their families. True Iranians love themselves. We don't give a damn about any Arab Spring in Iran. It isn't going to happen. Ever. You are here because you worked harder than everyone else and because you're smarter than everyone else. True Iranians are hard workers and intelligent." He paused and scanned the audience.

"Now I am told," he continued, "that we're maintaining production levels of MBD21. I don't want to maintain shit. Maintaining is what Americans do. We're going to increase production until we have enough bacterium to obliterate half the American population."

Some in the crowd let out their enthusiasm: "Yes!"

"We are true Iranians, and true Iranians don't wait for Americans to kill Iranian families. True Iranians protect their families by killing Americans first. You are the brightest people with the best equipment in the world. We can't fail now. We've come too far. We must never give up. We must never let the infidels win. I know it hasn't been easy, but don't let this moment fall into mediocrity. We must work harder than ever. Show the infidels what we can do. Become mean, insanely aggressive. Cut the infidels' hearts out. We must want this more than life itself. This moment will be the greatest for Iran. We must defend our families and country. In the same way I use bullets and bombs, you use science. Will you fight for your families and country with me?"

The scientists applauded: "Yes!" The Arab-Iranian scientist's response was weaker than that of the others. In contrast, the scientist with a crooked nose who sat next to him applauded louder than everyone else.

"Will you fight for your families?"

"Yes!" the crowd cheered. The Arab-Iranian scientist continued to respond weakly. Major Khan recognized him as a brilliant scientist who placed little value on politics and speeches.

"Your honor?"

"Yes!"

"That's the spirit. Let's do this! Maybe Iran will fall into mediocrity someday. But not today."

Major Khan stood and then walked over to the weakly responding scientist. All of the scientists were smart, but not all were wise. From beneath his jacket, Major Khan swung out his shoulder holster containing a sound-suppressed MPT-9KPDW, the Iranian copy of the German MP5K-PDW short submachine gun. The weapon remained attached to his shoulder holster and the folding stock remained folded, allowing him to fire quickly with the submachine gun still in its holster.

The Arab-Iranian scientist leaned back in his chair and put his hands out in front of his face. "No! Please, no!"

The crowd became silent.

Major Khan stood in front of the scientist, taking an angle that wouldn't injure others. Not that Major Khan cared about their lives—he cared only about the mission, and this mission needed scientists. Major Khan pivoted, and pointed his gun at the scientist with the crooked nose, the one who had applauded louder than the others. He waited for the man's eyes to register what was happening and then squeezed the trigger, firing a short burst. A single shot to the head would have sufficed, but the general had wanted something loud and exceptionally violent.

General Tehrani cleared his voice and patiently waited for the assembled scientists to direct their attention back to him. "Applauding loudly when I'm around is one thing, but slackening effort when I'm not around is another. It sets a bad example—it's bad for morale."

One of the scientists began applauding loudly. No one followed his example—they were too much in shock to move.

3

JANUARY 10, 2012

Alex Brandenburg wandered the aisles of the supermarket without noticing the food. His mind was on a mission. More specifically, the fact that he and the Outcasts' SEAL Team didn't have one. As the very sharp edge of Operation Bitter Ash, the black ops program that grew out of Operation Phoenix and the targeted killings of North Vietnamese communists during that war, Alex expected the missions would come fast. There was no end to terrorists looking to do America and her allies harm. Administering a lead aspirin at high velocity seemed just the ticket to cure what ailed these sick bastards, but so far the phone hadn't rung. Instead, just like when he was on the regular Teams, downtime stretched to seeming eternity while he waited for another chance to suit up.

Realizing he'd wandered into the cat food section, he decided to focus on the mission at hand—buying groceries. The food quality at the Navy Exchange and local supermarkets was okay, but Alex preferred the quality of foods available at Whole Foods. Until recently, the nearest one was located just outside Richmond, nearly a two-hour drive from his home in Virginia Beach, where he was stationed at SEAL Team Six. Of course, Alex could put the cold foods in a cooler to keep them fresh for the drive home from Richmond, but he was on standby, and if Team Six called, he had only one hour to get his ass on the plane and be ready for the brief—and driving over one hundred miles an hour down Interstate 64 didn't seem like a wise option. Thus, Alex eagerly attended the newly opened Whole Foods store in Virginia Beach.

Customers crowded the brightly lit store. Alex pushed his partly filled cart out of the cat food section and down an aisle that looked far more likely to have salsa. As he did he spotted an attractive blonde walking toward him. She was wearing a white silk blouse and black skirt under a red knee-length cashmere jacket. What made her attractive wasn't so much the shape of her face, the size of her breasts, or the calm, quiet way her hips swayed—there was a feeling about her. As she passed him in the aisle, she blew through him like an Indian summer, stopping his breath. As a frogman, he prided himself on breath control, but in that moment she'd taken that control from him. Alex placed the salsa in his cart and contemplated turning around to take another look at her, but he didn't. Maybe it would make her feel uncomfortable, or maybe he was too proud. It took him a moment to remember the other reason—Cat.

Alex headed to the dairy section. Once again, the woman in red appeared. Alex couldn't resist smiling. She smiled back. They both stopped in front of the milk. Some women didn't like the military, some did, and others didn't care one way or the other—he wondered which type she was.

Not that she'd recognize he was in the military. Alex wore his hair longer than regulation and paid conscious attention to walk rather than march to where he was going. If she asked what he did for a living, his cover was a manager for a company contracted to develop and test military equipment. After the attention from the killing of Osama bin Laden, Alex and his Teammates changed their covers again. When his fellow SEALs applied for car loans or credit cards, if asked for more details, they couldn't very well say that they worked for SEAL Team Six, so the Team provided them with cover jobs. A full-time secretary working for Team Six devoted her time to answering the phone in an off-base office that supported the cover.

Alex thought about what to say to her, but none of what came to mind seemed appropriate. He decided not to make an analysis out of it. "Hi," he said.

Her eyes smiled as well as her lips. "Hi."

Before Alex could say any more, his cell phone vibrated. Normally, he didn't wait to look at it, but this time he waited—until her eyes broke the gaze and looked at his phone.

That feeling of anxiousness crept through him: is this another training test, or is this the real deal? He looked down at the text message: *T-R-I-D-E-N-T-9-9-9*. Real deal or not, the clock was ticking and now he had less than an hour to get on the plane.

Alex forgot about the milk, but he remembered to say something to the woman in red: "Nice meeting you."

"Did we?" Her eyes continued to smile.

The cell phone had inconvenienced Alex before, but he'd never truly regretted it—until this moment. He turned and headed for a checkout counter. Alex stopped and turned to take one last look at her: now she was focused on getting a carton of milk. After putting the milk in her cart, she looked up to notice Alex staring. For a second, Alex thought about ignoring the cell phone—thought about telling SEAL Team Six *goodbye*.

The woman seemed puzzled. Alex turned around and headed to the cash registers. Long lines of people with full carts waited—Murphy's law: "Anything that can go wrong, will go wrong." He tried to judge which line was the shortest, searching for single men with near-empty carts, but the lines seemed filled mostly with women shopping for large families. He entered the nearest line, only to discover that a cashier was having problems with a customer's item.

It was as if something were trying to stop Alex from answering the call on his cell phone, but Alex chose to ignore the "signs," pushed his shopping cart to the side, and left it. Signs or not, he still had a job to do, and he still loved his job. A lot of SEALs he knew liked hunting terrorists but claimed they didn't like killing them. Alex liked killing terrorists. It wasn't a long-lasting joy, but it was still a joy.

He walked out the front door without any groceries and didn't turn back. When his warm breath hit the cold air, it created a puff of fog. He didn't yet know where today's mission would be, but it was probably somewhere that he wouldn't need salsa and milk.

Walking through the parking lot, Alex subconsciously scanned the area for trouble, but his spidey sense wasn't tingled. He opened his SUV, hopped inside, and sped away.

After leaving the parking lot, Alex drove along Laskin Road before turning right on First Colonial Road, which became South Oceana Boulevard. Snow covered the ground beside the roads. Five minutes after leaving the supermarket, he arrived at the Tomcat Boulevard base gate. The number "999" was the code in his text message that told him which gate to enter. Alex showed his contractor ID to the gate guard. The guard waved him through. On the base, Alex drove to the terminal and parked his SUV at the lot near the tarmac.

After locking his SUV, he hurriedly walked toward the plane. Even though Alex still had plenty of time, he walked hurriedly out of habit. Approaching a specially blacked-out C-130, he looked for Jet Assisted Takeoff (JATO) bottles on the plane, used for extra thrust on takeoff, especially useful when bad guys were shooting at Alex and his Teammates. There were no JATO bottles. Maybe this was just a training mission.

Alex wondered who'd be joining him. As a member of Red Team, Alex could be joined by Red Team SEALs. Alex also served on Black Team, the sniper team. Maybe this would be a sniper mission. Or possibly he'd be shooting solo.

On the plane, the white lights were on, running off an outside auxiliary power unit instead of the plane's valuable fuel. Alex didn't recognize the flight crew, but sitting near the cockpit was a bald Army lieutenant colonel. In conversation and informal writing, lieutenant colonel was shortened to *colonel*. The Colonel was from the Joint Special Operations Command (JSOC, pronounced *JAY-sock*). JSOC was headquartered at Fort Bragg and Pope Air Force Base in North Carolina. After the 1980 failed attempt to rescue fifty-three American hostages at the American Embassy in Iran, it became clear that the Army, Navy, Air Force, and Marines couldn't work together effectively on Special Operations missions. In 1987 the Department of Defense grafted all the military branches' Special Operations onto one tree—including Tier 1 units like SEAL Team Six and Delta. SEALs, Rangers, and Green Berets were special, but JSOC took only the best for the top tier: Team Six and Delta. JSOC was Team Six's boss, and the SEALs were careful not to bite the hand that fed them. The JSOC Colonel already had his portable projector screen and laptop hooked up.

Alex almost didn't notice John Landry sitting to the side quietly checking his gear. John was a handsome black man from New Orleans who spoke French and Creole. A former member of SEAL Team One, John was a devout believer in God, but John shot like the devil.

"Hi, John," Alex said.

John gave a quiet grunt—which was more than his usual response. *Progress.* As a regular Team Six member of Blue Team, John's presence suggested that this was an Outcasts mission. There were four Outcasts: Alex, John, Pancho, and Cat. Catherine Fares wasn't a SEAL, but she acted as a sister, girlfriend, or wife for the SEALs to aid their cover and help get them into countries where they didn't want to look like a bunch of military guys on a mission. She also spoke Arabic. The four of them had previously been in trouble with the Navy and been formed into a new unit: the Outcasts. Now their superiors could run the blackest of black missions—if the Outcasts were discovered, they'd take the fall. Alex had led their first mission, and the Outcasts succeeded in killing seven al Qaeda cadre vying to fill the leadership gap left by bin Laden's demise. He had fretted briefly about the mission's one loose end. Mohammed—the radicalized teenaged son of one of their targets—had managed to elude the Outcasts during a shootout in the streets of New York City. Alex would have liked to have had another shot at the blond terrorist.

Support personnel from Team Six had already loaded the gear belonging to Alex and the others on the mission. He checked his to make sure everything was okay.

"Where's your better half?" John asked.

Alex shrugged. During the last mission, Alex and Cat had developed feelings for each other that broke regulations. "She's on another assignment."

"Is she still one of us—the Outcasts?" John asked.

"I don't know."

John's right eyebrow shot up. "You waiting until she comes back, or are you seeing other women?"

Alex let out a breath. "Why so many questions?"

John paused. "I just like having her around."

Me, too. "No telling how long this separation will be. We agreed that it's okay to see other people while we're apart."

"Is that what you think?" John asked.

Alex didn't want to think about it. "Where's *your* better half?"

John frowned. "Has Pancho ever been early?"

Alex smiled.

A new guy Alex had never seen before stepped on board. He wore a military haircut and a nonmilitary goatee. "Uh, hi, guys. I'm Danny." He sounded friendly enough. "Danny Pieratti. From the Activity." The Activity was short for Intelligence Support Activity (ISA). The Activity gathered intelligence—especially for SEAL Team Six and Delta missions.

The bald Colonel fidgeted with his watch and strained his neck to look outside the plane. Suddenly, the Colonel stopped fidgeting and straining his neck.

Alex peeked outside.

Pancho strolled across the tarmac as if he didn't have a care in the world. Alex checked his Rolex Submariner watch: less than five minutes before drop-dead time. Even if the whole world was on fire, Pancho wouldn't care—the world would just have to wait.

"Pancho" was Francisco Rodriguez's nickname. A Mexican-American giant from Houston, he liked to wear shit-kickers and a big-ass rodeo belt buckle. Pancho was chewing on something, probably Red Man tobacco. He spit. *That's disgusting.*

Pancho had served with John on SEAL Team One before they both came to Team Six's Blue Team—also known as the Pirates. Although Pancho and John were friends, they were complete opposites. Pancho disliked religion and the heat. Although they generally avoided discussions with each other about religion, if there was a thermostat nearby, Pancho and John were always changing it. Pancho had seniority over John, but Pancho was the less mature of the two.

Pancho entered the plane and his eyes fixed on Alex. A big smile spread across his face. "Hey, Alex," he greeted. "You in charge of this rodeo again?"

"About to find out," Alex replied. "Good to have you back."

"Great to be here." Then Pancho greeted John but received no response. Pancho grinned.

The plane door closed and the crew switched from auxiliary power to the plane's own power. The interior lights switched from white to red. Cat wouldn't be on this mission.

The guys took their seats and buckled up for takeoff. Takeoffs and landings were the most dangerous parts of a flight. John opened a pocket-sized Bible and began reading it.

The C-130 taxied down the runway before lifting off.

"I heard that Hammerhead is banging Cat," Pancho said. "Guess that relationship didn't work out too well for you."

John looked up from his Bible and frowned at Pancho.

Although Hammerhead was a SEAL, Alex could never figure out how he'd managed to get into Team Six—he was a tactical moron and a shitty shot. "He isn't her type."

"Hammerhead said that you and Cat have some kind of agreement that it's okay to date other people while you're apart."

"Where'd he hear that?" Alex asked.

"From her, I guess," Pancho said.

"He lies a lot."

Alex noticed Danny listening in on their conversation. When Danny realized Alex noticed, Danny turned away.

Alex peered out a window. As the shapes of the buildings and roads on the ground became less distinct, Alex felt sad Cat wasn't going to be on this mission with them. He tried to rationalize: maybe it'd be safer for her not to be with them.

The plane ascended to a safe level. The guys took off their seat belts and walked toward the open area before the cockpit and sat down for the Colonel's brief.

Pancho turned to Alex and asked, "You're coming up on reenlistment in a little bit, aren't you?"

They were supposed to keep quiet and listen to the brief, so Alex, reluctant to speak, simply nodded.

"Who you going to invite?"

Now the Colonel was giving Pancho the dirty eye.

Pancho kept talking. "You got to have strippers. A good reenlistment ceremony needs strippers."

Alex hadn't heard of strippers at a reenlistment ceremony, but he hadn't attended Pancho's reenlistment celebration.

The Colonel's face was already red under the red lights, but now it was redder.

"Never know when to put a muzzle on it, Pancho, do you?" John muttered.

Pancho chuckled. "Muzzle on my mouth or muzzle on my—"

"Hey!" the Colonel shouted. "Am I interrupting something?!"

Pancho became silent.

"Because if I am," the Colonel continued, "I'll stop interrupting!"

The three Outcasts sat silent. "Please, we're ready for the brief," Alex said.

"Good!" The Colonel switched his projector and notebook computer from standby to run, then began his PowerPoint presentation. "Gentlemen, this is the real deal. The Iranian government is continuing its work on building nukes. STUXNET, the cyberattack that shut off the electricity to their centrifuges, slowed them down, but it didn't stop them."

The world knew about STUXNET now. A bunch of computer geeks in the United States and Israel created an electronic worm that actually sped up the Iranian centrifuges under the very noses of the Iranian scientists. While speed was often a good thing, in this case it served to destroy the centrifuges. Once the Iranians caught on they developed countermeasures and repaired the damage. What happened next wasn't known worldwide.

"Delta have gone in more than once and blown up power lines, disrupting their enrichment process and mangling more centrifuges," the Colonel said. "Due to certain political factors that I won't get into here, a government not ours has taken a more direct approach and assassinated several of Iran's nuclear scientists."

Alex looked around the group and saw knowing smiles.

"The success of these efforts has given the Iranians pause. We have intel that they are seriously concerned their nuclear enrichment program, also known as 'weapons,' won't pan out. And so they've created a backup plan."

The smiles vanished. This was something new.

"An asset code-named Leila has told us that the Iranians have been recruiting bioweapons experts from the former Soviet Union, North Korea, and other countries and set up a lab deep in the Lut Desert. One of the NSA's satellites picked up radio conversations confirming the lab. The NGA used their satellite to photograph a site that is two hundred klicks northwest of a small town called Abadi Abad. The lab appears to be well guarded." The National Geospatial-Intelligence Agency photographed a site that was 124 miles northwest of Abadi Abad. When Alex first joined the Navy, the military mixing of metric measurements with U.S. measurements seemed confusing, but the military used metrics to standardize operations with NATO countries, especially ground distance. Other measurements, such as altitude, remained unchanged. Now that he was a veteran, the metric mixing seemed natural.

The Colonel continued. "We aren't sharing this with our allies in the region at this time."

Pancho raised his hand. "Sir? Why not? The Israelis would have no trouble airing out a few biologists," Pancho said.

The Colonel shook his head. "Should an unnamed government get wind of this site there is a high probability that they would launch a strike against Iran just like they did when they hit Iraq's nuclear plant in 1981."

"Operation Opera," Alex said, remembering the details. "A bunch of F-16s and F-15s flew in and bombed the Osirak reactor just before it went online. Pretty much a success. One of the pilots even went on to become an astronaut."

"This isn't a game show," the Colonel said, huffing. "But yes, that strike was successful, most of all because it didn't set off a massive war in the Middle East. If a certain country were to try that again, however, the chances of the Middle East going up in flames are a lot more likely. And that, gentlemen, is something we're trying very hard to avoid, which is where you come in."

The Colonel clicked to the next screen, which revealed a map of Afghanistan.

"We're flying to Afghanistan, where you'll do a night HAHO from twenty-six thousand feet, then fly sixty miles to land in Iran." HAHO meant "high altitude, high opening." Alex and his men would jump out of the plane at high altitude, then quickly open their parachutes, so they could glide across the border to their landing point. They'd be too small to show up on radar, and Iran would never see or hear them coming.

The Colonel used a red penlight to indicate the drop point on the aerial image on the projector screen. "You'll land here, then hump ten klicks to rendezvous with Leila at her house." Ten kilometers didn't sound like much of a hike, but depending on the terrain and concentration of enemy in the area, it could be. An image of Leila appeared on the screen.

"She ain't ugly," Pancho said.

"Would you shut it," John said, elbowing Pancho in the ribs.

Alex agreed with Pancho: Leila was hot. She looked like the actress in the TV series *JAG*, all smoldering eyes and jet-black hair. When Alex had free time, which was rare, he sometimes watched education channels on his cable TV, but one day when flipping channels, he watched part of *JAG*. She captured his interest more than the show did.

The Colonel ignored Pancho and John and looked at the Activity guy: "Danny has been in and out of Iran a number of times and has been in direct contact with Leila. He'll take you to her house and knock on her rear window twice. She'll respond by knocking twice. Then he'll knock four times. The next evening Danny and Leila will insert your team near the target, you'll destroy it, Danny and Leila will help you extract, then you'll return to her house. From there, you'll proceed to Kandahar, where we will debrief you." The bald Colonel looked at Danny and asked, "Do you have anything to add?"

"Leila is solid," Danny said. "She's the most solid agent I've met. She's a triathlete and scuba dives, so she shouldn't slow us down too much."

The Colonel thanked Danny before continuing: "We can't support you while you're in Iran, but once you cross the border to Afghanistan, we can. Of course if your team is compromised, you're on your own. No one will avow responsibility for this mission."

The Colonel went on to brief them about enemy forces and the lack of friendly forces in the immediate target area. The nearest friendlies would be in Afghanistan, too far away to bail the Outcasts out even if the friendlies were allowed to. Because of the different time zones, the SEALs would lose seven and a half hours between Virginia Beach and Iran. As for the weather, there wasn't any place hotter—the Lut Desert was literally the hottest place on the planet. "Although the days are usually cool this time of year, right now the Lut is experiencing a record-breaking heat wave, with daytime temperatures exceeding one hundred ten degrees Fahrenheit," the Colonel warned. Locals passed on a legend that a load of wheat was left in the desert for a couple of days; the sun turned it into toasted wheat. Lut Desert was about to become even hotter.

The Colonel gave them maps and photos of the area, and a photo of Leila. Pancho nearly drooled on his photo of her.

John picked at his trousers as if there were lint when there was actually nothing—he did that when he felt troubled or annoyed.

"Why us for this mission?" Alex asked.

"Because you do the missions that are dirty," the Colonel said. "The missions that no one will take public responsibility for. And because you're expendable."

"I don't understand what's so special about this mission. Why no one wants to take responsibility for it."

The Colonel pulled out an olive drab case the size of a briefcase and set it between his feet and the Outcasts. He handled it like it was heavy. "You'll use this for the demolition: the Mark-2 SADM." SADM stood for Special Atomic Demolition Munition, sometimes called the "backpack bomb." The Mark-54 SADM was developed in the 1960s, but the one in front of the Colonel looked smaller and lighter. Congress banned the development of backpack bombs in 1994 but then removed the ban ten years later. "This weighs fifty pounds and packs a yield of one kiloton of TNT," the Colonel said. "You can imagine how upset people will be if they find out we nuked Iran."

Pancho's low whistle spoke for all of them. *A nuke!*

"I assume there's a good reason we won't be using conventional explosives for this," Alex said.

"There is," the Colonel explained. "We're not sure as to the extent of underground structures and how reinforced they are, and we're unclear as to how we'd disable the whole plant with conventional explosives or other methods, such as hacking their computers or cutting critical power lines. Also, all the scientists and their support live in the compound—we want you to destroy all the scientists."

"Who's the poor bastard who has to jump out of the plane carrying that?" Pancho asked.

The Colonel's eyes scanned the Outcasts before stopping at John. "John. You've been to SADM school for this very purpose."

"This just keeps getting better and better," John grumbled.

Pancho smiled. John's unhappiness made Pancho happy.

"I have a question," John said.

"Go ahead," the Colonel replied.

"I heard you got out of the military. You don't work for JSOC anymore, do you?"

"Good question," the Colonel said, avoiding an answer.

"If you don't work for JSOC," Pancho said, "who do you work for? The Agency?"

The Colonel gave away nothing.

"Bitter Ash?" Alex asked, looking for a reaction.

The Colonel shifted his weight.

Alex interpreted the shift to mean *yes*. The Phoenix Program of capturing and assassinating high-value personnel didn't truly end when the Vietnam War ended. Rather, it transformed into Bitter Ash. The Outcasts' previous mission to eliminate al Qaeda leaders fell under the command of Bitter Ash. Once again, it looked like Alex, Pancho, and John would be operating in the darkest shadows of blackness.

4

The inside of the C-130 remained darkened except for the red lights illuminating the interior as Alex, Pancho, and John took off their civilian clothes. Alex wore silk boxer shorts, and he wasn't the least bit ashamed. John, however, had on black Speedo swim jammers—formfitting nylon and Lycra spandex that extended from mid-waist down to mid-thigh, similar to triathlon shorts. Alex felt John should have been ashamed, and in the real world he would have, but then there was Pancho. Pancho, always the fashionista of their group, wore only his birthday suit. On this matter, Alex and John thought alike—if they ever got in too much trouble, they could always strip off everything except their shorts and make a swim for it, then walk onto a crowded beach and fit in like the other beach-goers. Pancho hoped he ended up on a nude beach—if not, oh well—can't blame a guy for hoping.

The SEALs put on polypropylene tops and bottoms in order to wick moisture away from their bodies. It wasn't simply a comfort thing. They'd be jumping from a high altitude in subzero temperatures and sweat would freeze.

Despite all the advances in material for extreme weather, they all wore wool socks. Scientists still hadn't managed to beat sheep when it came to putting something on your feet that would wick away moisture and keep them warm.

On his belt he carried a Swiss Army knife and a holstered Iranian Zoaf 9mm pistol, a knockoff of the SIG Sauer. The Zoaf was inferior to the SIG, but SEAL Team Six's expert armorers had customized this Zoaf with increased accuracy, phosphate corrosion-resistant finish on the internal parts, contrast sights, and a threaded barrel for mounting a silencer and the ability to hold fifteen rounds.

His main weapon would be an AKMS, similar to the AK-47 except this modern version had a side-folding buttstock, which gave Alex the option of making the weapon more compact for ease in parachuting and working in tight areas such as indoors. As with the Zoaf, SEAL Team Six's armorers customized this AKMS with improved sling attachment points, a Picatinny rail with low-profile holographic and laser sights attached, and an enhanced fire selector switch for easier use and more accurate firing. *When in Rome, look like the Romans, but carry a bigger stick.*

John carefully put the backpack nuke in his backpack. Of course, the United States could launch a missile with a nuclear warhead at the facility, but it would be difficult to disguise the source of the missile.

Danny is probably trustworthy, but shit happens, Alex thought. He double-checked the route to Leila's house and encouraged the others to do the same.

Pancho sat nibbling on Keebler cookies. "Can you name them?" Pancho asked.

Alex rolled his eyes.

"Name what?" John asked.

"The Keebler elves. All eighteen of them."

John corrected him. "All nineteen."

"Name them."

"Okay. J. J. Keebler, Ernie Keebler, Fryer Tuck, Zoot, Ma Keebler,

Elmer Keebler, Buckets, Fast Eddie, Roger . . ." John started to slow down.

"That's nine," Pancho said. "Don't forget Doc, Zack, Flo, Leonardo, and Elwood."

"Professor, Edison, Larry, and Art."

"See, that's only eighteen," Pancho said, grinning.

"There's one more. I just forgot his name."

Alex couldn't believe that two grown men were arguing about cookies and elves. After Alex made sure he was ready to go, he lay down on the cold deck, closed his eyes, and got some rest—he had no idea when he'd get a chance to rest again, so he didn't waste the opportunity. His adrenaline threatened to keep him awake, but he fought it and caught some sleep—only to be awakened by hunger, so he ate a Meal, Ready to Eat (MRE), also known as Meal, Refusing to Exit because the MREs had been known to cause constipation. More than the food, Alex made sure he drank a lot of water, saturating his cells with it.

They flew nine hours to Germany, stopped to refuel, then continued eight more hours to Afghanistan.

During a stretch of Alex's sleep, John woke him and said, "We're nearing ten thousand feet."

Alex put his helmet and mask on—special molds had been made so that each member's helmet and mask fit exactly. He connected the hose on his mask to an inline tube on the plane's wall (bulkhead) and started breathing pure oxygen to purge nitrogen from his bloodstream and avoid decompression sickness. Alex was also saturating himself with oxygen, so if he got low, he wouldn't black out as fast.

He had been through training that simulated a poor mask seal on his face, depriving him of oxygen—it made him feel euphoric. It was like being Superman. He really thought he could fly. If one guy broke seal, everyone had to restart the pre-breathing process, a process that could last thirty minutes to an hour and a half. Alex had seen a SEAL with a new mask that didn't fit properly. Fortunately it was a training op, and the guy passed out before he jumped. The commanding officer had to make a decision whether to abort the mission or carry on without him. They carried on the mission without him. And he'd heard from John about a training op where a West Coast SEAL had jumped, then gone unconscious. An Emergency Deployment Device (EDD) should have automatically deployed his parachute for him; however, the EDD failed, and he bounced off the ground before he ever woke. Immediately the guys radioed about their dead Teammate. Pancho had been on that op. While waiting nearly an hour for someone to come and help them take the body out, Pancho reached into the rubble of the dead SEAL's Playmate cooler, took his lunch, and ate it.

Pancho, John, and Danny joined Alex in pre-breathing.

After thirty minutes, the C-130 rose above ten thousand feet over Afghanistan. For each one thousand feet the plane ascended, the temperature dropped 3.6 degrees Fahrenheit. Alex put on overgloves, which covered his tactical gloves so his hands wouldn't freeze off.

As they reached eighteen thousand feet, a physiology technician monitored the SEALs and aircrew for signs of altitude sickness.

The plane rose higher and higher. Soon the loadmaster called out, "Thirty minutes!"

Alex's bladder had stretched tight from all the water he'd been drinking, so he relieved himself in a piss tube in the bulkhead.

"Ten minutes!" They were approaching the point of no return. Once they took that step off the plane, there'd be no getting back on.

"Five minutes!" The C-130's ramp lowered. Although there was no moon, there was still more light outside the plane than inside. The light entered the plane. The guys disconnected their breathing lines from the C-130's large oxygen tanks and connected the lines to their small individual tanks. Each SEAL checked and double-checked his oxygen bottle pressure and connections. They had duct-taped their masks onto their helmets so when they jumped, the wind wouldn't blast the masks off their faces. Alex also made a quick check of Pancho, John, and Danny. The PT watched them for signs of hypoxia. Burdened with his green oxygen tank on his left, rifle on his right, and more than a hundred pounds of gear in his backpack, Alex waddled behind the others, who also waddled to the ramp.

"Three minutes!" With all the wind blasting into the plane, Alex couldn't hear the loadmaster call out the time interval, but Alex recognized the man's three-finger sign and relayed it to his Teammates in case they hadn't seen it. Alex dropped to his stomach and slithered onto the ramp. He peeked over the edge and all he could see were clouds. He hoped the ground matched the aerial images the Colonel had shown them.

"One minute!" Alex slithered back away from the ramp and stood. He hoped the pilot and crew were on target.

"Thirty seconds!"

The light on the ramp switched from red to green. Pancho and John looked to Alex for the "okay." Alex pointed off the ramp: *go.* John was the lightest and would take the longest to reach the ground, so he jumped first. Danny went next. Pancho was heavier than Alex, but Alex had to make sure everyone got off the plane okay before he jumped. The three SEALs had distributed their gear so Alex carried more weight.

Alex brought up the rear, and stepped off the plane at twenty-six thousand feet above Afghanistan. It was the Superman feeling, mixed with fear and ecstasy. He longed to just fall through space, but the whole point to a high-altitude, high-opening jump was to deploy your chute right after jumping. Even more crucial, if he waited too long to pull his chute, he'd blast through Pancho's canopy below him and they'd both die.

A mere four seconds after stepping off the plane, Alex pulled his rip cord. He tensed up, even though he had done this hundreds of times before. Would the chute deploy? It was amazing to realize that your life literally hung from a bunch of string.

After what seemed an eternity, the chute opened at twenty-six thousand feet. The force was so abrupt and violent that Alex was certain he cracked a vertebra. Tensing really didn't help. He looked up and did a 360-degree check of his high glide ratio canopy to make sure it hadn't folded over itself like a giant brassiere. *So far, so good*— it had deployed properly and everything checked out fine. He suddenly wondered if, like so much else sold in the United States these days, the chutes had been made by a bunch of kids in a Chinese factory. They could take out a battalion of paratroopers just by skipping a few stitches.

"Damn it!" The temperature was 45 degrees below zero. He really didn't like HAHO jumps. You froze your damn ass off long before anyone got a chance to shoot it off.

He double-checked the canopy. Satisfied it was in full working order, he loosened the straps on his ruck hanging from his chest and let the ruck drop to the top of his boots to distribute the weight more evenly.

Floating while freezing, he began searching for the other jumpers in the night sky. With shaking hands he pulled down his night optical device (NOD) so that it rested in front of his eyes. Infrared (IR) chemlights glowed on the back of each man's helmet. Although invisible to the naked eye, the IR chemlights could be seen through the NODs. The Outcasts stacked up. John glided at the bottom and a large blob that was clearly Pancho was just below Alex. The large black space between them should have been Danny, but he wasn't there. *Where's his chemlight?*

Shit, shit, shit!

Alex looked harder at the empty space between John and Pancho. *Shit!* Danny drifted between them, his chute partially deployed and flapping in the wind! He was already too far away for Alex to tell if he was unconscious or not.

John spun his body and looked up to check his chute. Alex willed John to lunge after Danny and grab him, but he had already fallen past and was picking up speed. Alex did a quick calculation and tore at the release tab of his main chute. It detached and he was suddenly flying again, straight down. He angled his body into a high dive and blew past Pancho and John.

A cloud base at fifteen thousand feet rushed up to meet him. If he didn't get to Danny before then, he'd lose him. Alex was having a hard time maintaining the angle of his dive and realized his ruck was causing the problem. There was no way to cut it loose now. He strained and kept his dive. The wind ripped at his mask, trying to pry it off his face. The distance between him and Danny closed.

Five hundred feet. He started working out what he would do when he caught up to Danny. He'd try to get the unconscious man in a leg lock and bear hug. Then he'd pull his reserve and hope like hell.

Three hundred seventy-five feet. Danny must be unconscious. He was on his back, his arms flailing about in the wind. Grabbing him wasn't going to be easy.

Two hundred twenty feet. The top of the cloud base was looming close. This was going to be tight. Alex turned his focus back on Danny.

One hundred feet.

Forty-five feet. Alex reached out his gloved hands. He'd grab Danny first, pull him in tight, then wrap his legs around him.

Twenty feet. A piece of canopy from Danny's chute ripped loose and flew up into Alex's face. He desperately clawed at the cloth with his left hand while still reaching out with his right. He pulled the cloth away and was in the clouds.

Danny was gone!

Alex looked around, but he couldn't see anything. He had no choice. He pulled the D-ring for his reserve chute and a moment later felt the reassuring jerk as the harness straps bit into his body. No point looking up; he wouldn't be able to see a damn thing.

He tried to calculate how far off course he'd be when he landed. He was still ten thousand feet up, so he should be able to steer close to their original drop zone. If John and Pancho saw his chemlight they'd fly toward him. Alex said a silent goodbye to Danny. Murphy's law was a bastard.

Most of the buddies Alex lost, like Jabberwocky, he knew better than Danny. Some Alex didn't know as well. Experiencing so much death rubbed calluses onto his soul, but it didn't stop him from feeling—seeing a widow and fatherless children at a funeral always hurt him to the core, but now, Alex didn't have the luxury of mourning, feeling, or belly-button gazing. He had a mission to accomplish—a mission that could potentially save many lives. Now Alex was responsible for keeping Pancho and John alive.

Alex broke through the cloud layer and his vision cleared. It was nautical twilight, his favorite time to make magical mayhem. He saw shapes on the ground, the horizon, and stars in the sky to the east, where the cloud cover was broken up. Alex looked down at the tritium sighted glow-in-the-dark Silva Ranger compass mounted on his chest strap. He was off course. *No kidding.* Alex's shivering hands reached up to his parachute toggles and corrected course. Quickly he stuffed his hands under his armpits to protect them from the cold. The cold made his brain slow down. Thinking became difficult.

He spent the next thirty-seven minutes gliding and checking the sky above him for signs of Pancho and John. When he thought his head would fall off his neck from all the twisting he spotted a black shape a thousand yards above him. *Pancho!* He looked around and was amazed to see a chemlight just seventy-five yards below him, off to his left. *John!* They'd found him. The sense of relief was incredible. He wouldn't tell them, but a tear came to his eye. He checked his GPS and saw they'd traveled forty-nine miles from initial jump to their current altitude and position; 2,220 feet and forty-nine miles. Alex couldn't feel his hands or feet. He was ready to land in a volcano if it would warm him up.

John landed first—fortunately, his atomic backpack didn't explode into a giant mushroom cloud and take all of them with it. John was the fastest gun, but even he looked like his frozen body was moving in slow motion. Gradually he brought about his AKMS assault rifle and crouched into a covering position as Alex and Pancho came in to land.

Alex hit hard, the soles of his feet stinging as if they'd just slammed against an iceberg. He pitched forward awkwardly, ramming one knee into the dirt then the other as he did his best to roll and absorb the landing. He lay flat on the ground for several seconds, gulping for breath.

A loud thump a few yards away told him Pancho was on the ground. Alex picked himself up and without a word went about policing up their landing site, burying their parachutes and oxygen tanks and readying their gear. No one said a word about Danny. Alex hoped the enemy didn't hit them now because his fingers were so numb, he didn't think he could pull the trigger. Minutes later, they were ready, and Alex signaled Pancho to lead them out.

Pancho patrolled at the point, watching 180 degrees in front of them. His position was the most exhausting—trying to sense everything before it sensed them. Alex followed in the middle, wiping the frozen tears off his face, then alternating between covering the left and the right with his eyes and AKMS. John secured the rear by stopping occasionally to turn and check the 180 degrees behind them.

The desert evening was cold. During the day, the heat caused water to evaporate into the atmosphere, creating a barrier that trapped long-wave infrared radiation near the ground. As a result, the area became dry and clouds scarce. At night, when the sun disappeared, there was nothing to block the heat from escaping earth. After the heat fled, the desert became cold.

It felt good to be moving on patrol. Gradually, sensation returned to Alex's legs and arms. After three kilometers, the cold pain in his hands wore off, and he felt he had a fighting chance at being able to shoot someone. Two kilometers later, the patrol weaved around the bases of sandy dunes and rock formations. They came across a goat path and followed it toward the village.

After two kilometers on the goat path, Alex noticed something to his left. He couldn't tell if it was a bush or a human. As his eyes strained to see better, he almost ran into Pancho, who had stopped and crouched down. Alex stopped and crouched down, too. John did the same. Pancho pointed ahead to his left. Alex saw movement and aimed his AKMS in the direction of the movement. Pancho and John were aiming in the same direction. Whoever it was, they crouched low as they walked. The figure came closer until Alex recognized it—a goat.

Alex had to keep from laughing out loud. He was sure Pancho and John wanted to laugh, too. Keeping their silence, they resumed their patrol to the village. As they passed around a berm, the indistinct outline of the village came into view.

Continuing forward, they reached another berm—this one was just one hundred yards east of the village. Alex signaled for Pancho and John to stay behind while he went in to rendezvous with Leila. He left his cumbersome backpack with them so he could move more freely.

Alex kept low until he neared the edge of the village and dropped to a low crawl, which he continued until he reached Leila's house. A neighborhood dog barked. It was times like this that Alex hated dogs. Alex peered through Leila's back window—the curtain was closed and he couldn't see inside. He gave the coded knock: two knocks. No answer. *Is she asleep? Is she even here? Is this a trap?* He gave the coded knock again. Two knocks came back. He knocked four times. Now the window opened, and he recognized her. Leila looked even better than her picture.

He crawled through the window. Inside, he began searching the house.

"There is no one else here," Leila said quietly.

Alex continued with the search. He didn't know her well enough to take her word for it. It was a small, modestly furnished two-bedroom house. After clearing the house, rather than make noise by speaking, he broke squelch on his radio once, notifying Pancho and John that it was clear for them to come in. Alex stood guard, watching both the inside and outside of the house.

"Where is Danny?" she asked.

Alex hesitated. "He couldn't make it."

"But he said he was coming."

"He wanted to," Alex said.

"Something terrible happened?"

Alex wasn't sure what to say. He hadn't seen Danny die, but he knew he was dead. Alex didn't know how close Leila was to Danny. The only words that came out were "I'm sorry."

She turned her head away.

Pancho and John arrived. Alex let them in through the front door. With the three large men in the small house, the place became even smaller. Alex looked at his watch—it was already morning. Leila took them into a vacant room. "You can keep your things here and sleep today," she said quietly. "There is not enough dark left for me to take you to the chemical weapons lab now, but when evening comes again, I will take you."

The three SEALs stashed their gear in the room, then played rock, paper, scissors to see who'd stay awake for the first watch. John lost. Alex was tempted to volunteer to take the watch anyway because he was still too keyed up, but he knew John wouldn't go for it, so he stayed silent. Pancho collapsed and was snoring inside of a minute.

John went into the kitchen with Leila while Alex made himself comfortable on the floor. He could see the kitchen clearly through the open door. He half closed his eyes and focused on his breathing.

"Would you like a drink?" Leila asked.

"Water, please," John said. Alex thought he wouldn't mind a

martini, but he didn't need it dulling his senses now. And alcohol
would just make him piss, which would dehydrate him before the
mission.

Leila removed a pitcher of water from the refrigerator and filled
two cups. She sat down to drink with him. "I am sorry my English
is not good."

"Your English is great," John said. "How come you speak so fluently?"

She smiled. "It is not great. My mother liked English and she
taught me. When I was a high school student, I studied in the United
States as an exchange student for a year."

"Where?"

"Sacramento."

"That's great for just one year."

"Later, I majored in English at California State University."

"Wow," John said.

Alex rolled his eyes. No wonder John was single.

"It took me six years to graduate." She laughed.

"Maybe that's why your English is so good."

"I am embarrassed. It should be better."

"Two rooms but you live alone," John said. "Is that common
here?"

"No."

Alex wanted John to ask why, but John apparently decided to let
it drop.

After nearly a minute of silence, Leila explained: "The local
newspaper wrote a false article about my husband—saying he wanted
to overthrow the government. One day when he picked my son up
from high school, some agents abducted them. I tried everything
I could and asked the few people I knew for help. The authorities
released my son, but he had received such serious head injuries that
later he died. My husband remained in prison, and they tortured
him to death."

"I'm sorry," John said. His voice was quiet and Alex had to strain to hear.

"It is okay," Leila said.

"Did you ever find out why the newspaper wrote the false article?"

"It was a *basiji.*"

Alex understood. In 1979, Ayatollah Khomeini established a militia called Basij. Its members, *basiji,* were infamous for enforcing morals and obedience to the government.

"Reserve members do not get paid. Full members are paid. The special members are paid to be part of the Basij and Revolutionary Guard. He is a reserve member. His name is Emamali Naqdi."

Alex started to get up, but stopped. John was leaning across the table. He held Leila's hand in his.

"Why'd he target your family?" John asked.

"When my husband and I went out, the basiji man stared at me—he made me feel so uncomfortable, but my husband told me not to worry about it, so I did not worry. He looked at my husband with an evil eye, but my husband ignored him, too. The basiji disappeared for a couple of weeks. I thought it was finished. Then my husband was taken away. After my husband died, the basiji reappeared, watching my house late at night. Sometimes he just stood outside; other times he sat in his red Chinese SUV—he'd watch my house for hours. I reported it to the police, but they said that because I was living alone, he was protecting me, and they told me I should be careful not to irritate authorities."

"Didn't you have family or friends who could help you?"

"We had just moved here for my husband's work—we had only a few people. Two helped me free my son, but they were afraid to help my husband."

"And you hold your government responsible for what happened to your husband and son?"

"Yes. I love Iran, but I hate the government. It is not just what happened to me; it is what happened to so many other Iranians." She paused.

Alex understood her motivation, but he wondered if he could ever turn on his own government like that. Maybe if it was killing his family and friends and a theocracy, but luckily, the United States was still just a regular, messed-up democracy.

"Why do you do what you do?" she asked John.

"It's a long story," John said.

"We have time."

Alex tuned John out, thinking about his own reasons. It went back to when he was in high school. There was a man who had a hard time holding a job or connecting to society. He blamed the government for all his own shortcomings. One day, he blew up a post office. Both his grandfather and sister Sarah were killed in the explosion. It was an act of terrorism. Didn't matter what color the man's skin was or what god he believed in, he'd committed an act of terror. From that day on, Alex vowed to take people like that out.

"Not all Iranians are terrorists," Leila said, bringing Alex back to their conversation. "Very few."

"I know," John said. "It's the *few* we came for."

Leila excused herself and retired to her room to get some sleep. He heard her chair scrape across the floor and then the soft padding of her feet. A moment later there was a light thump on the table and the muffled sound of metal on metal. Alex smiled. John was field-stripping his AKMS. It wasn't a cold shower, but it worked.

The sun was just warming the house as the occupants began to stir. Alex stretched, sitting up in the kitchen chair after having taken the last watch. An early morning vehicle drove by outside. Alex thought about the red SUV Leila mentioned, but the vehicle was gone before he could peek out the window.

Leila walked into the kitchen and smiled at him. "I will make you breakfast," she said.

"You don't have to make anything for us," Alex said. "We brought some food."

"It is okay," she said. "I already bought extra groceries, and they will spoil if we do not eat. It has been a while since I have cooked for more than myself."

Alex didn't argue. It would be better than sucking on warm energy gel.

As Leila began preparing breakfast, over village loudspeakers came what Alex hoped was the call to morning prayer—not a call to kill the Americans.

5

Early Thursday morning, Major Khan returned home to Tehran for leave and donned his sheep's clothing. Sometimes he believed he was a sheep, but deep down inside, he knew he was a monster. Knowing what people do to monsters, he maintained an upstanding image in order to survive. At dawn, he said the Fajr prayer, the first of five that Muslims say each day.

Major Khan had breakfast with his wife, Daria; Mohammed, their eleven-year-old son; and Jasmeen, their nine-year-old daughter. His wife and children were excited that he was home. They ate nan flatbread with jam and feta cheese. After breakfast, they stayed at the table and talked.

"Where were you last week, Daddy?" Jasmeen asked.

"Working," Major Khan said. It was true.

"Working where?" she persisted.

"Somewhere special—doing special work for Allah," he said. Questions irritated him, but he'd learned the camouflage of patience.

Jasmeen soon lost interest in asking about his work and talked to her brother. Someday his daughter would learn like her brother and mother not to ask too many questions.

Major Khan's wife was a pious woman who didn't like violence, but she accepted his profession because of its necessity for Islam and

Iran. She knew that much of her husband's work for the Quds Force was secret, but she didn't know he kept secrets within secrets. *If she saw the full monster that I am, she'd surely want to leave me.*

Major Khan's cell phone rumbled. He answered it then listened for a moment before saying, "I'll be right there." Then he hung up.

"Do you have to go to work today?" Mohammed asked.

"I just have a few things to take care of."

The boy frowned. "How can they call it leave when you still have a few things to take care of?"

"I got to eat breakfast with my family. And I'll finish work early and be home for lunch."

"Your father is an important man," Daria said, defending him. "That's why he's so busy."

"Will you play soccer with me after school?" Mohammed asked.

"Yes, I promise." Major Khan kissed his children and wife before heading out the door. They truly seemed to love him, but his love for them was pretense. It had occurred to him that maybe their love was pretense, too.

He left his family and drove fifteen minutes to the Revolutionary Guard base and parked his car outside the Intelligence Division Detention Center. Inside, he checked in.

"The prisoner has been readied for you, sir," the Guard said.

"Yes, I came as soon as I could." Major Khan entered the interrogation room, where a young man with a swollen jaw sat on a chair with his hands tied and eyes blindfolded. In front of him was a small table with a baton on it.

"Good morning," Major Khan said.

The boy said nothing, turning in the direction of his interrogator's voice.

"I am told you're a member of the so-called Arab Spring movement."

"No," the boy said. "I told everyone *no*, but they don't listen."

"I'm listening. People tell me I'm a good listener. Not like the barbarians who brought you here," Khan said.

"Thank you."

"Are you thirsty?" Khan asked.

"Yes."

"Just a moment." Major Khan stepped out of the room and returned with a cup of water. He placed it to the boy's lips and poured slowly.

The boy drank until the cup was empty. "Thank you."

"What is it that you'd like me to know?"

"Pardon?"

"You said that no one listens to you. I'm here for you—to listen."

"I'm just a university student, and I don't have anything to do with the Arab Spring. Three men burst through my door at night, sprayed tear gas in my face, bound me, blindfolded me, punched me, kicked me, and brought me here. They kept asking me about the Arab Spring, but I told them I don't know anything. Then they hit me with a baton. I told them I don't know anything, but they don't believe me."

"I believe you," Khan said.

"You do?"

"Yes."

The boy became silent for a moment. "Can I go?"

"Yes, just as soon as we finish."

"Thank you."

"I know how you feel," Khan said, easing himself against the wall. "When I was your age, there was fierce competition in my neighborhood between religious sects. I was invited to convert from my sect to another—when I didn't, someone told the authorities that I was a spy, and intelligence agents captured me and interrogated me."

"How'd you get free?"

"My family had connections and eventually cleared my name. So you see, I do know how you feel." Major Khan walked behind the boy and removed the boy's shirt until it hung down from around his bound hands.

"What are you doing?" the boy asked.

"I'm making you more comfortable."

"You don't have to. I'm comfortable enough."

"Oh, I listened to what you said, but you didn't listen to what I said."

"I was listening," the teen said.

"Then you heard me say, 'I know how you feel.' I know you're not comfortable."

"But you're not making me more comfortable."

"But I am. You just don't understand. I'm going to teach you how to feel comfortable." With the boy's shirt removed, Major Khan began removing the boy's pants.

"No, please don't."

Now that the boy was nude, Major Khan picked him up out of his chair and leaned him over the table.

"You said you would let me go," the boy said.

"I listened to you, but you weren't listening to me. I said I'd let you go as soon as we finish. I haven't finished teaching you what my interrogator taught me." Major Khan unzipped his trousers.

"Oh, no. Please don't. Why are you doing this?"

"I'm teaching you a tradition so you can pass it down to the next generation." Major Khan dropped his undershorts. He didn't care whether the boy was a member of the Arab Spring or not. Major Khan cared only about liberating his own monster.

The boy screamed.

6

Thursday morning, after Alex's watch, the guys woke and ate breakfast together with Leila. Following breakfast, John showed his Bible to Leila and asked, "Do you mind if I read this?"

"Do you believe in God?"

"Yes. Do you?"

"I did. Before my son and husband were murdered."

"I know someone like that."

"Would that be Alex?" she asked.

John looked at Alex.

"If you all don't mind, I'm going to take a nap," Alex said. He retreated to the bedroom and lay down on the floor next to his kit. The walls were thin because he could still hear Leila.

"How about you?" Leila said.

"Me?" Pancho asked. "I'll believe Him when I see Him. Or, if that's too much, He could make me a believer by rescuing the poor."

"You lose someone, too?" Leila asked.

"No," Pancho said.

"If you do not do this for someone you lost and you don't do this for God, who do you do this job for?"

"John and Alex," Pancho said. "They're my brothers."

"They're not real brothers, are they?"

Pancho chuckled, causing the wall to vibrate. "No, not hardly. I grew up with six brothers, but not these guys."

"Seven boys. It must have been hard for your parents."

"I never knew my father. Rarely saw my mother. Grandma raised us boys in a shack that leaked. She fed us just enough to keep us hungry—did the best she could, and we loved her for it."

"That is why you do this job—to escape poverty?"

"I guess you could say that's part of it. My high school biology class took a trip to Corpus Christi, where I saw a sailor driving a red sports car with a pretty senorita sitting next to him. Later, I found out the Navy fed its sailors as much as they could eat and their ships didn't leak—I immediately signed on the dotted line. I loved being in the Navy, but I missed my brothers. When some SEALs deployed on my ship, I noticed the close bond between them, and I wanted the brotherhood they had."

"I wish I had a brother," she said.

"You do now," Pancho said. "You're part of our family now."

Alex drifted to sleep. He lost track of time until John's voice whispered, "Lunchtime."

Alex sat up, soaked in sweat. Somebody had turned on a fan, but it didn't seem to help. The house had heated up like an oven. It was hard to imagine, but the outside was probably hotter. Alex rose to his feet and walked over to the table, where he sat with the others to eat a thick stew served over rice.

After lunch, the guys helped Leila clear the table and do dishes. Then they sat down in the living room and Alex gave a final brief. Although JSOC hailed Leila as an excellent agent, Alex told her only what she needed to know: tonight she would drive them to a group of dunes southeast of the lab and wait there to extract the SEALs. Alex didn't tell her that they planned to take out the lab tonight, and he didn't tell her they'd be using a nuclear backpack.

7

After the "interrogation session," Major Khan showered. He washed the boy's blood off him, but he didn't feel clean. He donned his sheep's clothing, but he still felt like a monster. He arrived home to find his son waiting with his soccer ball. Major Khan took him outside to play. Major Khan had never shown his son or anyone else in his family his monster—and he never would. He was always careful. Later, they ate dinner as a family. At the end of dinner, his wife asked, "Aren't you going to spend some time with your friends? Aren't they playing cards tonight?"

"Yes."

"Why don't you go. We love having you home, but maybe you should have some time with your friends. They can't play Shelem without you." Shelem was an Iranian card game similar to Spades with a point system like Rook. It was a four-player game with two partners playing against each other.

The children grumbled, wanting to play with their father, but their mother furrowed her eyebrows at them.

"Are you sure?" Major Khan asked.

His wife nodded.

Her kindness made him feel disconnected from the world. The monster in him despised her, but tonight he despised the monster.

"Are you okay?" she asked.

"I'm fine."

"It's okay," Daria whispered. "I know."

Major Khan felt his stomach drop. He stared at her in disbelief.

"It's okay."

"You know?" he asked.

"I know you play Shelem for money." Gambling was illegal because it led men to believe in chance more than Allah. "Be careful."

He kissed her and the kids before he left.

Major Khan drove half an hour to Captain Rapviz's house. Inside, Rapviz greeted Major Khan before escorting him to the "guys' room," where Lieutenant First Class Saeed Saeedi was already seated. Saeedi was the most junior of the men and the most hotheaded.

Next to Lieutenant Saeedi sat a thin man, Captain Nasser Fat'hi. He was a strange one. He ate only one meal a day, but snacked incessantly on pistachios. Although many women adored Pistachio, he could take them or leave them. He wasn't married and never talked about his parents or siblings, if there were any—the Quds Force was his family, and he'd do almost anything for it. He wasn't a particularly violent man, but in the right environment, he could be—and hanging around Lieutenant Saeedi was often the right environment.

It looked like Pistachio and Lieutenant Saeedi would be partners in this game, so Major Khan sat across from Rapviz.

In the middle of the table sat a *galyan*, an Iranian hookah. Four mouthpieces decorated with sapphires connected to four hoses adorned with silk that led to a colorful pottery jar filled with water. A crystal pipe, held in place by a lid on the jar, rose from the water up to a bowl of sweetened tobacco. Above the tobacco sat a container of charcoal. Rapviz lit the charcoal. Because Major Khan was senior, Rapviz motioned for him to take the first drag.

As Major Khan inhaled through a sapphire-covered mouthpiece, he dragged air from the charcoal through the tobacco, vaporizing it. The smoke descended the crystal pipe into the water, which bubbled, cooling the smoke before releasing it into the space between the water and the water jar lid. The smoke continued through the hose to Major Khan's mouthpiece, then into his lungs. Even though he hadn't inhaled a second time, smoke pulled from the tobacco, via the water, to his lips again. Normally a smoke relieved him, but the burden of his monster weighed too heavily. He invited the others to join him. They smoked through their individual mouthpieces.

Rapviz dealt the cards and they played Shelem while smoking. The four joked around while betting their money. Pistachio cracked pistachios in his mouth and spit the shells in a plastic cup. At first Pistachio and Lieutenant Saeedi were winning. Lieutenant Saeedi bubbled like a giddy schoolboy. His emotions were easy to read, which made him easy to be around when things were going well. However, as the evening progressed, Pistachio and Lieutenant Saeedi began to lose. Lieutenant Saeedi didn't care much about money, but he did care about how he looked to others, and he hated looking like a loser.

Lieutenant Saeedi threw his cards down on the table. "This game sucks."

Pistachio complained. "Hey, what're you doing? We were having a good game of cards."

"It isn't a good game."

"Then what is a good game?" Major Khan asked.

Lieutenant Saeedi looked frustrated. Now he was losing even more face by not answering. "Russian roulette," he blurted.

"That's not a good game," Pistachio said.

Major Khan and Rapviz said nothing.

"Rapviz, what do you think?" Lieutenant Saeedi asked.

"Whatever you guys want to do," Rapviz said.

Lieutenant Saeedi mocked Rapviz: "Whatever you guys want to do. You're always so yellow-bellied, you never have a thought of your own." Although many Quds Force commandos were more concerned with skill than rank, Lieutenant Saeedi took the ethos to the extreme. While running death squads in Iraq, he butted heads with an incompetent superior officer. The next day, the officer was found dead—the official report said the superior officer was killed in action, but most people believed Lieutenant Saeedi killed him. Saeedi never confirmed or denied the rumor. Because he was the son of a powerful general, officers were hesitant to investigate. If Saeedi had kept his nose clean, he would've been promoted to captain like Rapviz and Pistachio—a constant source of irritation for Lieutenant Saeedi, but even Lieutenant Saeedi's powerful father couldn't help his son get promoted.

Pistachio put his hand on Lieutenant Saeedi's shoulder. "Relax. Have a smoke and relax."

"I want to play Russian roulette. Are you going to play with me or not, Rapviz?"

"Whatever you want," Rapviz said.

"I want to play Russian roulette."

"This is crazy," Pistachio said. "Don't."

"Hey, I'm not talking to you," Lieutenant Saeedi snapped at Pistachio. "Rapviz is a grown man. He can speak for himself. Go get that revolver of yours, Rapviz."

Pistachio shook his head. "Don't get your gun, Rapviz."

Rapviz left the room.

Lieutenant Saeedi turned to Major Khan and said, "You going to play Russian roulette with us, sir?"

Major Khan didn't like the way he said "sir," filled with envy and hate. They were friends, but now Lieutenant Saeedi was using Major Khan's rank as a way to manipulate him into proving his friendship over rank, but it didn't matter what Lieutenant Saeedi felt or said because Major Khan always did what he wanted to do anyway. Major Khan hated his own monster, hated himself, and in a rare moment of clarity, wanted to die. He verbally threw Saeedi's rank back in his face: "That's the smartest thing you've said all evening, Lieutenant. Of course I'd like to play Russian roulette."

"That's what I like about you," Lieutenant Saeedi said nervously. "You always say what you think." He said the words like he only half believed them. Of course, Major Khan knew the words were nonsense. Lieutenant Saeedi liked to hear only the things he agreed with, and Major Khan told him only a fraction of what was on his mind.

Rapviz returned with the revolver—and a bullet.

"Okay, let's get this game started," Lieutenant Saeedi said.

Major Khan saw a slight tremble in the corner of Lieutenant Saeedi's lips and smelled falseness in Saeedi's bravado.

"Okay, you're all badasses," Pistachio said. "Now put the gun away and let's play Shelem."

"I'll go first," Rapviz said. "Major Khan will go second. Lieutenant Saeedi will go last. Then we'll start again with me."

Major Khan calmly nodded.

Lieutenant Saeedi paused before nodding.

"There are no winners in Russian roulette," Pistachio said, trying to reason with them, but the boulder had already been pushed off the cliff and it was about to hit the ground.

Rapviz slid the bullet into one of the six chambers and spun the cylinder. Then he pressed the barrel to the side of his head, turning his head so that if the bullet fired it wouldn't exit the other side of his head and hit one of the guys or someone elsewhere in the house. He squeezed the trigger, causing the hammer to cock back until it slammed forward. *Bang!* His brains splattered across the floor, and he slumped in his chair.

"Allahu akbar!" Pistachio exclaimed. "Look what you did, Saeedi!"

"Me?!" Lieutenant Saeedi defended himself. "Rapviz spun the cylinder! Why'd he have to stop the cylinder on the bullet chamber?!"

"It was random! I'm not going to clean up Rapviz's brains!"

"I'll clean up his brains!" Lieutenant Saeedi snapped. "Give me a rag!"

Major Khan stared coldly. *I deserved to die more than anyone. Why couldn't it be me? It should've been me. Allah wants to torture me by making me stay in this world.*

8

At 2200 hours, Alex and Pancho stood in the main room of Leila's house wearing Iranian men's clothing. John and Leila each wore a black burqa, the Islamic women's garment, disguising them from head to toe.

Leila smiled at John. "Why are you wearing a burqa?"

John ignored her.

"There are not many blacks in Iran, but your skin is not so dark, and it's difficult to see at night."

"My father was African-American and Cajun, and my mother was French," John said. "And I'm not gay. I just think it's the best disguise."

"You are an interesting person," she said. "I asked you the other night why you do what you do, and you told me about the world as it is. But you didn't tell me what made you join."

John said nothing. He was a private person, especially with people he hardly knew.

"Should I tell her, or do you want to?" Pancho said.

John glared at Pancho, then turned to Leila. "I was reading poetry to a friend when her boyfriend showed up," he explained. "He was a control freak with a temper. The guy wigged out, went to his truck, and came back with a gun. He fired at us, so I picked up a chair and threw it at him, stunning him. Then I picked up another chair and killed him in self-defense. After that, I couldn't live in that town anymore, so I joined the Navy. At boot camp, our company commander made us take the SEAL physical screen test—I was the only one who passed. So I figured maybe my destiny was to become some sort of modern-day Paladin."

"What happened to your friend?" Leila asked.

"One of the bullets from her boyfriend's gun killed her."

"I am sorry." She put her hand on his shoulder.

John covered his face with the veil (*niqab*). Leila did, too.

Carrying their kit and an extra tank of water to keep in the vehicle, the SEALs and Leila left the house, walked through the darkness, and loaded into her car. It looked like a Peugeot with wide off-road tires and heightened suspension. Leila sat in the driver's seat and Pancho rode shotgun. Alex sat behind Leila with John next to him. The guys secured their doors, but Alex's wouldn't lock. "How do you lock this?" he asked.

"Lock is broken," Leila said. She started the engine—it purred. *Great, we're riding in a pussycat with a broken door.* When she stepped on the accelerator, the vehicle sucked Alex back into his seat. *I'm beginning to like this cat.* In spite of its power, the vehicle ran quietly.

Alex reminded Leila to exit Abadi Abad from the southeast so if anyone followed them, the followers wouldn't immediately know the Outcasts' true direction. Pancho kept a lookout ahead, Alex watched their left and right flanks, and John kept an eye on the rear.

Pancho asked, "What kind of car is this?"

"Samand," Leila said. "It is an Iranian car. *Samand* is a fast horse."

"This doesn't look like an average sedan," Pancho said.

"Danny customized it."

Just after the Outcasts left the village, John said, "We've got company."

Leila looked in her rearview mirror. "It is him."

"Him?" Alex asked.

She repeatedly glanced in the rearview mirror. "It is the basiji."

"Are you sure?" Alex asked.

"Yes. I think."

"You think. So it might be someone else."

"What should I do?"

"Just keep driving normal. Ignore him."

Leila did.

Alex glanced behind. The vehicle's lights came closer. Then the driver honked the horn and flashed the lights. *Not good.* As the vehicle neared, Alex could see it was a red SUV. The SUV pulled up beside them on the left, still honking and flashing its lights. The driver leaned out and shouted something in Farsi.

"It is him. He wants us to stop," Leila translated.

"Stop, but don't turn your car engine off."

She slowed to a stop. Leila kept the engine running. She seemed to be keeping her cool.

The basiji stalker stopped his vehicle, too, turned off the engine, stepped out, and approached Leila. Two other occupants remained in the vehicle. The basiji stalker was a handsome man. His eyes squinted at the SEALs, then at Leila.

Alex readied his AKMS rifle. He knew his Teammates were doing the same. A great SEAL op often didn't involve shooting. Usually a perfect op was one where the SEALs crept in, accomplished their mission, and sneaked out without anyone knowing. If this guy sucked them into a firefight before accomplishing their mission, the SEALs might not have enough ammo to reach the target, let alone enough ammo for going home. *This is looking less and less like a perfect op.*

Although Leila remained calm, the basiji stalker became louder and louder. He shook his fist. The calmer Leila remained, the more infuriated he became. The stalker moved over to Alex's window and started shouting at him and waving his AK-47. *I don't have time for this.*

The basiji stalker pulled on Alex's door handle, opening it.

"Leila, keep the engine running," Alex said. "John, come with me."

The basiji stalker's jaw dropped at the sound of Alex speaking English.

Alex fired a single shot up through the basiji stalker's jaw that burst out the top of his head.

The basiji stalker collapsed in the sand, and Alex fired a second shot in the stalker's head before walking toward the other vehicle. Alex had no idea who was in the red SUV, but they shouldn't have been out so late, and they shouldn't have been hanging out with the basiji stalker. *If you mix with crimson, you become crimson.*

The basiji stalker probably had the vehicle keys with him, and his friends couldn't drive away. Both were in the backseat. They could've stepped out of the vehicle and tried to make a run for it, but they didn't. If the one closest to Alex and John were armed, he could've shot at them through the window, but he began rolling it down.

Alex and John walked forward, shooting through the window at the silhouettes in the SUV. Alex fired so fast, it sounded as if he were shooting two-round bursts, but he controlled each shot. Although Alex fired fast, John fired faster. Alex pinpointed the bodies, but John pinpointed the pinpoints. The basiji's friends hip-hopped on the backseat like street dancers on cocaine. When the two SEALs reached the vehicle, the bodies were still twitching. Alex and John administered the coup de grace, each putting one final bullet in a head. The basiji's friends still held their AK-47s in their hands. Instead of shooting through the window, they'd tried to save it by rolling it down; but in the end, they lost the window and their lives.

Alex and John returned to Leila's vehicle. As soon as Alex and John were seated, Leila didn't wait for them to shut the doors; she sped away. Alex and John closed their doors.

"Take us back to the village, then exit from the southwest," Alex said. "That might confuse whoever tries to figure out who did this."

Pancho navigated with his GPS, giving Leila directional headings. Leila returned to Abadi Abad, then drove southwest out of the village. No one followed. When they passed beyond sight of the village, she headed off-road, west for a few kilometers, before driving completely off-road to their true course to the northwest. Leila drove carefully over spots of soft sand and around dunes, ravines, and other obstacles. She kept a steady speed for most of three hours until they arrived at their insertion site—five klicks away from their target. Leila parked in front of a group of dunes. Over time the wind had blown sand into piles that stood more than two stories tall, blocking the sight and sound of the Outcasts from the chemical lab compound. The SEALs stepped out and covered Leila inside her vehicle with a camouflage net. For a moment, Alex felt as if he were wrapping her in a death shroud. Now wasn't the time for feelings. He put his feelings in a box and closed it. Now was the time for killing.

The SEALs shed their Iranian garb—underneath they wore their cammies. They put the Iranian garb in their backpacks. John kept his backpack nuke and buried his main backpack in the side of a dune. Alex and Pancho buried their backpacks, too. They would need to move fast, and they didn't need the extra weight and bulk hindering their movements. They patrolled around the dunes and saw the lab, a complex of five multistoried buildings. Hunched over to make their profiles small, the SEALs patrolled toward the lab. Pancho signaled everyone to stop. They did. Then Pancho lay on the ground. Alex and John did, too. The sound of helicopter blades beat the air—probably coming from a helo pad inside the compound. Alex took out a pair of compact binoculars and scanned the area. He couldn't see the helo, but a guard stood inside one of the buildings facing Abadi Abad. Alex wanted to get near the complex's center to plant the bomb—he didn't want any reinforced underground floors surviving because they planted the bomb too far out. Alex put his binoculars away and signaled for Pancho to take them from the southwest corner to the southern edge.

The SEALs patrolled around to the southern edge and dropped down again. Alex looked through his binoculars. He couldn't see any guards in their direction. He motioned for Pancho to take them forward. They stood and crept forward.

Abruptly, a helo lifted from the lab complex and flew toward them with its floodlight brightening the ground below it. The Outcasts dropped to the ground and froze. The helo flew over them before turning and flying northwest. It continued northwest until it disappeared.

Alex tapped Pancho on the shoulder. He rose to his feet with Alex, followed by John. They resumed their trek and continued until reaching an earthen wall surrounding the compound. The three men climbed over it. Inside, they dropped to the ground and crawled on all fours. The compound floor was made of concrete. They low-crawled, slithering across the concrete like snakes.

All of the buildings were lit on the outside, but some were lit more brightly than others; and there were gaps in the light between buildings, creating shadows for Alex's team to use for cover. They crept in the shadows toward the center.

Suddenly, a siren blared and red lights flashed. *Was Leila captured? Did we trip an alarm? Are they watching us now?* Two armed Revolutionary Guard soldiers ran out of a building toward them. The SEALs stopped, lying flat on the concrete. Alex emptied his mind and imagined himself as concrete, hoping to defeat any sixth sense the soldiers might have. The two soldiers kept running, but they didn't aim their weapons in the SEALs' direction. One of the soldiers almost stepped on Alex's head as he ran past, but they continued on and entered another building. *Maybe we're okay.*

Then a third soldier came running out of the same building as the first two, heading in their direction. Again Alex imagined being concrete, but Pancho was a bigger piece of concrete than Alex, and the soldier tripped over him. The soldier picked himself up to see what he'd tripped over, and looked directly at Pancho. The soldier coughed nervously and raised his weapon in Pancho's direction. Alex, Pancho, and John fired at the soldier, and bullets from their sound-suppressed rifles drilled him back into the ground.

With the noise of the sirens, Alex hoped their shots hadn't been heard. Alex spotted a wooden walkway raised off the ground and dragged the soldier's body toward it while Pancho and John covered him. As Alex stuffed the body under the walkway, it occurred to him that if Leila was still alive, she might have abandoned them. Then it occurred to him: *Two hundred klicks is a long walk to Abadi Abad.*

The SEALs continued until they reached the center of the compound, where Alex noticed a cylindrical metal container standing two stories tall, mounted on a platform several feet off the ground. The two-story tank looked to be twelve feet in diameter. Alex looked at John, who smiled. Alex smiled, too. The space between the ground and the tank was ample for the atomic backpack bomb. While John set the bomb under the tank, Alex and Pancho covered the surrounding area. The same two Iranian soldiers from before exited their building and ran past the Outcasts. More soldiers poured out of the buildings. From the northwest part of the compound, more soldiers drove out in military jeeps and trucks. The soldiers on foot and soldiers in the vehicles spread out into the desert.

John stopped working on planting the nuke and turned around. "We've got three hours before we all end up in a four-mile-high mushroom cloud."

"And if the Revolutionary Guard tamper with the bomb before then?" Pancho asked.

"Boom," John said.

Alex looked at his Rolex watch: 0203 hours. It was time to get the hell out before getting vaporized—literally. The initial fireball would cover much of the lab compound. If Alex and his buddies were still around, they'd become particles of fallout along with everything else.

The Revolutionary Guard swarmed the surrounding desert like

angry ants. Even if the Outcasts succeeded in creeping past all of them, creeping would take hours. Alex and his men could use the uniform of the soldier they killed, but it was too small and that wouldn't disguise all three of them. Alex looked around for other options. His eyes stopped at the northwest, where vehicles had driven out of, probably their motor pool. Alex pointed, and then made a walking gesture toward it.

Pancho led them through shadows and behind walls until they reached the wall surrounding the motor pool. Alex and John stood guard while Pancho jumped up, grabbed the top of the wall, and pulled himself over it, taking a chunk from the top of the wall with him—*maybe it would've been faster if Pancho had walked through the wall*. Alex climbed over next. On the other side, Pancho stood guard as Alex came down. The motor pool sat empty except for a dark olive drab truck. Alex helped stand guard until John joined them. Then the three crept to the truck.

Alex and John stood guard while Pancho tried the door handle on the driver's side to see if it was unlocked. The door came open. Pancho slipped in. Alex checked the passenger side. It was unlocked, too. Alex hopped in and climbed into the back. John rode shotgun.

Because there was no key in the ignition and none hidden nearby, Pancho pulled out his Mission MPF1-Ti knife and flicked open the four-inch titanium blade. He inserted the tip of the blade into the ignition key hole, then used his herculean strength to ram the blade down deep. Then he twisted the handle. Something inside the ignition snapped, and the engine started. The technique was uniquely Pancho's, and Alex doubted he could repeat it.

Fifty yards ahead of their vehicle a barrel-chested man carrying a large wrench walked in front of the gate and faced them. He shouted at the Outcasts but the noise of the engine and the sirens drowned out his voice. Pancho put the vehicle in gear and rolled toward him. The man with the wrench became more animated. Pancho picked up speed. The man with the wrench stood his ground. Gaining more speed, Pancho ran over him. Alex heard only the clang of the wrench hitting the concrete.

Pancho drove out of the lab compound and north into the desert. He stopped, shifted into four-wheel drive, then proceeded. Alex hoped they reached Leila before the Revolutionary Guard. A squad of soldiers on foot walked in Pancho's way, but they must have heard the engine, because they scattered. Pancho drove a wide circle around to the southwest. Alex looked out the back to make sure their tail was clear.

Alex felt anxious about putting the first five hundred yards between them and the nuke. Within that first five hundred yards, the explosion would fry them with second- to third-degree burns and blast them with a hurricane of sand and other debris. The Outcasts passed the first five hundred yards. Now he worried about first-degree burns. They'd have to go another five hundred yards to get out of the danger zone—if his estimates were right.

"Oh, no," Pancho said.

Alex continued watching the rear. "What is it?"

Pancho didn't say anything.

Alex turned. In the distance, near the group of dunes where they had left Leila, a vehicle smoldered, its smoke rising high into the cold night air. Alex felt his heart sink, but he still had to watch their tail, which he did. After Leila lost her son and husband—then Danny's death—it didn't seem fair that she should die, too. *Life isn't fair.* Maybe now she could find peace.

Alex remembered when he and his sister Sarah were kids at his family's home in Annapolis, Maryland. They played in the infinity pool, where the water looked like it extended into the waterfront. Alex and Sarah dove in the pool for coins, shot a polo ball into a float ring, and raced each other the length of the pool. Alex beat her in the crawl and breaststroke, but Sarah, even though she was younger, always swam the butterfly faster. She'd practiced more and although Alex had more power, *smooth is fast.*

Pancho stopped the truck. The guys dismounted. Alex didn't want to see Leila's burned body, but he didn't want to put John through it. It was obvious John and Leila had connected on some level.

"I can do this," Pancho said.

John said nothing, just stared out into the desert.

"I'm coming with you," Alex said, fighting back the images of the day that had changed his life forever.

Alex thought back to when he was a high school senior listening to classical music, Grieg's "The Death of Ase," while sitting in his red Mercedes, an older model handed down to him from his parents. His car idled in the post office's west parking lot while he waited for his grandfather and Sarah to drop off a package. Then the explosion sounded. He couldn't understand what had happened until he saw the smoke. Suddenly it struck him—an explosion. Alex threw open his car door and raced to what was left of the post office building. The smoke was thick. It made his throat gag and his eyes burn. The whole face of the post office had blown out across the north parking lot, past the road, and into an empty lot. Bricks and debris blanketed the ground. Alex saw a severed arm but no body nearby. He forgot about Grandpa. All he could think about was finding Sarah. He searched the bodies—pregnant woman, baby, and others: bruised, broken, and bloodied. Somebody cried for help, but it wasn't Sarah. A female postal worker with blackened face and torn, blackened clothes limped out from what was left of the building. A man beside Alex was helping survivors. Alex found Sarah lying on rubble with her arm pinned under a section of the fallen roof. Alex tried to pull the roof off, but it was too heavy. He tried to pull her out from under it but couldn't. "Sarah, I'm going to get you out of here. Just hang on, okay?" But Sarah didn't respond. "Sarah, can you hear me? You're going to be okay." No answer. He pulled at the ceiling again, but it didn't budge. He'd never felt so helpless in his life. *Where are the firefighters? Where are the police?* "Somebody help me!" he called.

Since that time, Alex had cried out the sadness. In the empty space that remained came rage, something he didn't share with the world—he reserved that for the terrorists. Alex couldn't do anything about the domestic terrorist who'd killed Sarah before committing suicide, but Alex could do something about other terrorists—killing them before they shed innocent blood. The hunt had consumed his life.

"She isn't here," Pancho said.

"Where is she?" John asked. He'd followed them to the car.

"Damn good question," Alex said.

9

Alex searched the surrounding area, but there was no sign of her. "Leila," he called, but no answer came. He wasn't being stealthy, and he didn't care. Part of him hoped the Revolutionary Guard would come, so he could unleash his rage. "Leila!" he shouted.

"Alex?"

He looked in the direction of the voice.

From beneath a pile of sand on the side of a dune Leila scrambled to her feet. The dirt poured off her, and she stumbled toward them.

"Are you okay?" John asked.

"I am fine," Leila said.

"What made you hide in the dunes?"

"I heard engines and voices, and I saw how well your bags were hidden. Then I looked at how poorly I was hidden."

"What did the Guards do when they found your vehicle empty?"

"They threw some firebombs on it before they even checked if anyone was inside."

"Thank you for not leaving us."

"Thank you for not leaving me."

The SEALs retrieved their backpacks buried in the side of the dune. Nothing in Leila's vehicle seemed salvageable. Alex hated losing their backup supply of water. If their truck broke down, they could all dehydrate.

They piled into the truck, its engine still running.

As Pancho drove them south, a small Revolutionary Guard jeep came around the dunes and headed straight at them, flashing its lights and honking.

"What does he want?" Alex asked.

"Probably selling something," Pancho replied.

"Not interested," John said.

Pancho picked up speed, heading straight for the jeep.

"What is this called?" Leila asked excitedly. "In English what do you call it? Chicken. Yes, this is a game of chicken."

"This is a different game," Pancho said. "It's called Rules of the Road. The biggest truck rules the road."

John laughed, sucking air through his nose.

Pancho's joke wasn't funny, but John's laugh was. "Buckle up," Alex warned Leila as he fastened his seat belt.

She did.

Pancho plowed head-on into the jeep. The jeep's passenger, who looked like a high-ranking officer, flipped out of his seat and landed on the jeep's hood, and the driver's head smacked the steering wheel, knocking him out. The front of the jeep folded like an accordion.

Pancho stomped the accelerator. The truck pushed the little jeep forward. The officer fell off the crumpled hood before the jeep veered backward out of Pancho's way. Then Pancho zigzagged through the desert to throw off anyone who might try to follow their tracks later. They had cleared the danger zone of the nuke, but they still had to travel several more klicks before they were safe from radiation.

As Pancho drove through the darkness, Alex undid his seat belt so he could turn around more easily and watch their rear. The desert air was cold. Leila took off her seat belt, then moved closer to John. Alex did his best not to smile. *Good for them.* She put her head on John's shoulder. *Maybe she's tired. Maybe she's lonely.* She was attractive, and John was a good man. Alex thought about pulling John aside when he had a chance to remind him they still had a mission to accomplish, but he doubted John had forgotten.

After about ten klicks, the truck stopped. The rear wheels spun in the soft sand, but the truck went nowhere. "I liked Leila's driving better," John said.

Alex couldn't see Pancho's face, but he imagined he was giving John a dirty look.

Leila woke. "What is wrong?"

"We're stuck."

She crawled into the back and rummaged around until she found a shovel. Then she got out and dug sand out from in front of a rear wheel. The SEALs got out. Pancho grabbed the shovel and took over the digging.

"Could someone get the sand mats?" she asked.

Alex went into the truck and looked in the back, where he found two wide strips of metal with holes in them. He brought them out and laid them next to the vehicle.

"I'm sorry," she said. "I need two ropes."

John went into the truck and came back with twenty-five feet of rope. "If this is long enough, I can cut it in two," he said.

"Yes, two of those would be perfect," she said.

John cut the rope in two.

Pancho had finished digging the sand out from in front of both rear wheels.

Leila laid one of the sand mats down in front of one rear wheel, and Alex laid the other sand mat down in front of the other wheel. Then she tied one end of a rope through one of the holes in a sand mat and the other end of the rope to the truck's rear bumper. Next, John did the same to the other mat. "Okay, we are ready to go," she said.

Pancho put away the shovel and the four of them returned to their seats in the truck. Pancho drove over the sand mats and beyond.

Behind the bumper trailed the two sand mats tied to the bumper, skiing over the dirt. "When you a hit hard stretch of land, you stop, and I will get the sand mats and rope," Leila said.

The truck stopped. "This sand is too soft," Leila said.

"I didn't mean to stop," Pancho said.

"You have to pick up speed to third gear, but not too fast."

"I was trying."

John laughed, sucking air through his nose.

Leila started to get out of the vehicle, but Alex told her, "I got this." He grabbed the shovel, dug out the rear wheels, then put the sand mats in front of the rear wheels. Alex returned inside the truck and gave his best Donald Trump impersonation: "Pancho, you're fired." He turned to Leila. "Leila, drive us out of here."

John laughed again.

"Shut up," Pancho said.

John laughed more.

Leila drove until she hit a hard stretch of land and stopped. Alex pulled in the sand mats and Leila resumed the drive to Abadi Abad.

They had traveled sixty klicks from the lab when the black sky became dark gray and the air felt slightly warmer. The truck stopped. "What're we stopping for?" Alex asked.

"We are out of gas," Leila said. "This truck must have a leak."

"I was looking forward to a hundred-forty-klick walk through the hottest desert on earth," Pancho said.

"I wasn't," John said.

Pancho smiled.

"Can you fix the leak, Pancho?" Alex asked.

"Probably," Pancho said. "Then what? You hiding a spare tank of gas up your ass?"

Although the hike sounded impossible, Alex was happy to be out of the danger zone of the nuke.

Boom! The earth shook. Alex thought it was an earthquake, but he looked at his watch: 0503 hours. "Whoa," he said.

The four hurried out of the truck and looked toward the sound of the explosion. A mushroom cloud rose in the air above the biological weapons lab. It was a beautiful and terrible sight.

"Orgasmic," Pancho said. He high-fived Alex, then high-fived John.

Alex smiled at John, who smiled back. Out of the corner of his eye, Alex noticed Leila standing there, staring at the mushroom cloud. She wasn't smiling. "Was that a bomb?" she asked.

Alex thought before answering. "Yes."

"Is the lab destroyed?"

"Yes."

"What about the people?"

"The people, too. There's nothing left."

She seemed to be pondering what she'd just participated in. She'd probably never given anyone a death sentence before, and now she'd helped wipe out a whole biological weapons compound and all its personnel.

"Will there be survivors? I mean, will anyone suffer?"

Alex didn't see the point in sugarcoating it. "No survivors, no suffering."

"No one should have to suffer like I suffered. Not even my enemies," Leila said.

"Well, now we don't have to worry about them coming to look for us," Pancho said.

"I'm thinking we should rest today and do our traveling at night," Alex said.

John nodded.

"Sounds like a plan," Pancho said.

Alex looked around. They were in a sea of sand with occasional dips and swells that the wind had blown ripples into like waves— their vessel dead in the water. "This truck sticks out."

"Like a turd in a bowl of cereal," Pancho said.

"Don't see much in the way of shelter from the heat," John said.

"The truck sticks out, but right now I'm more concerned about the heat than the Revolutionary Guard."

"I agree," Alex said. "We'll lose water trying to stay hydrated if we lose the shade of the truck."

The SEALs took turns standing watch and sleeping. It was common for them to sleep during the day and work at night. They were living the vampire lifestyle long before vampires became popular.

The sun crawled up the desert sky, raising the temperature. Sweat covered Alex. He couldn't survive long without water. Before becoming thirsty, he drank. If he waited until he was thirsty, his body would already be dehydrating. Thirst was a late warning signal. The heat continued to increase.

Alex imagined he was in a sauna at a country club—he was actually enjoying it. Ironically, Leila seemed to have the most trouble with the heat, but she didn't complain. From her backpack, she pulled out a civilized breakfast of nan with jam. In contrast, Alex sucked energy gel from a tube.

The Lut Desert was too hot for plants or other living organisms. In the summer, scientists had left uncovered sterilized milk out and it stayed sterile—the desert was too hot even for bacteria.

The sun shone directly above them, taking away the shade from the side of the truck and threatening to kill the four of them. Alex dug out a trench under the truck. He lay down in the trench—it was cool. Soon the others dug trenches and joined him.

Later, as the sun set and air cooled, Alex and his team prepped themselves for the first leg of their 140-kilometer trek. The easy thing about leading SEALs was that a leader didn't have to tell them everything to do. The difficult thing about leading SEALs was that they ate weak leaders for breakfast.

"We good to go?" Alex asked.

They nodded.

"John, you okay to watch out for Leila?" Alex asked. "Leila, you follow Pancho, and I'll be right behind you." With those words, Pancho and John understood that if she did something to betray them, John would be the one to put a bullet through her skull. Leila wouldn't know unless she betrayed them, and then it would be too late.

"She's fine," John said. He didn't sound happy.

"I'll keep an eye out for her," Alex said.

"I am fully capable of taking care of myself," Leila said.

John sighed. "We know, but I'll keep an eye on you all the same."

"Let's go," Alex said. They moved out in patrol formation with John bringing up the rear.

The air became cool—then cold. Alex started to shiver. Pancho picked up the pace, and he warmed up. They continued a couple of hours until Leila slowed down significantly. She was their slowest member and the SEALs could move only as fast as she could. Although Alex didn't want to, he stopped for Leila to take a break, drink some water, and make sure her feet were okay. Not only did they lose time and momentum, but Alex started shivering again. John and Leila shivered, too, but Pancho seemed fine. Leila repeatedly apologized for slowing them down, but the SEALs were patient with her—anything else but patience would wear her down and slow them even more. They could leave her in the desert, but that would be inhumane.

Leila stood up, ready to move again. The four continued through the evening, hours of walking, with short breaks in between. When they walked, Alex was happy; when they took breaks, Alex exercised patience. In the morning, Alex checked his GPS. They'd covered forty kilometers and had one hundred more to go. It was discouraging to think they hadn't even covered one-third of the distance, so Alex stopped thinking about it.

Pancho gave Leila a pep talk. Meanwhile, Alex and John talked alone.

"What do you think the odds are that we'll make it out of this?" John asked.

"What do you think the odds are?"

"Not good. What do you think the odds are that Leila will make it?"

Alex shook his head.

10

On the third day, the silhouettes of soldiers faced Alex and his crew. The SEALs readied their weapons, but as they neared the soldiers, they realized it was just a sandy rock formation. The SEALs and Leila were dirty, ragged, and broken down. They dug their trenches in the shadows of the sand soldiers. As the four lay in their trenches, sweat permeated their skin, soaking their clothes. Wind blew across their bodies and evaporated their sweat. More sweat leaked through their pores to cool their dry, burning skin. Then the wind removed the sweat again. Alex's team drank more water to stay hydrated. The vicious cycle continued, robbing them of precious fluids.

In the afternoon, Alex's head hurt. It was a burden to stand up and walk away from the group to take a piss, but he did. His piss had decreased in volume and was dark. He was dehydrating. Alex drank the last of his water before returning to his trench to rest.

Leila was quiet but seemed okay.

"Pancho, if you hadn't rammed that jeep head-on, we'd be in Abadi Abad by now," John complained.

Pancho laughed. "You seemed to think it was a good idea at the time."

"Now do you think it was a good idea?"

"Are you upset?"

"Of course I'm upset," John said. "We're walking across a desert."

"I thought Jesus did that," Pancho said.

"You're thinking of Moses," John said, "and that's only because he was leading the Jews out of Egypt. If he'd had a perfectly good truck he wouldn't have rammed into one of the pharaoh's chariots."

Pancho laughed.

Alex didn't have the energy to break them up, but for now their bickering wasn't straying into anything that would lead to a brawl. The more they dealt with dehydration, however, the more that could change.

In the evening, Alex's shivering came more quickly and violently, and he was having difficulty thinking. John shivered the most violently. It was a burden to talk, so Alex just stared at Pancho. Pancho got the message and they moved out. All four of them moved in slow motion, but the cold was killing John, who had the least body fat. When John stumbled the first time, Alex stopped the patrol and took a look at him. John's face had become pale and his lips were blue.

Pancho tried to offer John his jacket, but John refused.

"Don't stop," John pleaded. His teeth chattered. "Gotta stay warm."

"We won't stop," Alex promised. True to his promise, Alex continued without stopping. Leila would just have to suck it up—and she did. Alex had to be careful to look back at John and slow down for him occasionally so they didn't leave him bumbling around in the desert night alone. In spite of traveling nonstop, their pace had slowed, and they traveled only thirty kilometers—thirty more to go.

On the fourth day, at noon, Alex knew he should leave his trench to take a leak, but no piss was left in him. Just the small walk to relieve his bladder would wind him, so he was happy not to have to move. Alex felt his heart race. His mouth was dry and his tongue had swollen. He wanted to puke, but he couldn't afford to lose the body liquids. Alex also wanted a drink, but he had no more water, and he didn't want to take valuable water from the others—who were probably worse off than he was. He had known the desert was more deadly than the Revolutionary Guard, but it occurred to him now that the desert might succeed in killing him.

Out of the corner of Alex's eye, he noticed Pancho stand up, then fall down. Pancho stood up again. Alex caught a glimpse of Pancho's eyes, which seemed far away. Pancho stumbled away from the group like he was going to take a leak. Then Pancho yelled. Alex first thought that a snake had bitten him, but nothing lived in the desert. Leila stood and walked over to Pancho. Before she reached him, he fell. "Pancho, are you okay?" she asked.

Pancho was silent for a moment. Suddenly he broke out laughing, but not the earth-rumbling Pancho laughter—this laughter was feeble. He was delirious. He had the most meat on his bones, so he heated up the fastest and the dehydration affected him the worst.

Leila encouraged Pancho to stand up. Then she helped him return to his trench. She gave him a drink of her water. Alex thought Leila must be part camel not to have drunk all her water yet, but he was grateful to her for helping out Pancho. Alex felt embarrassed about feeling so weak and sorry for himself that he hadn't been the one to help Pancho.

Alex looked out across the desert and spotted water. Then he realized it was only a mirage. The heat reflecting off the surrounding sand seared his eyes, so Alex reached into his backpack and pulled out an Iranian shirt. Then he sank back into his trench, closed his eyes, and covered his face with the shirt.

Later the sun disappeared, giving everyone relief. Alex and his team were slow in getting up, but John started shivering, so Alex and the others hastened to move out. Even though they hurried, they moved like turtles.

The cool air, their weakened condition, and uneven terrain all worked against Alex—his left ankle twisted and a horrible pain shot through his body. Alex didn't think he'd broken it, and he hoped he hadn't torn ligaments—maybe he'd only strained them. He limped.

"You okay, chief?" John whispered.

Alex's swollen tongue and deteriorating physical condition turned talking into torture. Alex saved his breath by ignoring John. Hot pain throbbed up Alex's leg.

They pressed forward into the night.

Pancho stumbled, Leila slowed, and Alex continued to feel the pain in his ankle. Alex looked back and saw John shivering more violently—hypothermia. *Shit. At this rate, we're all going to die.*

On the fifth day, the sun had risen and Alex was lying on his back in a trench. *I don't even remember digging this—my grave.* He looked forward to seeing Sarah but realized his anger at God might prevent him from doing so. It was time to make peace, so he said a short prayer in his heart. *God, I'm sorry for being angry at You all these years. I still don't understand why Sarah had to die. I still don't understand Your ways, but I want to be patient. If I survive this, please help me be patient with the things I can't understand. If I don't survive this, please help me see her again. Amen.*

When evening came, somebody said they had ten more kilometers to go. Alex wasn't sure because his GPS was fried and he didn't have the energy to ask Pancho or John, who also had GPSs—and he was too tired to count his paces and record them with knots on parachute cord. The four of them marched through the dark like zombies. At first, Alex's left ankle hurt and he shivered, but after a couple of hours, the pain and the shivering stopped. Alex blacked out, and when he came to, he was walking alone through the desert. The others stopped him.

He couldn't go any farther, and he was sure no one had the strength to carry him.

"Just another kilometer," Leila said.

Alex hadn't realized they were so close. He could walk another kilometer, so he pressed on. As time went on, he complained, but he could manage only a whisper: "We've been walking more than a kilometer."

"Just half a kilometer," Leila said.

Alex figured he could last five hundred yards more, so he forced one foot in front of the other. After a while, he was sure they'd walked more than half a klick.

"Just a little bit farther," Leila said.

Alex realized she was tricking him into pushing forward just a little more. Because he'd persisted this far, he figured he could persist farther. He might not make it all the way to Leila's house, but he wasn't going to give up until he passed out or died—whichever came first.

The sun had begun to brighten the sky, and Alex saw the squat cluster of buildings—Abadi Abad. Maybe he was dreaming it. He continued forward until he reached the village. Pancho led them along the outskirts until they reached Leila's house. After Alex entered her house, he collapsed on the floor. Leila held his head up and gave him water. Alex's mouth and throat were so dried up that he felt like the water was tearing up his insides. Being severely dehydrated, the water gave him cramps, cinching his gut so tight that he passed out. He'd been so focused on his own survival that he'd forgotten about his men—he didn't even know if Pancho and John had survived.

In his unconscious state, Alex's mind began to work overtime. Alex abruptly sat up. "Where are Pancho and John?" he asked.

Leila turned from the kitchen sink and walked to him.

"Where are Pancho and John?" Alex repeated.

Sadness filled her voice: "I'm sorry. Pancho didn't make it."

Alex's soul sank. Maybe Pancho was still alive. "Where's his body?"

"In the back room. I'm sorry."

Alex heard a vehicle stop in front of Leila's house, car doors slam, and voices. "You expecting visitors?"

"No," Leila said.

Alex looked down at his hands—no weapon. "Where's my weapon?" he whispered.

"Behind you."

Alex turned around and grabbed it.

"Is the door locked?"

"Yes."

The front door flew open with a bang. Four Iranian men dressed in plainclothes poured in, wielding pistols.

"Contact front!" Alex yelled. He fired two rounds into the chest of the first man. Beside him, another aimed in Alex's direction, and Alex gunned him down. Meanwhile, the two others fired. Rounds hit the floor next to Alex's face—too many enemy too close firing too fast. Alex picked one off just before a round tore through his right hand. *Shit!* The remaining agent aimed carefully at Alex's head. The agent looked like he was smiling until two bullets struck him above the nose.

Alex turned to see where the bullets had come from. John stood in the hallway. "Thanks, brother," Alex said.

John looked troubled.

"What's wrong?" Alex asked. He followed John's eyes to Leila, who had fallen to the floor. "Leila."

She didn't respond. Blood spread across her blouse like a blooming rose.

With his left hand, Alex felt the carotid artery in her neck for a pulse. There was none. Leila was dead. Alex didn't have time to mourn. He pulled gauze out of the blowout kit in his thigh pocket and bandaged his bleeding hand. The blood soaked through almost immediately. He stood, walked to the sink, grabbed a thin towel, and wrapped it around his wound.

Alex turned back to John.

"We need to get out of here," John said. Suddenly a loud crash sounded from behind John and his forehead exploded. John fell dead on his face.

No! Alex could feel the words, but he couldn't say them. Instead of making his escape out the front door, Alex wanted payback, so he rushed to the guest room. Inside, one Iranian agent stood in the room while another crawled through the window. Holding his AKMS in his left hand, Alex gunned them both down. Alex looked outside for more, but there were none.

The pain in Alex's hand shot through him like bolts of electricity. He donned his backpack and dragged John's and Pancho's bodies out the front door, hoping to find a vehicle nearby. Alex discovered a black Mercedes sedan idling, then loaded Pancho and John into the vehicle before jumping in and speeding off.

Iranian police lights lit up Alex's rear. He stomped on the accelerator. Gunshots blasted through his rear window. Alex wanted to return fire, just to get them off his back, but his right hand was useless, and he needed his left hand to steer. He raised his left knee to steer and grabbed his AKMS with his left hand. Before he could return fire, a bullet struck him in the back of his head. His upper body hunched over the steering wheel and his eyes closed.

Alex opened his eyes and sat up. He was in Leila's living room on the floor and Leila was doing something in the kitchen.

"Where are Pancho and John?" he asked.

"They went out to find a vehicle."

Alex closed his eyes briefly, reflecting on how real the dream was and how close to delirium he must have been. He felt a weight lifted from him, knowing that they were all still alive, but his ankle still hurt when he walked.

He changed into his Iranian clothes. Somebody had already filled Alex's CamelBak with water. As he grabbed a jug full of water, he heard a vehicle drive up near the front door.

Alex checked the door to make sure it was locked and readied his weapon. The door unlocked and a figure stepped inside. Alex aimed. It was Pancho. "Great to see you, too, amigo," Pancho said.

Pancho and John entered the house wearing their Iranian clothes.

"We brought you a Christmas present," John said.

"A car," Alex guessed.

Pancho closed the door. "Ah, you peeked."

"You both got water?" Alex asked.

"We're all filled up," John replied.

"Then let's roll," Alex said.

The SEALs and Leila grabbed their things and exited her house. Outside, an unmarked black Mercedes SUV sat idling. On the roof above the driver's seat sat a single blue police light that appeared removable.

"Leila, I need you to drive," Alex said. Pancho might look less conspicuous as a driver, but if asked questions in Farsi, he wouldn't be able to answer. Besides, Alex was anticipating having to shoot his way out of Abadi Abad, and he wanted both of Pancho's hands on his gun, not on the wheel.

Leila nodded.

The SEALs and Leila loaded their kit into the SUV, then climbed inside with Leila in the driver's seat, Pancho sitting next to her, and Alex and John in the back.

Leila had been driving east for only a minute when a white and green police car turned the corner and followed them. The car didn't flash its lights but continued following.

"We've got a police car behind us," John said.

"Stay calm and turn right at the next intersection," Alex said.

Leila calmly turned right at the next intersection. The police car followed. Fifty yards ahead was what appeared to be a police car parked in the middle of the road.

"No side streets, and we're heading straight for another cop," Pancho said.

"Turn on the police lights and siren," Alex said.

"What does *siren* mean?" Leila asked.

Forty yards.

Pancho looked at the center console, where a line of four small red switches rested. Pancho tried one, but nothing happened. "I can't read which is which; it's all in Iranian."

Thirty yards.

Leila reached over and flicked all the switches but still nothing happened.

Twenty yards.

Above the line of small red switches was a big red switch. "The big red switch," Alex said.

Ten yards.

Pancho flipped the big red switch and the SUV came alive with siren blaring and blue light, front lights, and rear lights flashing. "Don't slow down," Alex said, hoping that in the world of Iranian law enforcement, an unmarked black Mercedes SUV reigned over white and green police sedans.

Five yards.

Leila drove around the police car. Even though the road had stopped, Leila drove off-road, heading south. Both police cars' lights and sirens came on, and the police followed her. They turned off their lights and sirens. Alex didn't want to kill law enforcement officers, but if he had to defend himself and his team, he would.

"Just keep driving straight," Pancho calmly advised Leila.

A voice spoke out of a police car's speaker.

"He is telling us to stop," Leila translated.

Pancho laughed.

One police car pulled up next to Alex's team. The SEALs readied their AKMS rifles. Over the loudspeaker came a voice again, followed by the driver waving his pistol. *Enough is enough. Somebody is going to get hurt, and I don't want it to be me.* "Pancho and John, tell him in Spanish and French that you don't understand Farsi, then shoot out his tires," Alex said.

Pancho and John rolled down their windows and spoke Spanish and French. The policeman looked at them strangely. Pancho and John opened fire. The loud noise in the small area of their car's interior made Alex's ears ring. A hot shell from one of the weapons bounced off Alex's arm, making him wince. Terror flashed on the policeman's face and his tires on the SEALs' side blew out. The police officer had difficulty maintaining a straight line as he skidded to a stop. The other police car stopped beside the one with the blown-out tires. They probably didn't get paid enough for fighting SEALs.

When Alex was sure no one else was following, he told Leila to turn east and head for Afghanistan. She did.

Soft sand and barren desert had given way to hard sand and occasional trees and plants. Alex and Pancho drank constantly, replenishing their depleted cells. Leila avoided small Iranian villages by driving around them. Alex and Pancho continued to drink until their cells were saturated, but they were running low on water again. Hours of driving fatigued Leila, so she stopped and switched places with Pancho.

Pancho drove them east out of Iran and across the border into southern Afghanistan. Soon they reached a lake, so Pancho stopped and they replenished their water supply. The SEALs popped in iodine tablets to disinfect the water. After thirty minutes, they drank some. It tasted like iodine, but they didn't care.

Night fell before they neared the small Afghanistan town of Bandare Wasate. The four abandoned their vehicle several kilometers outside the village and walked into town, where they stayed the night.

In the morning, they found an Afghani local to drive them nearly five hundred kilometers to Kandahar. Alex loosened the laces on his left boot—since they finished their death march through the desert, the swelling and pain had gone down, but after sitting in the car for a couple of hours, the swelling and pain returned. He remembered his nightmare. Alex was relieved that Pancho and John were okay.

11

A week after the biological weapons lab was destroyed, Major Khan stood outside General Tehrani's office. He studied the lobby for signs of an ambush. The destruction of the lab wasn't his fault, but he was the ranking officer at the Russian roulette game where Captain Rapviz decorated his game room with his brains. The penalty for such lapses in judgment often meant death. Of course Major Khan didn't fear death itself, but he did fear dying on someone else's terms, and he would fight to die on his own terms, even if it meant killing the general.

The general's assistant asked, "Are you carrying any weapons?"

Major Khan was armed, but he wasn't about to disarm himself. He stared through the assistant.

"Please remove any weapons before entering the general's office."

Major Khan stood still.

The assistant seemed uncomfortable but persisted. "Are you carrying any weapons, sir?"

"Do you see any?" Khan asked.

"No, sir."

Major Khan cracked his knuckles with impatience.

"General Tehrani will see you now," the assistant said.

Major Khan entered the general's office.

General Tehrani finished up a call on his black cell phone before putting it away. "Sit down," Tehrani said to Major Khan.

Seated to the right of the general was Lieutenant First Class Saeed Saeedi, Major Khan's friend—the hothead who started the Russian roulette game in the first place. The irony that Lieutenant Saeedi was sitting next to the general instead of standing in front of him wasn't lost on Major Khan.

To General Tehrani's left sat the other friend who was present at the Russian roulette game, Pistachio. When the general wanted to get rid of a commando, he used the commando's closest friends to snuff him. Both of Major Khan's best friends were here now. Major Khan knew he could take Pistachio and Lieutenant Saeedi separately, but he didn't think he could beat both at the same time.

"What's wrong, Major Khan?" Lieutenant Saeedi said with his chest puffed out. "The general offered you a seat."

Major Khan didn't like the disrespectful tone of Lieutenant Saeedi's voice. Sitting would give them more of an advantage if this was an ambush, but they were all seated, and maybe General Tehrani was simply being polite.

"Maybe you're afraid we're here to, oh, how do the Americans say it—terminate your command?" Pistachio said with a chuckle.

Major Khan remained standing. Pistachio's probe for a weakness—fear—irritated Major Khan even more, and he thought he would like to kill Pistachio first.

Lieutenant Saeedi chuckled. "That's a good one. Terminate his command."

"Please, sit down," General Tehrani said. "We're all family here. No one, save perhaps me, is in danger of losing his command."

Major Khan felt like he didn't have a choice. He sat down, but he didn't let his guard down.

"Major Khan, you owe me."

"Yes, sir."

"Can you tell me why?"

"I was the ranking officer when the Russian roulette game took place, and I was responsible for the senseless death of Captain Rapviz." Major Khan's gaze shifted to Lieutenant Saeedi. Lieutenant Saeedi lowered his head and stared at his shoe tips.

"Do you realize how much money goes into training a man like Captain Rapviz?" General Tehrani asked.

"More than a billion rial."

"Yes. Now I am going to tell you how you're going to repay me," the general said. "Someone destroyed our secondary biological weapons lab, and I want you to obliterate the bastards who did it. They think they can act with impunity against us, but they are wrong. The Supreme Leader wants this. I hope you understand how important that is. So I want you to find them and cut them into little pieces so we can feed them to their mothers. I have called in your two best friends here so we can get to the cutting soon. I know you three have had successes together in the past, and this will be your next success."

Major Khan took it as an insult: *The general is telling me that I don't have what it takes to finish the job by myself. What would the general say if I rejected his plan? Maybe Pistachio and Lieutenant Saeedi will try to kill me right here and now. I'd like to see them try.*

"With all due respect, sir, I think I can handle this alone," Major Khan said.

Pistachio and Lieutenant Saeedi shifted uneasily in their seats.

"Are you questioning me, son?" General Tehrani asked.

Pistachio tried to mediate. "I think Major Khan understands what a great addition we would be to the Team, sir."

"Shut up!" General Tehrani shouted.

The four men sat in silence for a moment.

"Was it the Zionists?" Major Khan asked.

"Them, or their American Satanist overlords," the general said. "In the village of Abadi Abad, three basiji were found murdered just before the biological weapons plant was destroyed. You will hopefully find some answers there."

"Is a helicopter available, sir?"

"I can have a helicopter fly you to Abadi Abad right now."

"Then, if it pleases the general, I'll take Pistachio and Lieutenant Saeedi to Abadi Abad and we'll find whoever bombed our biological weapons plant, sir. Then we will cut them into little pieces."

"You're damn right," General Tehrani said. "The Supreme Leader and I are counting on your success."

Major Khan exited the room as quickly as he could. He wasn't afraid, he was angry, and it took every bit of his willpower to not kill Pistachio and Saeedi. Instead, the three men boarded the waiting helicopter and flew to Abadi Abad. The helo landed just outside the village, where a fat police chief met them. The police chief escorted them to his police car and drove. Pistachio held a plastic cup in one hand and with his other put pistachios in his mouth.

"Do you need something to eat?" the police chief asked.

"I don't think he needs anything to eat," Lieutenant Saeedi said, utterly tickled with himself.

"Were you talking to me?" the police chief asked.

"No," Major Khan said. "We've already eaten."

Pistachio spit pistachio shells into a plastic cup.

The police chief explained about the three murdered basiji. Next, he told them about the stolen black Mercedes law enforcement SUV and the shots fired at a police officer's vehicle.

"Didn't anyone try to follow them?" Khan asked.

"At the time, we thought they were government agents, so we let them go."

"You pursued them because they were government agents. They shot at you. Then you stopped pursuing them because they were government agents. Is that what you're telling me?"

"We tried to follow the tracks, but by then the wind had blown them away," the chief said.

The man is a disgrace. "And now you're insulting my intelligence."

Like lightning, Lieutenant Saeedi punched the police chief in the side of the head and knocked him out. The chief fell over like a frozen block of ice. Lieutenant Saeedi kicked him on the ground. "Hey, fatso. Wake up. Wake up!" He kicked him again.

The police chief stirred on the ground.

"Don't insult Major Khan," Lieutenant Saeedi warned.

"You said they were heading south?" Major Khan asked.

"Yes," the police chief said, groaning as he regained consciousness.

Major Khan surveyed the area. "Whoever did this wasn't an amateur."

"Who do you think it was?" Pistachio asked.

"The Israelis," Major Khan said. "America wouldn't be so bold. This looks like the work of the Mossad."

Pistachio cracked a pistachio shell with his teeth. "Where do you think they went?"

"No telling. Just because they drove south out of here doesn't mean they drove south all the way. There's nothing south of here unless they rendezvoused with an aircraft or went farther south and got picked up at sea. I don't think they'd find many friends in Pakistan, so they could've driven to Afghanistan."

Lieutenant Saeedi became impatient. "We need to start searching south or toward Afghanistan before they get away."

"We can search where they went and hope to catch up, or we can think about where they'll strike next," Major Khan said.

"Where do you think they'll strike next?" Pistachio asked.

"One of the scientists got appendicitis and was flown out to a hospital in Tehran before the biological weapons compound exploded. If I were the Mossad, I'd go to Tehran."

12

On Friday, a week after blowing up the lab, Alex, Pancho, John, and Leila had their driver drop them off at the Armani Hotel in Kandahar. It would have been easier for them to ask to be taken straight to the airport, but doing so would also make it easy for the enemy to follow them. The SEALs and Leila stepped into the hotel and sat down for a few minutes, then stepped out again and caught a taxi. Splitting up would be more discreet, but the Taliban were still active in Kandahar and the SEALs chose safety over discretion. Their cabbie drove them ten kilometers to the U.S. military base on Kandahar International Airport. Alex paid the driver, then he and his crew walked up to the gate. The gate guard looked suspiciously at them. Alex gave the cover name of a supply unit they worked for. After thirty minutes of waiting in a visitors' area, a geeky-looking sergeant drove them to a classified corner where JSOC was based. Inside the classified area, they left Leila with an escort at a VIP lounge while the SEALs crossed the street and entered a three-story building that looked like a porcupine because of all the antennas sticking up from the roof. On the third floor, the geeky sergeant spoke to a muscular sergeant standing guard outside one of the rooms. The muscular sergeant ran his ID through the card reader lock and opened the door, letting them in. Inside, the walls appeared soundproofed.

Minutes later, their debriefer arrived. Alex was surprised to see Captain Kevin Eversmann, the commanding officer (CO) of SEAL Team Six—the skipper. Like half of the SEAL officers in the Teams, the skipper had been an enlisted man and risen up through the ranks to become an officer and now a CO. He knew about combat from experience. He and Alex were both six feet tall, but the skipper's salt-white hair was cut short in comparison to Alex's longer dark hair. The skipper was also a longtime member of Bitter Ash.

Alex, Pancho, and John stood at attention.

"At ease," the skipper said.

The Outcasts stopped standing at attention, but Alex didn't relax. Although SEALs were fearless about most things, they feared getting kicked out of the Teams, and a skipper held the power to do the kicking.

"How are you, Skipper?" Pancho asked, his face beaming.

Alex wished Pancho would just keep his big mouth shut, and he was sure that John felt the same.

"Well, Pancho, I think I'll be fine if you can shut that blowhole of yours. You think you can handle that, son?"

"Yes, sir," Pancho said, all evidence to the contrary.

"Great, I'll tell you when to open it. By the way, I came to Iraq and Afghanistan to visit our Teammates here, but the timing is no accident—I personally wanted to debrief you on your mission. Let's have a seat, gentlemen, and Chief Brandenburg, why don't you begin telling me how things went."

The four SEALs sat down. Alex summarized the bald lieutenant colonel's brief, losing Danny during the HAHO, rendezvousing with Leila, taking out the lab, the deadly hike through the desert, stealing an Iranian police SUV, and escaping from Iran.

"The loss of Danny was tragic," the skipper said. "We have a team out searching for his remains. You did the right thing by proceeding with the mission. Congratulations on blowing up the lab. The Iranian government is furious. They claim that someone bombed a pharmaceutical plant, but the world's media outlets are reporting that Iran's secret nuclear weapon facility blew up. Because of all the radioactivity, the Iranian government is having a hard time going in to analyze exactly what happened. Abadi Abad is the closest village to the explosion, and they haven't seen any significant increase in radioactivity, but they suspect a secret nuclear facility blew up. Well done, gentlemen. There's only one piece you left unfinished."

Alex, Pancho, and John looked at each other.

"What didn't we finish, sir?" Alex asked.

"One of the scientists, Dr. Sheema Khamenei, had appendicitis and was medevac'd out of there by helo. That was probably the helo you observed as you neared the biological weapons lab to plant your nuke. NSA intercepted email communication saying Dr. Khamenei is in a hospital in Tehran. She is one of the senior scientists there. Trained in Russia. With her alive, their bioweapons program remains alive. I need you to go in and finish the job by killing Dr. Khamenei."

"Yes, sir," the SEALs replied.

"We've given Leila an Army uniform to help her blend in while she's on base. We asked her to help us out on this one, too. Go ahead and clean your kit, eat some chow, then meet me back here in two hours for the brief."

"Yes, sir," they said.

The skipper left.

The three SEALs went to the armory and cleaned their weapons. Alex made sure his AKMS was unloaded and on safe before removing its bolt carrier group. Sand grains spilled out onto the wooden table in front of him.

As Pancho cleaned his AKMS, he turned to Alex and said, "I heard the BUD/S XO asked you to become an instructor there." Basic Underwater Demolition/SEAL (BUD/S) Training was what began the transformation from sailor to SEAL. The executive officer (XO) was second in command, under the CO.

"Where do you hear all this stuff?" Alex asked.

"People talk," Pancho said.

"When do people have so much time to talk?"

"Is it true?"

"Yes."

"Are you going to do it?"

Alex thought for a moment.

"You have to think about it," Pancho said.

"We have to eliminate Dr. Khamenei." It was officially a capture-or-kill mission, but Alex rarely captured anyone, and his superiors already knew that.

"We're brothers, man. You can't break up the family."

John stopped cleaning his rifle. "Alex is a big boy. He can do what he wants."

Alex didn't know whether to thank John for defending him or complain that John was trying to get rid of him.

They finished cleaning their gear, then went to the chow hall. Alex almost didn't recognize Leila wearing an Army uniform and sitting by herself eating dinner. The trio joined her.

After the four finished dinner, Leila went to take a rest in the VIP lounge while the SEALs returned to the soundproofed room where the skipper briefed them for their next mission: "You'll assume new identities and take separate military flights from here to Germany, Azerbaijan, and France." Alex spoke German fluently, and he often used the cover of German businessman, so he guessed he'd be going to Germany. John spoke fluent French, so France seemed the natural choice for him. Pancho spoke Spanish, but the Spanish airlines didn't fly to all the countries that German and French airlines did—besides, it would be easiest to send the bulk of their gear via military aircraft.

The skipper continued: "Alex, after taking a military flight from here to Frankfurt, you'll go undercover as a German businessman with your assistant Leila and fly via Lufthansa to Azerbaijan. Pancho will take most of your mission gear and hop on a military flight from here to Azerbaijan. John, you'll fly from here to Paris, then, posing as a French-Canadian minister, fly from Paris on Air France to Azerbaijan. In Azerbaijan, the four of you will link up with the Azerbaijan Navy's Tiger unit, made up of its top members from the 641st Special Warfare Unit. The Tigers will take you via fastboat across the Caspian Sea and insert you just north of the Iranian coast, where you'll swim to the beach. From there you'll rendezvous with our agent, who will escort you to a safe house in Tehran and update you on Dr. Khamenei's current location. Then you will capture or kill Dr. Khamenei. Finally, the Tigers will extract you by sea."

"I'm assuming there's a good reason for us using a similar insert-and-extract method, sir," Alex said.

"Yes," the skipper said. "Right now the Iranian government isn't too popular at home or abroad, so they're executing people just for sneezing—as frogmen, the water is your best chance for getting in and out. Intelligence has found a number of weaknesses along the Iranian coast, and you're going to take advantage of those weaknesses."

After the briefing, Alex cleaned up and helped Leila prepare for her role. Early Saturday morning, they wore dark blue Armani suits and carried dark brown leather satchels. Disguised as a German businessman and his assistant, they boarded a military flight to Frankfurt.

While sitting in the airport lounge, Alex's eyes followed Leila's long black hair from the top of her head to below her shoulders. His eyes followed down her skirt, tracing her dark blue curves. His eyes continued past her hemline. She had firm thighs, and her calf muscles were athletic, yet feminine. She reminded him of Cat. Alex needed someone to trust—someone he could ask whether he should stay in the Outcasts and Team Six or take the XO's offer to become a BUD/S instructor. Cat was someone he could trust and ask about such things, but work in the Teams had divided their paths, and she wasn't here. Through the years before he met Cat, there'd been other women, but again, they gave up trying to compete with the Teams. Even if Alex got to know Leila, she would give up, too. Alex didn't blame them. He was the one who chose the Teams over them.

Being a BUD/S instructor would demand a lot of time, but it wouldn't demand as much time as operating in the SEAL Teams. In the Teams, for months he trained individually at Professional Development/Schools (PRODEV) before returning to his troop for months of Unit Level Training (ULT). Then Alex and his Teammates would fly to one of the hot spots around the globe and fight bad guys for six months or more. After that, he'd return to the States and begin the cycle again with PRODEV. In contrast, as a BUD/S instructor, Alex would be able to return home almost every night. If he met a woman he liked, he would have time to share with her. Alex had enjoyed his work with Team Six and the Outcasts, but now he wanted something more.

Leila saw Alex looking at her, and she smiled.

He remembered the smile of the woman in red in the supermarket and how she blew through him like an Indian summer.

If Alex asked Leila, she would probably tell him to take the BUD/S instructor position. Cat would tell him the same. So would his sister Sarah. In that moment sitting in the Frankfurt airport, Alex decided: *After killing Dr. Khamenei in Tehran, I'll go to Coronado to become a BUD/S instructor.*

Soon Alex and Leila boarded their Lufthansa flight and flew to Azerbaijan. Azerbaijan was strategically located, with Iran to the south, the Caspian Sea to the east, Russia to the north, Georgia to the northwest, and Armenia to the west. Although predominantly Muslim, Azerbaijan led other Muslim countries in its openness to other cultures. In 1920 the Soviet Union invaded Azerbaijan, and in 1991 Azerbaijan took back its independence. Its people spoke

Azerbaijani, similar to Turkish, and held a close relationship with Turkey. Azerbaijan also held a strong relationship with the United States and had supported America and its allies fighting in Kosovo, Afghanistan, and Iraq. In addition, they worked closely with the U.S. Navy on security issues related to the Caspian Sea.

Early in the afternoon, an Azerbaijani wearing a civilian gray wool beret met Alex and Leila at the airport. "Welcome to Azerbaijan."

"Good to be here," Alex said. Their exchange seemed natural, making it ideal as a coded exchange to verify identities.

"The car is waiting."

"Great."

The man in the gray beret drove Alex and Leila in a civilian sedan twenty kilometers southwest toward Baku, where the Azerbaijan Navy base was located, but instead of stopping at the base, the driver continued south.

"I thought we were stopping at the naval base," Alex said.

"No, this way better," the driver said in broken English.

"Where are we going?"

"Neftcala."

"Do the others know this is where we're going?"

"Your SEAL friends go same place. No one else need know."

The change in plans made Alex uneasy, but the skipper was no dope, so Alex trusted that the skipper had put him in the proper hands. He tried not to worry about it.

They traveled south more than 150 kilometers before arriving at the port of Neftcala. The driver pulled into a parking lot on the pier and stopped. The other vehicles in the parking lot were civilian—no sign of military anywhere. Alex stopped trying to be calm—now he was nervous. He looked around for weapons of opportunity and paths of escape.

The driver escorted Alex and Leila into a warehouse. Secluded, it would be a good place to torture them or kill them. Being on the wharf, it would be easy to hose off blood and other body fluids, removing any evidence of what had happened.

Inside the warehouse, Pancho and John sat on a couple of crates next to their duffel bags. John read something, probably reviewing his cheat sheet about the mission or rereading his Bible. Next to Pancho were bags of the SEALs' gear. Pancho laughed it up with one of the Tigers. The Tigers were dressed in civilian clothes, and on the deck around them rested stuffed civilian duffel bags and backpacks.

The inside of the warehouse wasn't really a warehouse; it was a covered slip with a fastboat sitting in the water. Day or night, the fastboat could be docked ready to go, yet remain undetectable by satellite or prying eyes.

Alex breathed more easily. When the Tigers noticed Alex, they stood up. Alex appreciated the respect, but he felt embarrassed by it. Normally such a courtesy was only for a commanding officer in a formal setting—Alex was far down the totem pole from commanding officer, and this was a real-world operation, not a formal dog-and-pony show. "Please, relax," Alex said.

The Tiger who appeared to be the leader approached Alex and said, "We ready when you ready. I am Lieutenant Zadeh." Lieutenant Zadeh had long, black curly hair and a handsome face, like a rock star. His men looked more like pirates.

"You can call me Alex."

"I know."

"Let's do this," Alex said.

13

At night, the SEALs, Leila, and the Tigers changed into dry suits. With the Caspian Sea's temperature in the fifties on the Fahrenheit scale, and considering the possibility that Alex's team might have to spend much time in the water, the dry suits would keep them warmer than wet suits. Alex showed Leila how she would need to hold on to her mask with one hand while somersaulting out of the back of the fastboat while it was still moving.

The SEALs traveled light, carrying small waterproof backpacks and their customized Iranian Zoaf 9mm pistols. Leila carried no weapon. "Does she need a weapon?" Lieutenant Zadeh offered his firearm.

"Never used one before," she said, "and I don't know how."

"She'll be fine," Alex said.

Each Tiger carried an Israeli TAR-21, a bullpup assault rifle that fires 5.56mm NATO rounds. The bullpup design imbedded the weapon's action in the buttstock, conserving space. Although the TAR-21 was small like a carbine, it fired with the velocity of a rifle.

SEALs and Tigers loaded into the boat. The Tigers cast off the fastboat's lines and the coxswain started the engine. The coxswain eased the throttle forward a bit and the fastboat floated out from underneath the covered slip. Then the coxswain pressed the throttle forward. The boat responded by leaping forward, spitting a rooster tail of water behind it. Light dotted the land, water, and sky. Alex and the others lay on the floor of the boat, keeping a low profile. Not only did the fastboat's bulkheads hide them from sight, but they also protected Alex's crew from the cold wind that tried to bite their faces. They sped south.

After four hours of being knocked around on the deck of the fastboat, Pancho peered over the bulkhead to see where they were. They must have approached within three kilometers of the Iranian shore, because Pancho looked at Alex and the others. Alex nodded. Pancho somersaulted off the back, plunging through the rooster tail into the Caspian Sea. Alex motioned for Leila to jump; she executed a perfect somersault. Alex was next. John would be right behind him. Alex tumbled through the speedboat's wake and held his face mask to keep the water from ripping it off his face. He didn't know which way was up until the water settled and he floated to the surface. Alex recognized the outline of the Iranian shore from the photos in the skipper's brief. Between the shore and Alex, an Iranian patrol boat headed straight for him. The bow might crack his head open before the propellers chewed him up. Alex dove underwater. The buoyancy of the dry suit made it more difficult to dive, and Alex didn't want to kick his feet and splash a signal to the Iranians. He furiously breast-stroked with his arms until his fins submerged—then he kicked as hard and as fast as he could. The Iranian patrol boat passed, and he tasted its motor oil.

When Alex emerged, he saw the patrol boat race northward after the fastboat, which seemed to run full throttle. Little by little, the gap widened between the Tigers' speedboat and the Iranian patrol boat, but the patrol boat continued to give chase. *Better them than me. Give 'em hell, Tigers.*

Alex searched for his Teammates until he accounted for each one. Everyone seemed okay. Pancho and John led them south in a swim for the beach. Using only gestures, Alex helped Leila keep a low profile so she didn't splash. Although the dry suit kept Alex dry, he still felt the cold. Swimming fast kept him warm, and Leila had little trouble keeping up.

After an hour of swimming hard, they stopped. Ahead churned the surf zone, where the waves broke and rolled to the shore. Pancho donned his NODs and held an infrared flashlight. He pressed the flashlight button, signaling shore. No one could see the light with their naked eye and they couldn't see the response from shore. When Pancho began swimming through the surf zone, Alex followed. John swam next to Pancho and Alex and Leila followed. Inside the surf zone, small waves pushed them to shore, making the swim easier. They continued until their bellies hit bottom. Covered and concealed by water, they stuck only their heads out enough to breathe. Underwater, the SEALs took off their swim fins and hooked them to bungee cords strapped to their backs. Leila didn't finish as quickly as the SEALs, so Alex helped her.

Pancho crouched low and moved inland to the tree line on the eastern edge of the Sisangan National Forest. Alex and Leila followed. After checking their rear, John joined them.

Alex squatted among the trees and shook hands with their contact, an Iranian-American named Reza, who was working for the Activity—his nickname was *Razor*. Razor led them across a highway paralleling the beach, then farther into the woods, where a big gray SUV, a Toyota Land Cruiser Prado, sat off the road. Everyone piled into the vehicle. Razor drove out onto the highway to the east. With the black Caspian Sea to their left, black forest to their right, and black sky, the world seemed black. Soon the forest ended and the land brightened up with a few lights shining from scattered houses, assorted buildings, and large farms. Alex and his crew changed into their Iranian clothes.

"It's about one hundred and fifty klicks from here to Tehran," Razor said.

I must be crazy, Alex thought. *We just escaped from Iran, and now we're going back in.*

With the sea still on their left, the Toyota Land Cruiser passed several small towns on the right. Razor drove over a bridge before turning right at a larger town. They traveled southeast on Expressway 22 until it became Expressway 77 and took them around a city that looked about half the size of Virginia Beach.

"What city is this?" Alex asked.

"Amol," Razor answered. "This city has been around since at least the third century. It was a capital city until the Mongols invaded. Today it mixes the past, present, and nature. A lot of people have summer homes just south of here."

Leila put her head on Alex's shoulder and closed her eyes. He thought about nudging her head off, but she looked so peaceful—and beautiful—that he did nothing. He looked to see if John was paying attention, but he was focused on the road.

Alex and his crew passed Amol and after riding ten kilometers south, their Land Cruiser climbed up the Alborz mountain range. The Land Cruiser groaned and Razor shifted into a lower gear, relieving stress on the engine. After a while, they descended the other side, and the engine raced. Razor shifted back up into drive, calming the engine. The Land Cruiser traveled around, up, and over smaller mountains. When they rounded the last mountain and headed west, Alex saw some scattered lights in front of them. Abruptly the lights became a sea of orange, yellow, and white—Tehran.

In the city, on top of a six-floor lobby that looked like a saucer, stood a tower that rose more than fourteen hundred feet in the air. At one thousand feet, a twelve-story pod looking like a giant Fabergé egg perched on the slender column of the tower. Above the pod, the tower was topped off by an antenna.

"That's the Milad Tower," Razor said. "The antenna is the Islamic Republic of Iran telecommunication antenna used for television and radio. Adjacent to the east of the tower is the Milad Hospital, where your target is located."

Razor took an exit off the Expressway 77 and zigzagged through Tehran until he came to the parking lot of an upscale condo. He pulled into an empty space and stopped. When they had all exited, Razor pressed the key remote, locking the SUV's doors. He handed the keys to Alex. "This is yours. The SUV has no connection to me or our friends. It's clean, so you can do whatever you want with it. This other key on the key chain is for that green van." Razor pointed to the van. "The smaller key is to your condo, which is also clean. The condo key also opens the gate to the stairs, but the gate is low, and you can jump over it, if needed—it isn't burglar-proof, but it helps to keep unwanted visitors out."

Alex and his team followed Razor into the lobby, where they walked across a granite floor. They stopped in front of a locked glass door to the elevator, where Razor typed "8888" into a number pad. The locked glass door opened. "I didn't choose the combination," Razor defended himself, "the building manager did. This isn't the most secure condo in the world, but it's one of the most secure in Tehran—and one of the nicest."

The group rode up the elevator to the seventh floor, where Razor showed them to unit 701. Alex used the key Razor had given him and opened the door. Inside, he took a look around. The four-bedroom condo was well furnished. The refrigerator was packed with food. On a table was a notebook computer that probably had hidden software for secretly communicating with JSOC. Even the closet had local clothes and hospital uniforms for the SEALs and Leila. The glass balcony doors afforded a view of Milad Tower and Tehran. "You done good," Alex told Razor.

"The view is to die for," Razor quipped.

"What's the phone number for room service?" Pancho joked.

Razor smiled. "If room service comes calling, you've worn out your welcome."

Alex used the notebook to quickly report to JSOC that his team had arrived in Tehran. Meanwhile, the others grabbed food out of the refrigerator and made an early breakfast. Then everyone ate while Razor briefed them on their target's location and relevant information. Finally, Razor departed. The SEALs and Leila decided they'd do a reconnaissance of the hospital the next afternoon, when there would be a lot of people and confusion—if the opportunity presented itself, they'd hit Dr. Khamenei. On this day, they took turns sleeping and standing watch.

As evening approached, everyone was awake. Leila started to make dinner, but the guys told her not to. "The *koobideh* is ready," she argued. "We must eat it tonight."

Alex had no clue what koobideh was and he could tell by the looks on Pancho's and John's faces that they didn't, either. After she finished cooking, they all sat down for the meal. Leila served them plates of buttered Persian rice with grilled tomatoes on the side. Then she brought out two kebabs in her left hand. On one stick were skewered Persian-style barbecued lamb and onions. On the other was Iranian minced meat that she called koobideh, made from beef and mixed with parsley and chopped onions. In Leila's right hand she held one piece of nan flatbread. She placed the kebabs on Alex's rice and used the nan to hold the food in place as she pulled out the skewers. Then she did the same for Pancho and John. Alex waited for the guys and Leila to get their food before eating. In Alex's mouth, the hot meats tasted of an exotic mixture of salt, black pepper, garlic, celery, olive oil, sumac, and saffron.

While everyone ate, Leila served drinks. As she gave Alex his drink, her breast brushed against his shoulder. He looked again at John, but either the frogman was oblivious or doing one hell of a dumb act. The drink was a deliciously sour mix of yogurt, carbonated water, salt, and dried mint—*doogh*.

While eating and drinking, Alex noticed Leila looking at him. When she realized he'd noticed, she looked down. Alex resumed eating, then he noticed her looking at him again. This time she stared longer before lowering her eyes. He watched her devour her food. *This is nuts.*

Finally, Leila served dessert: Persian ice cream flavored with frozen chunks of cream, rosewater, and saffron—sandwiched between thin crispy waffles. As she gave Alex his dessert her hand discreetly brushed against his. This time he was sure it was no accident. Alex felt lonely, but he didn't want to risk the mission by getting romantically involved with her.

After dinner, the SEALs cleaned up while Leila took a shower. Although there were four bedrooms, there was only one shower. Alex showered next, followed by John and Pancho. Then Alex took a long look through the glass balcony doors at the nighttime view of the Milad Tower and the sea of lights that was Tehran—its beauty had caught him by surprise. In the reflection of the glass, he saw Leila—she was catching him by surprise, too. He went to his room, stripped down to his black silk undershorts, crawled into bed, and tried to sleep, but he was too anxious about the mission—and Leila. He lay in bed awake for a couple of hours. Then his door slowly opened.

Alex kept his pistol under his pillow, but he hadn't heard anyone break into their house, so it had to be one of three people. Maybe it was Leila, but this seemed too bold for her. Or Pancho was about to play a practical joke on him.

Alex looked and saw Leila walk across his room toward him. She lifted his sheet and crawled into bed with him. *How far is she going with this?* After a few minutes, Leila moved closer to him and pressed her body against his. "I do not usually do this," she whispered in his ear.

Leila's thin T-shirt did little to cover the touch of her curves. Alex's mind wanted to tell her *no*—he didn't want to endanger the mission. If he spoke, he was worried Pancho and John might hear and know that she was in his room. He worried that he was eroding his leadership in his men's eyes. Just because he could, didn't mean he should. Alex knew that John was attracted to Leila, and he felt a momentary pang of guilt. In spite of the red lights, his body signaled green. He wrapped his arms around her. She felt firm, yet soft. Her nose nuzzled his face. Alex's lips found her lips. Her lips parted slightly and he kissed her more deeply. Her lips parted more. Alex's temperature rose. Leila's hand caressed his cheek. Her hand continued down to his shoulders, then his chest, making him warm. Alex removed her T-shirt and explored her naked body with his hands—her skin was warmer than his. Leila felt his right bicep before returning to his shoulders and chest. It became so hot that Alex removed the bedsheets. He kissed her neck. Her hands descended to his abdomen. Alex and Leila's bodies combusted, burning into the night.

14

I n the morning, Leila, who had gone back to her own room, acted as if nothing had happened. Alex did his best, but he worried that Pancho and John could see through them. Alex checked his computer to see if there were any messages—there was one from Razor: "Today target is checking out of hospital at 1700."

Alex updated Pancho, John, and Leila and told them to get ready to hit the target ASAP. Then Alex sent a secure email to JSOC to tell the Tigers that he needed the extract for his team tonight.

Leila put on a black skirt and gray blouse with a doctor's white coat. She covered her hair and neck with a black scarf called a *maghnaeh*. Although the burqa and niqab were seen in Iran's southern rural areas such as Abadi Abad, headscarves and maghnaeh were popular throughout the rest of Iran. Alex, Pancho, and John wore dark slacks, gray shirts, and doctors' white coats—and Zoaf pistols. After breakfast, they went downstairs and loaded into the SUV.

Leila drove them to the hospital. From the hospital parking lot, they entered a side entrance to the main building and passed a handful of armed Revolutionary Guards milling among the crowd of patients and staff. The Revolutionary Guards stared at John, then Alex. The SEALs and Leila stepped into the elevator and the door closed. Pancho pressed the button to the tenth floor. The four of them put on their surgical masks. On the tenth floor, they stepped out and walked down the stairs to the eighth floor, where their target was. Riding the elevator up was easier than walking up stairs, and getting off on the wrong floor tricked anyone who might be watching.

They walked down the hallway. Outside their target's door, two Revolutionary Guards stood with their AKMs, modern versions of the AK-47 rifle, slung on their shoulders. One Guard's uniform was wrinkled and his hair was uncombed. The other Guard had an ironed uniform and his appearance was neat—they looked like the odd couple. When Alex's crew neared the Guards, they became rigid and alert.

Alex led his posse into the room two doors before the target's room and waited for the odd couple to relax a bit. Inside the room, a patient lay asleep, another sat reading a book, and another lay in bed staring at Alex. Alex pulled the curtain, so the patients couldn't ogle him and his crew. Because their target would be checking out at 1700, doing the hit at night was no longer an option. They could wait for another day, but that day might never come. Alex led them out the door.

The four walked down the middle of the hallway. The odd couple was alert but not rigid as the two watched Alex and his team. *Good.* Alex took one step in front of the odd couple then turned sharply, walked between them, and proceeded into the target's room. Alex reached into his right pocket, which had been cut out, and pulled his sound-suppressed Zoaf pistol from its holster. Behind him, the odd couple chattered loudly in Farsi. Alex trusted Pancho and John to protect him—if the odd couple went for their weapons, Pancho and John would dispatch them.

Inside the room, a sleepy Revolutionary Guard sat in his chair. His AKM leaned against the wall. The Guard reached over and grabbed his rifle. Alex aimed and shot him twice in the upper torso and once in the head. The Guard tumbled out of his chair and onto the floor. Alex continued forward into the room. Two of the three beds were empty. Alex recognized the middle-aged woman in the third bed as his target, Dr. Sheema Khamenei. Alex wheeled his pistol around in the scientist's direction.

Eyes wide open, Dr. Khamenei babbled in Farsi. Alex didn't understand it, but her lips slurred like she'd been drugged.

Alex aimed his pistol at Dr. Khamenei's forehead and squeezed the trigger. *Click.* Alex's pistol malfunctioned. Alex tapped the magazine on the bottom and racked the slide to fix the malfunction, but the slide didn't return forward properly. Probably two rounds had tried to enter the firing chamber at the same time—a double feed. *Damn!*

Dr. Khamenei's voice rose in pitch, volume, and speed.

Leila had followed Alex into the room. "She says there is another biological weapons lab," Leila translated. "More secret than the one near Abadi Abad, but in another location, and close to launching an attack on the United States."

Alex pressed his magazine ejection button and pulled out the magazine. He racked his slide again. Then again. The jammed bullet popped out and the weapon was clear.

Dr. Khamenei's voice squealed louder and faster. She looked at the ceiling and cried out. Alex recognized only one word: *Allah.*

"Dr. Khamenei says a Russian, a North Korean, and Iranian scientists are at the top-secret lab," Leila translated. "Dr. Khamenei didn't want to do this job, but the Iranian government is holding her husband hostage. God save me."

Alex reloaded his magazine, tapped the bottom of it with his hand, and racked the slide. He aimed at Dr. Khamenei's forehead. "Where is the lab?"

"You must rescue my husband first," Dr. Khamenei said in English. "Then I will tell you where it is. I will even take you there, if you want."

"You're not in a position to negotiate," Alex growled.

"Let Allah's will be done. I can't continue living this hell while I know my husband is dying in prison. If it's my time to die, I will die."

"Shit!" Alex exclaimed. He turned to see what happened to Pancho, John, and the odd couple outside the room. Pancho and John had already dispatched the Guards and were putting them in two patient beds. There was a puddle of blood on the floor and blood spatter on the wall. Alex had been so focused on the Guard he shot, his weapon malfunction, and the target that he didn't even hear Pancho and John fire their pistols. Pancho covered the bodies with bedsheets while John guarded the door. "Guys, we're taking the doctor alive," Alex said. "She's going to lead us to another lab."

Pancho took off his bloodstained white jacket, strapped on one of the Guards' AKMs, and put on his jacket again. Then Pancho relieved John at the door. Alex and John armed themselves with the remaining AKMs and concealed their weapons with their white coats. Now Alex and his team had to get Dr. Khamenei out of the hospital. And out of Iran.

PART TWO

We are going to have peace even if we have to fight for it.

—DWIGHT D. EISENHOWER, U.S. PRESIDENT

15

Pancho headed out the door of Dr. Khamenei's room. Leila followed, helping Dr. Khamenei walk. Alex fretted, debating whether to just scoop the doctor up. She wasn't much faster than a two-legged tortoise. Although there were no Revolutionary Guards, there were people in the hall, and some of them were staring. Alex and his team couldn't run faster than their slowest person.

"Faster," Alex said quietly. "Dr. Khamenei, you've got to walk faster so we can get out of this hallway and down the stairs."

The doctor sped up a little, wobbling like she'd been heavily sedated—probably on purpose to keep her from escaping. Maybe the Guards had been there to prevent that just as much as to protect her. *Damn, she's slow.*

Alex's eyes scanned the hall for a wheelchair, but there was none. He realized that walking down the stairs was going to be so slow, it would put them in more danger than taking the elevator. Also, if going down the stairs popped the doctor's stitches, they'd have even more problems. When Pancho turned back to see how they were proceeding and check for any communications, Alex said, "Take us to the elevator."

They entered the elevator and went down to the second floor. "Stairs," Alex said. When the elevator doors opened on the second floor, Pancho led them out and through the doors to the stairs. The doors closed behind them. On the stairwell, they were protected from eyes in the hallway.

Alex gestured for Pancho to take a look on the first floor. Pancho went downstairs and peeked through the door window at the first floor. He climbed back up the stairs, looked at Alex, and shook his head. The first floor was too dangerous. Alex turned to John and said, "Take us to the elevator."

John took them out of the stairwell, into the hall, and to the elevator. When the elevator door opened, two armed Revolution-ary Guards stood inside—with similar heights and appearance, they looked like twins. The Guards noticed Dr. Khamenei, grabbed their AKM rifles, and proceeded to aim. John didn't hesitate. He lifted his pistol and fired. Alex had seen more than his share of close-up head shots, but two heads exploding in the space of an elevator was a shock even for him. The two soldiers slid down the back wall of the elevator, where their bodies slumped on the floor.

Alex and his crew stepped onto the elevator. The floor was slick with blood. Alex stood on one of the twins so everyone could fit in the elevator more easily. "Fourth floor," Alex said.

Pancho pressed the number four.

"We can follow the fourth floor to another wing and find an exit there," Alex explained.

The elevator stopped at the third floor and opened. A young couple started to enter the elevator when they noticed all the blood. Pancho put up his hands, gesturing for them to stop. Leila told them something in Farsi, and the couple backed off. The elevator door closed. Up it went.

The elevator stopped on the fourth floor, and Alex's team stepped off. A group of women waiting to ride the elevator stared at Alex and his crew in shock. With blood all over the SEALs' white coats and their surgical masks, the SEALs looked like they had just finished performing surgery. They passed the group of women. After a moment, one of them screamed—she'd seen the twin Guards.

"Come on, Dr. Khamenei, you've got to move it," Alex pleaded.

Dr. Khamenei tried to hurry, but she stumbled, almost falling—Leila held her arm, steadying her. Alex, using a fireman's carry, hoisted the scientist on his back and carried her. Although now they could move faster, if they came under attack, Alex wouldn't be able to return fire quickly.

The fourth floor was almost as crowded with people as the first floor, but fortunately there were no Revolutionary Guards in sight.

Enemy AK fire sounded.

"Contact rear!" John shouted.

Alex wanted to turn, drop to the deck, and open fire, but he couldn't drop Dr. Khamenei without busting her stitches and spilling her guts all over the floor, so he hid around a nearby corner in an alcove. Pancho and John fired their sound-suppressed pistols while the enemy made a terrible racket with their AKMs. In the alcove next to him were two beds. He noticed the beds had wheels. *Hot damn!* Alex put Dr. Khamenei on a bed. There was a wet spot on the side of her stomach—blood. There was no gunshot wound; she was bleeding through her stitches. Alex looked around for gauze, but there was none. He folded the bedsheet into a giant bandage, placed it on Dr. Khamenei's bleeding spot, and told her to hold the sheet there with her hand. "Keep pressure on it," Alex said. He grabbed the sheet off another bed and covered Dr. Khamenei, including her face, to hide her identity.

The firing stopped. Alex poked his head out into the hall. Bodies lay on the ground in the distance, a number of them civilians. Alex, Pancho, and John played dirty, but they didn't kill innocent bystanders. The civilians were mowed down by the Guards, who were now dead. Alex wheeled Dr. Khamenei out. "I need you to push this," he told Leila.

She did.

Alex's team resumed their escape, but now they were moving at least ten times faster. *We just might make it out of here.* They passed a tall woman lying facedown on the floor—her blood formed a small puddle around her head. An elderly man walked in a daze with a bloody shoulder.

"Contact rear!" John shouted.

Damn! Alex and Pancho quickly turned about-face.

"Pancho, take Leila and Dr. Khamenei, go to the first floor, and wait," Alex said.

"Aye," Pancho said.

"Be careful," Leila said to Alex. Then she hurried off with Pancho.

A shot popped the air next to Alex's head. Either it was a lucky shot, or these guys weren't the average Guards—Alex suspected the latter. About thirty-five yards in front of Alex, three combatants in plainclothes used walls for cover while firing at the SEALs—the bad guys were firing in a rhythm, so that when one reloaded, the others fired. There were no lulls in the heat they delivered. John had already taken shelter behind a wall, and Alex followed his example. Just as Alex took cover, a chip of wall hopped out near his face.

Alex popped out and fired back, trying to shoot the bad guys in the upper torso, shoot them through the wall, and skip rounds off the wall to take them down. Alex thought he recognized one of the three—an adversary he'd fought years ago in Iraq: Gholam Khan. John fired a staccato of bullets at Khan and his men.

Alex took cover in an alcove and removed his jacket. He unslung his AKM and brought it up to his shoulder. The desire to kill Khan pumped adrenaline through Alex's arteries.

"Reloading!" John called out. Alex knew John would be taking cover while he was reloading.

"Die, you slick bastard!" Alex cried as he swung around the corner. In the absence of John's shooting, Khan and his men advanced confidently—three against two, and submachine guns versus pistols. Khan and his men moved like they had superior firepower on their side. But Khan and his men had no idea who they were up against, and they had no idea that Alex and John were armed with AKM assault rifles. In contrast to Alex's quiet sound-suppressed Zoaf pistol, his AKM assault rifle roared—and in contrast to the Zoaf, the AKM delivered a wicked bite. Alex fired three rounds in rapid succession. The first round struck low and to the left of Khan. The second caught Khan in the chest, knocking him back a step. The third went high and right. Khan stumbled backward over his men trying to find cover from Alex's onslaught.

John appeared with his AKM firing in rapid succession. Khan staggered into a side room, and his two buddies must have realized how exposed they were, because they followed him. John skipped a round off the wall that nailed one in the right ass cheek—he howled in pain.

Alex wanted to stay and fight Khan, but even if Alex killed him, reinforcements were surely on their way. Alex's ammunition wouldn't last long, and dying in Tehran was not a mission objective. "John, drop smoke," Alex said.

"Dropping smoke," John repeated. He stopped firing and popped a smoke grenade directly in front of their position. Soon the hallway filled with white smoke and Alex could no longer see Khan and his men.

16

Pistachio pulled his wallet out of his back pocket. "I can't believe they shot me in the ass." He looked at his wallet: the hole went completely through. He grunted. "And the bullet is still in my ass!"

Major Khan looked down at his chest—a metal piece of GPS electronics stuck out of it. When he lifted his arm, electronics shifted in his chest pocket like loose change. The major pulled the bloody piece of metal out. He remembered the face of the man who just shot him. He knew the shooter from Kahar, Iraq, when the major had the green-faced devil in his sniper sight. Green-Face moved just before he took the shot. He was the same green-face who slaughtered his Shiite militia, the same man who had killed his beloved Abubakar. Major Khan's militia reported that this green-face's name was Alex Brandenburg.

Major Khan looked at the smoke ahead of him in the hall—he couldn't see anything beyond it. The major could charge through and hope he didn't run into an ambush or booby trap, or he could be cautious and wait until the smoke receded before proceeding—not that he was afraid of death. On the contrary, part of him welcomed death. Major Khan simply wanted to die under his own terms.

"That bastard shot you," Lieutenant Saeedi said. "Nobody shoots my friend and lives to tell about it—nobody!" He rushed down the hallway toward the smoke.

Major Khan appreciated Lieutenant Saeedi taking the lead. The major followed, staying just far enough back in case the shit hit the fan. Major Khan glanced back to see Pistachio limping behind him.

"You hear that, you bastards?!" Lieutenant Saeedi called into the smoke. "I'm coming for you!" He ran into the smoke. "Come on," Lieutenant Saeedi shouted, "they're getting away!"

Major Khan entered the smoke, and when he exited the other side, he saw Lieutenant Saeedi but no Alex. He caught up with Lieutenant Saeedi, and they picked up speed.

17

Alex and John, with their weapons concealed in their white coats, frantically searched the first floor for Pancho, Leila, and Dr. Khamenei. In the lounge corner of the lobby, Alex and John found them. The first floor in the wing was crowded, but there were no Revolutionary Guards, and, for the most part, Alex and his crew were able to blend in. "We're going to have a hard time returning to our vehicle," John said quietly.

"Follow me," Alex whispered while continuing forward. He had no idea where he was going, but he knew he didn't want to be in that lobby—especially when Major Khan and his gang came looking for them. At the first corridor, Alex turned left. He looked back to make sure his team was with him—they were. Up ahead, people flowed into the hospital from what looked like an emergency entrance—it gave him an idea. He dodged people like a race car as he hurried forward. Then he exited the emergency entrance. In the parking lot, he saw what he'd hoped for: ambulances. The ambulances had the word for "ambulance" written in reverse on their fronts. They had orange stripes along the side and Farsi writing.

"Contact rear!" John shouted.

Alex turned. Two more Guards came running out of the hospital. Shots whistled past his head and drilled into the nearest ambulance.

John fired off two short bursts and the Guards tumbled to the pavement, where they lay still. The clatter of their AKs hitting the ground made a terrible noise.

Alex ran to the ambulances and frantically looked inside. On the third try he found one with keys in the ignition.

Alex opened the driver's side and looked at Leila. She nodded and stepped into the driver's seat. Pancho rode shotgun. "Get us out of here now!" Alex told Leila and Pancho. Alex, John, and Dr. Khamenei loaded into the back. Alex covered Dr. Khamenei's eyes with a black hood—she didn't need to see their safe house. Alex found some bandages in the ambulance and used them to dress Dr. Khamenei's stitches. John kept a lookout to their rear.

Leila stomped on the gas and drove them out of the hospital area. Pancho turned on the lights and siren, and Leila picked up speed. The downside of the lights and siren was that they drew attention. On the upside, Alex's crew could quickly put more distance between them and the bad guys. Also, if the bad guys ran surveillance on the SEALs, they could spot the surveillance team driving faster than the vehicles around them.

Leila drove out onto the expressway. Minutes later, John said, "We got company."

A black sedan followed behind, speeding faster than the vehicles around it but staying behind the ambulance. Alex and John prepared their AKMs without showing them through the back window. The two SEALs waited for the man in the black sedan to make his move. Maybe he was just using the ambulance to drive through traffic faster.

Without using her turn signal, Leila made a quick exit off the expressway. The sedan didn't follow. Pancho cut off the lights and siren. Without the noise of their own siren, Alex heard sirens screeching throughout Tehran.

Pancho told Leila to take three consecutive right turns, to make sure they weren't being followed. No one came. They were clean.

Leila pulled into the condo parking lot, stopped, and turned off the ignition. Alex pulled the condo key off his key ring and handed it to Pancho. Pancho took the key, pulled down his surgeon's mask, and left behind his AKM as he hurried with Leila into the condo lobby.

Alex laid his AKM on the ambulance bed, grabbed Pancho's AKM from the front, and laid it down next to his AKM. Then he motioned for John to hand over his.

"You're not getting rid of these, are you?" John asked.

"Just need to conceal them so we can move them to the van," Alex replied.

John looked longingly at his AKM and then handed it over.

Alex wrapped it with the other two AKMs in the bedsheet. "You bring the doctor."

John nodded. "You're bleeding."

"Where?"

"Your ear is bleeding."

Alex touched his ear, then looked at his finger—it was bloody.

"Looks like a round sliced your earlobe."

"Is it still attached?"

"Yeah, but it's going to need a few stitches. Let me put something on it." John grabbed rubbing alcohol, poured it on some gauze, and cleaned Alex's earlobe. Then he taped it with some gauze.

Alex had been so focused on fighting and jacked up on adrenaline that he didn't realize a shot had grazed him. "Thanks." Alex looked through the window to see if anyone was watching. He didn't see anyone, so he pushed open the back doors and hopped out with the AKMs wrapped in a bedsheet. Alex opened the rear door of the van and loaded the weapons inside. He held the door open for John and shuttled her into the back of the van. Alex and John entered the van and sat.

Alex looked anxiously out the van window for Pancho and Leila. It seemed like it was taking them too long. Maybe they were in trouble, but Alex didn't hear any shots. When he saw Pancho and Leila exit the building with their bags, he felt relieved.

After loading their bags in the back, Leila got behind the wheel of the van. Pancho drove the ambulance and Leila followed. Several blocks away from the condo, Pancho parked the ambulance on the side of the road and left the keys in the ignition with the door unlocked. Hopefully no one would connect the ambulance to the condo. If someone stole the ambulance and broke it down in a chop shop to sell the parts, that would be even better.

Pancho sat up front in the van next to Leila. She drove west and entered Expressway Two, then exited on Chalus Road, which took them north through the Alborz mountain range and all the way to the resort town of Chalus on the Caspian Sea. East of Chalus was a Revolutionary Guard base.

Alex took off Dr. Khamenei's black hood. She looked relieved. John checked the AKM magazines—one had less ammo than the others, so he redistributed the ammo in the magazines so each weapon had twenty rounds.

From Chalus, Leila turned west and followed the Caspian Sea for a little over thirty kilometers, passing the town of Abas Abad. To the left appeared a forest. Pancho directed Leila to drive off-road into the woods far enough so they couldn't be seen from the highway. There they waited for darkness.

"Dr. Khamenei, where is your husband being held hostage?" Alex asked.

"In Lebanon."

Alex bit off a curse. Of course he wouldn't be held somewhere close.

"Who is holding him in Lebanon?"

"Hezbollah. My husband was teaching Farsi in Tripoli. At the beginning of last year, some of his students became swept up in the Arab Spring, and they encouraged him to join them. His students supported Lebanon and opposed Syria's interference in Lebanon's government. Of course, Syria was not happy. Syria's close ally Iran was not happy, either. Both Syria and Iran continue to fund Hezbollah in order to take control of Lebanon. The Iranian Revolutionary Guards trained Hezbollah and continue to train them. Naturally, Syria and Iran have told Hezbollah to squash the Arab Spring. Hezbollah tortured my husband and many of his friends. Other friends of his were executed. I didn't want to do the work I do, but the Iranian government told me that if I did, they would make sure Hezbollah didn't torture my husband. They would make sure Hezbollah wouldn't kill him. My government said that when I completed my work, they'd get my husband released from prison. Hezbollah didn't kill my husband because Iranian leaders know that if my husband dies, I won't help them with their biological weapon. But I found out that Hezbollah still tortures him. I need you to free him as soon as possible."

"Then you'll tell us the location of Iran's biological weapons lab?" Alex asked.

"Gladly."

"Just what is it that they're researching at this top-secret lab?"

"They're researching a more deadly strain of the bubonic plague—Black Death. In the fourteenth century it started in China and killed thirty percent of their population—twenty-five million people. Rat fleas carried the plague and lived on rats that sneaked onto merchant ships that sailed to Europe, where it killed about half of Europe's population. In total, the Black Death killed four hundred fifty million people.

"Recently our scientists went to Madagascar to study a strain that resists streptomycin, tetracycline, and six other antibiotics. The scientists brought back the Madagascar Black Death bacterium and crossbred it with pneumonic plague, creating a hybrid that can be carried by fleas *and* infect the human respiratory system. Our scientists also treated the hybrid with small doses of other drugs so the bacterium would become resistant to all antibiotics. The scientists completed the twenty-first strain. They called it Madagascar Black Death Twenty-One, or MBD21. Our government plans to infect rat fleas with the virus, so we are raising superior breeds of rat fleas that reproduce more fleas and live longer. Then the scientists will infect the rat fleas with MBD21 and infest the United States. Because the bacterium carries the characteristics of pneumonic plague, it can also be transmitted from human to human by coughing or sneezing. You can imagine, with all the advances in travel since the fourteenth century, how quickly the virus will spread today. The scientists calculate with ninety-nine percent reliability that MBD21 will destroy at least half the U.S. population."

"We better shut these guys down, pronto," Pancho said.

At 0145, Pancho and John slipped out of the woods and across the highway into the trees bordering a construction site. Next to the trees were houses, but the lights were out as if everyone had gone to sleep. Then at 0200, Pancho flashed an infrared signal into the Caspian Sea. Pancho was busy signaling and looking for a reply, and he couldn't pay attention to what was happening around him, so John watched their immediate surroundings, guarding Pancho.

Ten minutes later, Alex escorted Leila and Dr. Khamenei out of the woods, across the street, and into the trees next to the construction site. There they linked up with Pancho and John. Alex could see a few white lights on the sea—none of them would belong to the Tigers.

Minutes later, Alex noticed a dark shape approaching them from the sea—the Tigers quietly paddled to shore. As they came closer, Alex recognized Lieutenant Zadeh, the rock star. He brought two men with him. It was no small feat to paddle the big black rubber boat using only three men. Alex and his crew met the Tigers, who'd dismounted in the shallow water. They helped Leila and Dr. Khamenei into the middle of the boat.

Then the SEALs and Tigers, half on the starboard side and half on the port side, held on to the boat and walked it into deeper water.

The front two Tigers, one starboard and one port, jumped into the boat first, grabbed their paddles in the boat, and started paddling. Alex and Pancho continued to push the boat to sea until water came up to their knees. Alex jumped inside the boat on the starboard side and Pancho on the port side. Alex sat with his right knee resting on the outer rib and his left knee inside the boat on the deck. He grabbed his oar and paddled, as did Pancho. Similarly, John and Lieutenant Zadeh continued pushing the boat out to sea until the water rose too high up their legs for them to maneuver effectively. Then they hopped into the boat and started paddling. Lieutenant Zadeh also served as coxswain, steering them.

Silently the SEALs and Tigers paddled out to sea. Lights from one of the vessels headed toward them. The SEALs and Tigers couldn't paddle faster than the approaching vessel's engines. Lieutenant Zadeh tried to fire up their motor. It didn't start. He tried again—nothing. On the third try it started. The engine was a special stealth motor, quieter than most boat engines, but it wasn't as quiet as the oars. Lieutenant Zadeh twisted the throttle, and their black rubber boat jumped forward. The SEALs and Tigers stopped paddling and put their oars in the boat. When their boat hit waves, it caught air—which was thrilling for less than a second—then the boat came back down on the water hard, smashing Alex's left knee. Even though Leila and Dr. Khamenei were in the middle of the boat, Alex didn't know how they kept from getting bounced out. They were probably so scared that they were holding on for dear life. Soon their boat sailed out of the path of the approaching vessel. The vessel didn't follow.

Two more lights floated ahead of them: one to the west and the other to the east. Lieutenant Zadeh cut between them. Again, neither vessel followed.

"Someone coming at us from the rear," John said.

Alex looked behind and saw a boat approaching them with what looked like a searchlight—it was too far away to be sure.

Lieutenant Zadeh glanced over his shoulder. "Iranian patrol boat." That was what Alex didn't want to hear. The SEALs' and Tigers' little rubber boat with small weapons would be no match for a huge Iranian hunk of metal with big guns.

Up ahead to the north, in the middle of the sea, floated another vessel with its lights out. Lieutenant Zadeh steered east of it, passing the boat. The boat didn't follow, and the Iranian patrol boat steered straight for the vessel with its lights out.

Lieutenant Zadeh continued north. The Iranian patrol boat stopped near the vessel with its lights out. Lieutenant Zadeh made a sharp turn left and headed east. Gradually, the land appeared closer and closer. Their boat slowed down and motored into the covered slip that looked like a warehouse from on land. Five and a half hours after launching their boat off the coast of Iran, they arrived safely in Neftcala, Azerbaijan.

Alex contacted JSOC to let them know they'd arrived with their precious cargo (PC): Dr. Khamenei. Alex relayed the information the doctor had given him about the top-secret lab and requested permission to rescue Dr. Khamenei's husband. JSOC told Alex to "stand by." Hoping to receive approval to launch a rescue, Pancho and John flew with their PC on a military flight to Stuttgart, Germany. Alex and Leila resumed their business cover and flew on Lufthansa to Frankfurt, then Stuttgart.

18

Tuesday, snow descended on the grounds of Patch Barracks, Stuttgart, Germany. Pancho and John turned over Dr. Khamenei to JSOC for holding before joining Alex for the debrief. JSOC told Alex that he'd get a new team member for the possible rescue op, but the rescue op hadn't been approved yet.

On base, the SEALs and Leila each checked into separate rooms at the Schwabian Inn, an above-average hotel by American standards that charged discounted military rates.

In the morning, Alex gave Leila the morning off to relax and shop while he, Pancho, and John went to JSOC's intel "shed" for maps and information about the prison, such as door locks, window fasteners, skylights, alarms, and security.

Alex requested information about Dr. Khamenei's husband and the Arab Spring movement in Lebanon. Alex also asked for intel on Gholam Khan and his two comrades at the hospital in Iran.

The SEALs discussed infiltrating Lebanon disguised as a documentary film crew there to film UNESCO World Heritage sites. They put together identities for each member of their team and asked JSOC to help them with weapons, supporting documents, equipment, and a safe house. At lunch, they gave Leila her identity and camerawoman role to study. Then the SEALs went back to the intel shed for the latest dump, which included photos of Dr. Khamenei's husband. The SEALs continued with their planning.

After dinner, as Alex was finishing a hot shower, a knock came at his hotel room door. Steam rolled out of the bathroom with him. Expecting the new team member, Alex threw on shorts and a T-shirt. He looked through the peephole. There stood Leila, appearing calm as usual. Alex opened the door. She walked in and embraced him. Her enthusiasm was contagious.

After the door clicked shut behind her, Leila pulled off her blouse—she wasn't wearing a T-shirt or bra. The rush of combat still lingered in Alex's blood, and he was primed for action. Alex took off his T-shirt and they kissed. Leila dropped her skirt—she wore nothing but smooth skin. Alex dropped his shorts, and they embraced. A knock sounded at the door. Alex ignored it.

"Alex," a familiar female voice called. It was Cat.

Alex was confused as to why she was there, and the memory of his relationship with her collided with his feelings for Leila. Without thinking, he picked up his shorts and put them on.

"Who is she?" Leila whispered.

The knock sounded again.

Alex put on his T-shirt. "Cat."

"Who is Cat?" Leila asked quietly.

"Alex?" Cat said.

He picked up Leila's clothes and handed them to her.

Concern filled Leila's face as she took her clothes and put them on.

"Alex, are you okay?" Cat asked.

No, I'm not okay. He was free-falling without a parachute. He was about to hurt two women at the same time. Lower and lower he dropped—soon he would crash and burn. "Just a moment," he answered. Alex opened the door.

Cat burst in with a big smile on her face. She looked like she was about to hug Alex, until she noticed Leila. Cat's smile disappeared.

"Cat, this is Leila," he said.

Cat's eyes examined Leila's blouse; part of it was untucked. Cat spoke Arabic to Leila.

Leila responded in English, "I am Iranian. I speak Farsi, not Arabic. Are you Arab?"

"My grandmother is Lebanese." Cat's blond hair and fair skin didn't pass for Arab, but when she put on a dark wig and dark makeup, she became Lebanese. Cat's eyes shifted to Alex and she asked, "What are you dressed for?"

"I just stepped out of the shower," Alex said.

The three of them stood quietly for an awkward moment.

"What brings you here?" Alex asked.

"Am I not welcome?" Cat asked.

"I didn't say that," Alex said.

"You're not making me feel welcome," she said.

"I wasn't expecting you," Alex said, feeling totally out of his depth.

"I can see that."

Alex struggled to come up with something to say. "We agreed it'd be okay to see other people." The moment he said it he knew he should have thought longer.

Cat's eyes went steely. "That seems to have worked well for you."

"I heard you and Hammerhead were seeing each other," Alex said, letting his jealousy take over.

Cat looked at the ceiling and huffed. "Hammerhead? Oh, please. Who in their right mind would believe that?"

Alex was about to say he did, but realized that when you're in a hole you stop digging. "I didn't."

"Really?" Cat said. "Because from the looks of things, it appears that you used it to justify something."

Alex longed to be back in combat. "Leila is a good friend."

Now Leila huffed. "Is that what I was?"

Alex didn't know what to say without pounding himself deeper into the ground.

"Maybe a better question would be 'What am I now?'" Leila said. Alex looked at Leila then Cat. "I need some time to think."

"Time!" Cat said. "I wasted a lot of it on you. What you need is to take those feelings out of those little boxes you keep sticking them in. What you need is to learn how to love. Without love, you'll keep living in that lonely little dysfunctional world of yours."

Alex glared at her.

"Don't give me that look," Cat said. "I'm the one who should be pissed. Go ahead and be pissed. It's one of the few emotions you do well—and I wouldn't want to take that away from a man suffering in emotional poverty."

"Are you finished?"

"I'm reporting for duty. JSOC sent me. There's no one else. So when you're finished laying Leila, let me know. My room is across from John's." She turned to Leila and said calmly, "You can have him." Cat quietly walked out the door.

Alex wanted to slam the door on Cat. *I know how to love. My world isn't dysfunctional. And I don't live in emotional poverty.* "I'm sorry," Alex said. "I need some time."

Leila put her hand on Alex's shoulder. "Just call me if you want to talk." Leila walked out of his room.

I know how to love. My world isn't dysfunctional. I don't live in emotional poverty. The more he thought it, the less he believed it, so he stopped thinking it.

He didn't know what to do about Cat and Leila, so he left his room and went to John's room. The two sat down and Alex told him about his relationship with Leila and about Cat's visit. Alex half expected John to throw a punch at him, but he just listened and nodded.

"What should I do?" Alex asked. "I've let enough relationships slip through my fingers, and I don't want it to happen again. I cared about Cat; hell, I still do. And Leila, man, I'm sorry. I should have said no. And now that Cat is here, I'm confused."

John laughed. "Oh, to have your problems!"

"Then what should I do?"

John thought for a moment. "Look, if this was a tactical situation I'd have your back one hundred percent, but I can't tell you what to do. Yeah, I like Leila, but I mean we were just talking. I barely know her. You barely know her. Cat, on the other hand, Alex, she's one of us. She understands life in the Teams and is probably better equipped to cope."

Alex was amazed. John understood this better than Alex did himself.

"So what do I do about Leila?" Alex asked.

John smiled. "Leila is her code name. Do you even know her real name?"

Alex shook his head. "Do you think she and Danny had a romantic relationship?"

John shrugged. "I don't know."

"I sure know how to make a mess of things," Alex said.

"But you usually find a way to make it right," John said, picking up his Bible and reading.

Alex continued thinking for half an hour. He didn't need any more time. He'd wasted enough already. "Thanks."

John grunted.

Alex stood, left John's room, walked over to Leila's door, and knocked. She opened it. "Come in."

Alex walked inside and his head began to spin. He tried to read her face, but his head was too dizzy to read anything. "Can we sit?"

She nodded and they sat down.

He didn't know what to say, so he tried to start from the beginning and kept going. "The first time I saw you, I couldn't help thinking how beautiful you are. When you told me what happened to your husband and son, I wanted to help you. We had some tough times on this mission, like the death march through the Lut Desert, but you stayed calm, you helped us, and we made it through. Every time. You're intelligent, talented, and honest, and I wanted to know more about you."

"But," she said.

"I have to fix things with Cat," Alex said.

"She seems like she does not want to fix things."

"I have to try. I have to believe I can. It's time to up my game."

"Up your game?" Leila asked.

"Do better. I should've done better a long time ago."

"I was afraid of this."

"JSOC still wants you on this mission. The guys and I want you on this mission."

"I want to continue."

"And I want to stay friends with you."

"When she came through that door, I was afraid of this."

"I'm sorry." He paused. "I don't know how to say this, so I'll just say it. Tomorrow, if we're still waiting for the rescue mission, I need to spend some time with Cat."

"What if she does not want to spend time with you?"

"I have to believe she will. And I don't want you to have to stay in this hotel room alone all day. I'm thinking maybe Pancho and John can show you around Germany, if you like."

She scratched her head. "I do not want to see Germany. I want to see you. Just let her go."

"I can't."

"Yes, you can."

Alex said nothing.

"My real name is Shalah Farshid," she said. "Farshid was my family name before I married."

Alex remained silent.

Leila became quiet, too. Finally, Leila broke the silence. "I envy her."

"I'll tell Pancho and John to take you out tomorrow."

"I do not want to go out."

"I'm sorry."

Alex turned to go, but Leila stopped him. "Just one more thing," she said. "Kiss me goodbye."

He hesitated like he was standing in front of the railroad tracks—the red lights flashed and the bells rang.

"Please do not tell me you are sorry," Leila said. "Show me with a kiss."

The red lights continued to flash and the bells continued to ring—and now the crossing gates began to lower as he stepped onto the tracks. He leaned in and tilted his head. He let the tension out of his lips before they touched hers. Leila's lips were smooth. Alex put one hand on her hip and the other slowly sifted through the back of her hair. His closed lips touched the top of hers. She closed her eyes. He softly kissed one eye then the other. He kissed her bottom lip. His lips traced hers in a slow circle. Alex opened his lips slightly. She opened hers. Leila's breath was minty. He kissed her gently. She kissed him back. His tongue touched inside the edge of her lip. Her tongue touched his tongue, stimulating it. His right hand descended her neck and stopped between her shoulder blades, holding her. Leila's hands touched his face.

The train illuminated Alex in its lights as it blasted its whistle. Alex was too entranced to step off the tracks. He took a step forward. Leila took a step back. Kissing her deeply, Alex walked forward, easing her backward. When they reached the bed, Leila sat to keep from falling. Alex continued forward, pushing her onto her back. He picked up her legs and put them on the bed. Alex lay near the middle of the bed, next to her. They kissed. Leila rolled on top of him. Then Alex rolled on top of her. She wrapped her arms around him. He lost himself in the sensuousness of her mouth.

Red lights flashed, bells rang, the light shone bigger and brighter, and the whistle blew louder—now it was too late to step off the tracks. Alex rolled off her and lay on his side next to her. He placed his hand on her belly, and when her head turned to face him, he kissed her. His consciousness disappeared into Leila. His hand caressed her body. She pushed his hand away and sat up, breathing heavily.

"*Mamnoon,*" she said. Thank you.

Alex stared at her for a moment, not understanding.

"Thank you," she said.

He was in a daze.

"I think you better go now."

Alex sat up, still looking at her.

"Please, go."

Alex stood and walked to the door. He stopped and turned to look at her.

"Wait." She rose and walked over to him. Leila held his face in her hands and kissed him sweetly. Then she stopped.

"*Mamnoon,*" she said with tears in her eyes.

He walked through the door and turned around, but Leila closed the door in his face. Alex returned to his room, but his legs could only move sluggishly. Although he should already be at his door, he was still in the middle of the hallway. Finally, his hand pulled out his key card and unlocked the door. He grasped the door knob, but his hand seemed to move in slow motion. The door opened and he entered. Just walking to the bed exhausted him. He sat down, but he knew he wasn't finished. He felt terrible about bringing tears to Leila's eyes, but he had to put her out of his mind.

I have to try to fix things with Cat. But how can I talk to her with the same lips that just kissed Leila? I could wash my face, but that wouldn't wash away Leila's memory, and her scent would still be on me. I could shower, but then I'd smell like I was trying to wash away something. No matter what I say to Cat, she'll still be angry. No matter what I do, I'm damned. Damned or not, I already made up my mind. I already wasted enough of Cat's time without being able to make any kind of commitment to her.

Alex pulled himself out of slow motion and quickly walked out of his room, hurried to Cat's room, and knocked on the door. No answer. He knocked again. No answer. He thought about returning to his room, but he knocked again. The door opened and there stood Cat. Her eyes were red.

"Can we talk?" Alex asked.

"I already told you, I'm through with you," Cat said.

"But you said to come back when I was finished with Leila."

"Did you screw her?"

"Can I come in? People might hear us."

"Why? I want the whole world to hear what you are—a jackass."

"No, we didn't have sex."

"I'm not just talking about tonight."

Alex didn't say anything.

Her face became hideous with anger. "That's what I thought!" Cat slammed the door in his face.

Alex heard laughter. He turned to see who it was.

Pancho and a redhead in a black raincoat stood arm in arm in the hallway. The raincoat was buttoned in the middle, but so many buttons were open at the top and bottom, and she showed so much skin, that it appeared she wasn't wearing anything under the raincoat. Pancho laughed at Alex. At six feet two, Pancho was tall, but his date was the same height as him. "Sorry, amigo," Pancho said, "but that shit is just too funny."

Alex wanted to punch him.

Pancho strained to stop laughing. "Come on, Xenia, let's see how fast we can drive on the autobahn." He broke into laughter again as he led Xenia into his room.

Bastard.

19

Alex slept on and off—mostly off. When Wednesday morning came, he was already awake. He checked his secure email. Although his team needed to launch the rescue mission as soon as possible, he secretly hoped for another day to try to fix things with Cat. When he saw there was no email, it gave him hope. He needed to show her that he was serious. All he needed was a chance.

He called John to ask him to give Leila shooting lessons. Who knew, maybe the two of them would be able to rekindle whatever they'd started at the kitchen table.

Alex showered, shaved, picked up a large manila envelope with information about Cat's role on the mission, and headed out the door. On his way to Cat's room, he spied a DO NOT DISTURB door hanger lying sideways on the carpet in front of Pancho's room. *Bastard.*

Alex knocked on Cat's door. There was no answer. He knocked again. The door opened. "Why can't you just leave me alone?" Cat asked.

"This is important."

"You just keep dragging my heart on a chain tied to your SUV."

Alex didn't like the imagery. *Am I really that cruel?* "Please."

"I know if I let you in, you'll hurt me again," Cat said. "You always do."

"Just give me this one chance," Alex said. "If what I have to say hurts you, I won't bother you anymore."

"So you can make a fool out of me?"

"Please."

She shook her head and opened the door wide. Alex walked in and they sat on stuffed chairs in her room.

"What is so important?" she asked.

"I never should've let you go. I never should've agreed to seeing other people while we were apart." He gulped. "I was a fool."

If his admission had an effect on her, she didn't show it. "I go where I want, and I see who I want."

"I should've tried harder."

"It doesn't matter. You're committed to the Team, and I can't compete with that."

"I know." He handed the envelope to her. "We're planning a rescue mission. And then we'll take out an Iranian biological weapons lab."

Cat threw it on the floor.

Alex didn't pick it up. "Just listen. Please. After this mission, no more missions for me. I'm coming up on my reenlistment. I'm going to request a transfer to become a BUD/S instructor. I know the XO at BUD/S—he wants me out there. I'll have most nights off. Weekends and holidays, too."

Cat looked down at the envelope and then back at him. There were tears in her eyes. "Do you realize what you're saying?"

Alex nodded.

"You can only be satisfied if you're killing terrorists."

"I've killed enough," Alex said. He meant it, too.

"What about Sarah?"

A tear came to Alex's eye. "I've done enough for Sarah. You told me that once. I think, no, I know, Sarah would agree."

"Have you told the guys?"

"Pancho doesn't want me to leave, but John says I should do what I want."

"But you'd be in California, and I'd still be in Virginia. We'd be on opposite coasts."

Alex had thought about that. Regular relationships were hard enough. Long-distance ones were pretty much impossible. "If you're willing, I'm sure I can get you transferred to Coronado with me. I want you to. I'm coming up on my reenlistment—the Navy wants to keep me. What we've done as the Outcasts has gone a long way in restoring all of our careers. They might say we're expendable, but I think that's just so they don't have to pay us the big bucks."

Cat started to smile, then stopped.

"You're really serious about this, aren't you?"

"Deadly. I've thought about what I want, and I want you. After this mission, you are my number-one priority."

She shook her head. "You hurt me, and I let you make a fool of me." Tears welled up in her eyes, but she didn't let them fall.

"You don't have to decide anything now. I just want you to know that I'm really sorry. And I'm serious about us."

"I don't know."

Alex wanted to take her out for the day, but that would be too much for her to agree to all at once, so he simplified it: "Can we eat breakfast together?"

"I've been crying and I look terrible."

"You look beautiful," Alex said, realizing that on a planet with more than three billion women, she truly was the most beautiful in the world.

"My eyes are all red."

"You can wear sunglasses."

She didn't say anything.

"Please," he said.

"I'm not very hungry."

"Lunch?"

"I guess."

"Any requests?"

"You know Germany better than I do."

"How about the Black Forest?"

"There's a restaurant called the Black Forest?"

Alex smiled. "In the Black Forest. Would you like to find a restaurant in the Black Forest?"

"Is it far?"

"It's a little over an hour from here."

She nodded.

Thirty minutes later, they rode a taxi off base. They left the snowy, vine-covered hills of Stuttgart and traveled southwest for an hour and a half until they came to the Black Forest. "With all the snow, it looks like the White Forest," Cat said.

Alex smiled.

"Why do they call it the Black Forest?" she asked.

"Because when the Romans saw it, that's what they called it. Compared to Rome, I guess the Black Forest was thicker and darker than what they were used to. Over time, man and nature took away many of the trees, but the forest still stands."

"Yes, there are more open areas than I expected, but it's beautiful."

The driver stopped at the Liftverbund Feldberg.

"Looks like a ski resort," Cat said excitedly.

"It is. I thought we could eat lunch here."

"You didn't tell me there was a ski resort."

Alex paid the driver, and they walked inside the main lobby. "We're a little early for lunch. Would you like to ski a little before we eat?"

"Yes!"

They rented ski equipment and went outside.

"Beginner, intermediate, or advanced?" Alex asked.

"You choose."

He didn't want to start out on something that was too challenging for her, but he didn't want to insult her, either, so he chose the intermediate slope.

As they rode the ski lift high off the ground, it exposed them to the chilly wind, but Cat was smiling. It felt good to be near her and especially to see her smile again. When the lift reached the ramp at the top of the ski run, Alex and Cat skied off. She skied effortlessly, but Alex had to work in order to keep up with her.

After skiing the intermediate slope for an hour, they took off their skis and stood in line for the gondola leading to the advanced runs. When Alex and Cat reached the front of the line, their gondola came around, and they put their skis in the rack. Then they hopped inside and sat on a bench. Another couple joined them in the gondola. They sat on the opposite bench and held hands. Alex and Cat turned around and looked through the window at the view behind their gondola. As they rose higher and higher up the mountain, they could see the snow-covered resort, scattered houses in the distance, and roads through the Black Forest. It reminded Alex of the snowy streets of downtown Zermatt, Switzerland, where he first kissed Cat.

Cat still seemed happy. Alex put his hand on hers. She pulled her hand away. He glanced at the couple, but they were so absorbed in each other, they didn't seem to notice. Cat was enjoying skiing in the Black Forest, but she wasn't enjoying him.

Near the top of the mountain, they departed the gondola, took their skis, and carried them past a pile of chopped wood, where they put their skis in a rack outside the restaurant. Inside, they sat between a warm, crackling fireplace and an enormous window that gave a panoramic view of the Black Forest from the mountain to the valley in the distance. Speakers filled the dining room with the music of Bach.

They ate Black Forest ham for lunch.

"It's so red," Cat said.

"They cold-smoke it with a fir tree's wood and leaves. That's why it keeps its red coloring." Salt, pepper, garlic, berries, and other spices seasoned the ham. With the ham they had *Kartoffelsalat*, a warm potato salad made with vinegar, oil, and bacon bits.

She tasted it.

"How is the kartoffelsalat?"

"It's really good."

They drank German hot chocolate, which was thicker and heavier than American hot chocolates. For dessert, Alex and Cat ate Black Forest cake.

"This cake tastes divine," Cat said. "Chocolate cake, cream, sour cherries—and something else. What is it?"

"A sour cherry brandy called Kirsch, short for *kirschwasser*, meaning 'cherry water.'"

The environment had everything for romance—warmth of a fireplace, a panoramic view, tasty food, good music, and a beautiful woman—all except for the passion.

"How'd you learn to ski so well?" Alex asked.

"My father." Alex knew she grew up in Idaho, but she never talked about her family. "We lived in Ketchum, which is right next to the Sun Valley ski resort."

"When you go back home, do you still ski together?"

Cat drank her hot chocolate. "When I was fourteen, he was killed in a car accident."

"Oh."

"I really miss him."

"I'm sorry. It must've been hard on your mom, too."

"She was a perfectionist, and after Dad was gone, she just got worse. Every night, she rode me about my homework. If I didn't get straight A's, she would yell at me and ground me. Dad and

I liked the outdoors, but Mom didn't. After he was gone, she wouldn't let me go out hardly at all. For four years, I just became numb. I felt like a zombie. I never told anyone. Then I joined the Navy."

Alex didn't want to say the wrong thing, so he kept quiet.

They finished their drinks, went outside, and grabbed their skis. From the restaurant, they skied down a gentle slope. Ahead of them in the trees, a bird chirped.

"Is that a cuckoo bird?" Cat asked.

The Black Forest was famous for cuckoo bird clocks, but Alex didn't know what a cuckoo bird looked like. "I don't know."

The gentle slope turned left, and they skied down the advanced slope. Cat sped off, leaving Alex in her mist of snow spray, and she didn't look back. He tried to catch up to her, but he realized he was trying to ski beyond his ability. If he broke a leg, he'd be off the mission. *Maybe I should be off the mission.* He thought about hurting his ankle in the Lut Desert. Then he thought about Leila, but he quickly blocked her out of his mind. He wanted Cat, and he wasn't going to let himself get sidetracked.

Alex continued alone making runs down the advanced slope for the rest of the afternoon. As Cat passed him, the sunlight illuminated the tips of her blond hair sticking out of her white wool hat and blowing in her wake. Her speed looked so effortless.

Later, as the ski lifts neared closing, Cat rode the gondola with him to the top. Instead of leaving him in her dust, she skied down the mountain with him. Even though now they were physically together, Cat remained distant.

They returned their ski rental equipment, and Alex called a taxi. Soon Alex and Cat rode it out of the ski resort.

"I enjoyed skiing in the Black Forest," she said.

"Thank you for coming."

During the hour-and-a-half ride back to Stuttgart, instead of resting her head on his shoulder, she rested it on the side of the cab. The distance between them was palpable to Alex.

When they arrived in Stuttgart, Alex took her to a nice restaurant. Although the dinner was first class, eating with Cat was awkward. He just wanted to go back to his room and forget about the day. The magic between them was gone.

20

Alex woke Thursday to see the morning sun enter his room around the curtains' edges. He checked his secure email. There was a message from JSOC. *Mission approved. Phase One: rescue the scientist's husband, Hassan Khamenei. Phase Two: locate Iranian biological weapons lab and destroy. Phase Three: capture or kill General Behrouz Tehrani. Attached are the photos of the general. Note: After Phase Two is completed, don't worry about any scientists who might escape. We can deal with them later. Focus on the general.* Alex opened the attachment and looked at the general's photos.

Alex hurriedly made one last visit to the intel shed before gathering the Outcasts and Leila. The five of them met in one of JSOC's secure meeting rooms, where Alex gave the mission brief. John and Leila entered the room talking and smiling. Cat and Leila avoided eye contact with each other, and Alex avoided prolonged eye contact with either of them. Pancho showed up last, hungover.

"Before I begin the mission brief, intel gave us photos of the three enemies we ran into in the Tehran hospital: Major Gholam Khan, Captain Nasser Fat'hi, and Lieutenant Saeed Saeedi," Alex said. "Any one of them is bad news."

Alex gave the Outcasts the mission outline JSOC gave him,

including copies of the general's photos. Then he continued with the rest of his brief.

". . . SIGINT reports that Hezbollah terrorists and the Iranian Revolutionary Guard are holding Dr. Khamenei's husband, Hassan Khamenei, hostage in the Sheikh Abdallah Barracks in Baalbek, which is located in the Bekaa Valley of Lebanon, just across the border from Syria. The Activity has reported that cardboard has been used to cover up the windows of a building north of the compound. Hezbollah has used this building to hold hostages before. JSOC believes the hostage is being held there now."

Alex showed them a digital three-dimensional building plan. "This is what JSOC's architects and engineers generated. No one has seen the inside of that building, but JSOC used sophisticated software to generate this model." JSOC had a computerized database of thousands of properties.

"Considering the situation in Lebanon, and considering that JSOC can't or won't give us additional team members, we're going to need some help from the locals for this rescue. Of course, we won't get help from the Shiites or Hezbollah supporters there, but Tripoli is nearby, and it's the home of Lebanese Sunnis. JSOC has provided us with information for a Sunni contact there.

"Cat, Leila, and I will fly into Beirut on a civilian flight as the advance team of our film crew. Then we'll check into an apartment in Tripoli and meet up with our Sunni contact. Pancho and John will travel separately, disguised as hospital corpsmen attached to a Marine unit that will launch from the USS *Kearsarge*, anchored off the shore of Lebanon. Pancho and John will come ashore with their unit to train with the Lebanese Army. Once on land with all our goodies, Pancho and John will change into civvies, separate from the Marines, and link up with us at the apartment in Tripoli. At Byblos, Lebanese marine commandos will extract us using their boats—the extract team will think this is part of the training exercise, and we need to try to keep them thinking that way. They'll take us to the USS *Kearsarge*." The USS *Kearsarge* was a Landing Helicopter Dock (LHD) amphibious assault ship that could carry almost nineteen hundred Marines. It was like a small town on water—with an armament that included a variety of missile systems. Also, the *Kearsarge* had dental and medical services, including emergency operating rooms.

"Nurses," Pancho said. "I feel another Purple Heart coming on."

"The last time we were in Lebanon," Cat said, "we almost didn't make it out alive."

"This time will make last time feel like lifeguarding at the kiddie pool," Alex said.

A FEW HOURS LATER, Cat wore a black wig and brown contact lenses. She rode with Alex and Leila in a chartered van from Stuttgart to Berlin, where they boarded a Lufthansa flight. Cat and Leila engaged in superficial chitchat, but they still seemed uncomfortable with each other. Riding the plane with both at the same time made Alex uneasy, too.

The three landed at Beirut–Rafic Hariri International Airport, named after the Lebanese prime minister assassinated by Hezbollah in 2005. On their last visit, Alex and Cat had passed through immigration without any trouble, but this time Alex noticed an older immigration officer, who looked like the boss, standing behind the other officers. The boss looked no-nonsense as he swooped into an immigration booth and escorted an arriving person into a side room.

When Alex reached the front of the line, he stepped forward and handed his passport to the young immigration officer in front of him.

"Are you three together?" the officer asked.

"Yes."

The officer pointed to Cat and Leila. "Tell them to come here."

Alex motioned for them to join him.

"What kind of work do you do?"

"I'm the producer and director of a documentary we're filming," Alex said.

"What movie name?" the immigration officer asked.

Alex looked up to the ceiling for effect before answering. "Wonderful World Heritage Sites."

"Bad title."

"Well, it's a working title."

"Need better working title." He looked at Cat and Leila. "Passports."

Cat and Leila handed him their passports.

Alex felt anxious, but he pushed it deep down inside himself. He knew their passports were immaculate. Cat had done this before, so she would be okay. Leila seemed cool under pressure, too. Even though he knew they should be okay, deep down inside he was anxious.

Suddenly, the older officer with the no-nonsense attitude hovered near the officer in front of Alex. *Is something wrong?*

The young officer examined Cat, then her passport photo. "What your job?"

"I'm his assistant."

"What does assistant do?" the officer asked.

Cat purposefully avoided speaking Arabic so the officer would be at more of a disadvantage and tire more easily. "Whatever he needs."

The officer leered at her and let out a creepy snicker.

"Within reason," Cat added, forcing a smile.

The officer leered at Leila. "Are you assistant, too?"

"No. I am the camerawoman."

"Do you take pictures of director and assistant?"

"No."

"You take my picture."

"I have to pick up my luggage."

"Can I be in movie?" he suddenly asked.

"That is not my decision."

The boss moved in closer to the Outcasts. *What's wrong?*

"Okay," the young officer said. He turned to Alex. "You director. Can I be in movie?"

Alex pretended to give it some thought. He just wanted to get past immigration, but maybe having a government minder with them would be a blessing in disguise. Who would suspect them then? "In Hollywood, anything is possible."

The young officer beamed. "Great."

Standing behind the young officer, the boss cleared his throat. The young officer noticed and quickly waved the Outcasts through.

Outside the airport, taxi drivers stood by their cabs offering rides to the Outcasts. Rather than let one of them choose him, Alex chose a cabbie. "How about this one?" he asked Cat.

Cat shook her head and pointed to another cab. They walked over to it, and she spoke to the driver in Arabic. "This one," she said. "He said it'll cost about fifteen thousand Lebanese pounds from the airport to Tripoli."

Alex made a shortcut calculation in his head by dropping the zeroes—roughly fifteen dollars. His shortcut wouldn't be acceptable in a bank for converting money, but adding or dropping zeros made it quick and easy to mentally process currencies around the world. "Okay," Alex said.

Cat sat next to the driver, so Alex sat in the backseat. Leila joined him. The cabbie drove north through Beirut then north along the western coast of Lebanon. Alex enjoyed watching the sun setting on the Mediterranean Sea. The first sunset he'd seen in Lebanese waters was when he and Cat sat alone on a yacht, kissing as the sun melted into the water. Later on that mission, they rendezvoused with

Pancho and John to begin reconnaissance of their target. Days later, they took out their target and were running and gunning for their lives, driving up the same road they were on now. Alex wanted to say something to Cat about the memories they shared, yet he wanted to be sensitive to Leila's feelings, too. Moreover, this was a military operation, not a vacation. So he kept his mouth shut. Maybe the driver sensed the mood, because he was quiet, too.

After thirty minutes, they passed a Christian town named Amsheet, where Alex, Cat, Pancho, and John had hidden from the enemy.

Alex looked at Cat. She looked at him. Leila noticed them looking at each other and they stopped.

Amsheet was as far north as Alex had ever traveled in Lebanon. Another thirty minutes later, they arrived in Tripoli, Lebanon. Buildings here appeared to be a mix of Arabic and European architecture. Strings of lights descended from towering buildings like loose cords from the tops of tents, out to posts in the ground. The driver turned east into the city, which was bathed in illumination of various shapes and colors: crescent moons, stars, rainbows, reds, magentas, violets, and more. There was so much to take in and the cabbie was driving so fast that Alex couldn't process it all.

The driver stopped in the parking lot of their apartment building. The three exited with their luggage and Alex paid the driver. JSOC had already rented their apartment, furnished it, and left the key with the building manager. The Outcasts located the manager's apartment on the bottom floor behind the front office, and Cat retrieved the key and a large envelope, probably containing their contract, insurance, and other paperwork.

Inside their apartment were three bedrooms. The apartment was clean and furnished. "This looks like the best room in the house," Cat said. "Leila, would you like to share it with me?"

Leila paused, staring at Cat. Leila nodded.

Alex took one of the other rooms. While lying in bed, he heard the sound of talking coming from Cat and Leila's room, but it wasn't loud enough for him to make out the words, so he wondered. Then he put Cat and Leila out of his mind. Tomorrow he'd be meeting with their Sunni contact.

21

Major Khan, Captain Fat'hi, and Lieutenant Saeedi flew on Iran Air from Tehran to Damascus International Airport in Syria. It was a far more dangerous flight than it had been before the civil war now tearing Syria apart. Khan had little sympathy for the plight of the Syrian people. They were not of his faith and so their deaths meant little to him. Not because of his faith in religious principles—Khan knew he was damned. He knew that the other religious groups constantly jockeyed for power, and he didn't like being jockeyed with. Islam had two major denominations, Shia and Sunni. Major Khan was a Shiite, a member of the Shia, the most popular denomination in Iran. Within Shia there were various sects, the Twelvers, which he belonged to, being the majority. Twelvers believed in the twelve imams, those directly succeeding the Prophet Muhammad. Only eleven were known to date, but Khan knew, as all Twelvers knew, that the twelfth and final imam, Muhammad al-Mahdi, would soon appear. On that glorious day, peace and justice would reign. Until then, Khan would gladly kill anyone who wasn't a Twelver. He wished his government had the courage to destroy the other sects because he believed that deep down inside, they wanted to destroy the Twelvers—it was only a matter of time.

Outside Iran, the Sunnis outnumbered the Shiites, and Major

Khan hated it. When he was a child, it was a Sunni who framed him, sending him to jail, where he was tortured and raped by a prison guard—the beginning of his transformation.

A Syrian soldier drove them to a checkpoint on the Lebanon border. With the civil war still raging, the border looked like a desperate outpost made for last stands. Khan doubted they would have gotten through if arrangements hadn't been made ahead of time. The Lebanese guards passed them through after checking their papers. All the guards at that checkpoint were Lebanese, but they were loyal to Syria. Their Syrian driver continued to Beirut, where he dropped them off at a hotel. It would have been faster to ride straight from Damascus to their final destination in Baalbek, but they didn't want the Syrian soldier or anyone else to know their final destination.

After checking in and renting a car, the three sat in their hotel. "B018," Lieutenant Saeedi said.

Pistachio smiled.

Major Khan stared at them. "What's B018?"

"Nothing," Lieutenant Saeedi said. "I was just thinking out loud."

Major Khan ignored him and continued with his meal.

"We should go to B018 tonight," Lieutenant Saeedi said.

"It's a great club," Pistachio added.

"Great?" Lieutenant Saeedi said. "It's better than great."

Khan shook his head. This was no time for debauchery. "No. We go out to dinner, and then back here. We leave here tomorrow at oh-seven-hundred to lay an ambush for Alex and his friends at the Sheikh Abdallah Barracks," Major Khan said.

Lieutenant Saeedi frowned.

Pistachio sighed, then nodded.

They walked to a local restaurant and took a table at the back. It was a simple place, the walls dull from smoke and dirt. Khan knew Pistachio and Saeedi were unhappy with him, but he didn't care. They could play all they wanted after the mission was over.

"Just an hour?" Saaedi asked.

Khan ignored him.

"It's not that far from here. It's in the Karantina district."

The Quarantine district. During the French occupation, ships' crews and their cargo were quarantined before being cleared to enter the country. Later, Armenian refugees camped there before settling inland. After that, Palestinian refugees arrived and stayed. During Lebanon's civil war, more refugees settled in Karantina, until fighting broke out between the Palestine Liberation Organization (PLO) and Christian militias, who massacred the PLO and their neighborhoods.

Khan had been there before. The place always smelled like death.

"No."

While the other two sulked, Khan studied the restaurant. Seven tables, a single narrow door at the front, no windows, and the kitchen in the back. It was simple, but the smell of the food told him it was good.

What did concern him was that there seemed to be only one exit, the stairs they entered from. This would be a bad place to be caught in an ambush.

Pistachio and Saeedi ordered the local Almaza beer, but Major Khan didn't drink what he called the *foreign poison*. Instead, he drank bottled water.

"How are we supposed to meet ladies here?" Pistachio said out loud.

"Maybe this will help," Saeedi said, pulling out his pistol so Pistachio and Khan could see.

"What're you doing that for?" Pistachio asked.

Saeedi put his pistol away. "I'm just joking."

"It isn't funny," Pistachio said.

"You guys brought yours, too, right?"

"Yeah, but we're not flashing them around."

"I'm not flashing it around. I only showed you two."

Pistachio shook his head.

Saeedi laughed. "You worry too much. You're going to get a heart attack. Just relax."

Pistachio popped a few pistachios in his mouth and cracked the shells with his teeth. "I'm trying to relax."

A group of three women walked into the restaurant and were seated at the table next to them. Saeedi immediately began talking up the women. Khan ignored it. It was hard enough pretending to be attracted to his wife without having to pretend to be attracted to strangers, too. He didn't have to come with his friends, but he tried to act sociable and let them have their fun.

Two of the girls invited them to sit at their table. One had straight brown hair and the other had curly brown hair. Khan motioned for them to go. It would leave him in peace. The curly-haired girl sat on the opposite side of Pistachio. Saeedi clapped his hands, a smile stretched across his face so wide, it looked like his skin might split.

Pistachio and Saeedi laughed and talked with the girls in Arabic. They joked and teased and seemed to be having a great time. The women appeared to enjoy the attention as well, judging by their squeals of delight. More drinks were ordered. Khan heard his name whispered a few times. He swiveled his chair around so that his back was to his friends and the women.

The waiter came up to his table with another bottle of water. When he put it down his hand brushed Khan's. Khan looked up at him. He was young, maybe twenty-two. His skin was smooth and his dark eyes were so inviting. He had the build of a swimmer.

Khan looked away, terrified his own eyes would reveal the desire he couldn't defeat.

"Your friends are having a good time," the waiter said.

Khan watched Pistachio and Saeedi. They were fools, but they were open with their desires. Why should they enjoy this life and he be denied its pleasures?

"Where is your restroom?" Khan asked, keeping his voice low.

The waiter motioned with his head toward the back of the restaurant. Khan nodded and then looked away. The waiter disappeared while Khan casually watched his friends. They were completely enthralled by the women.

"I think that airline food did a number on my stomach. I'll be back in a few minutes," Khan said, getting up from his table.

"What? Sure, we'll be here," Pistachio said, barely looking at him.

Khan paused, then walked to the back of the restaurant. He found the door leading to the restroom and strode in. The young waiter was there, pretending to be tidying up.

"I—" the waiter started to say, but Khan grabbed him by the throat and pushed him against the wall. The waiter's eyes went wide.

"I don't want to hear another word out of you," Khan said, bringing his face in so that their noses touched. "Get on your knees, now."

Khan let go of his throat and pushed the waiter down. He remembered the door and was turning to lock it when it swung open and Pistachio walked in.

"Thought I'd better check . . . see how you are," Pistachio said, looking from Khan to the waiter and back.

Khan stepped back from the waiter and furiously brushed at his suit. "The spilled water," Khan said.

Pistachio looked at Khan's suit then up at him. "Look, it's none of my business."

He knows! Rage and guilt roiled Khan's stomach. "It's no one's business," Khan said, pushing his way past Pistachio and going back to his table. A few moments later Pistachio returned.

"I see you managed to save our sick friend from getting lost," Saeedi said, laughing as he casually put an arm around one of the women. "You've got a career as a shepherd, Pistachio," Saeedi said. The women giggled.

Khan realized he was reaching for his gun when the door to the restaurant banged open. A large man walked in. He wore an expensive blue sport coat over a white T-shirt and designer jeans. He didn't wait to be seated, but walked right over to Pistachio and Saeedi.

"You dishonor our family by associating with these pigs," the man said. He was at least six foot two and well over two hundred pounds. Khan figured most likely a brother of one of the women.

The curly-haired woman stood up. "You do not own me, Talal! I can do what I want."

"Filthy whore!" Talal shouted, slapping her face and knocking her down. Saeedi jumped up with his pistol drawn and swung it at Talal, but for a big man he moved quickly and easily dodged the blow. Someone screamed.

Talal cocked his right arm, ready to land a haymaker against Saeedi, but Pistachio stepped in and dropped him with a punch to his temple.

The door opened and a man charged in. He looked the spitting image of Talal. Khan got up from his chair and went to intercept him, but before he got to him the waiter darted between them.

"Please, no fi—" Khan brought up an elbow and slammed it into the waiter's temple. The man went down like a sack of rice. The twin threw a punch at Khan, but Saeedi got there first, hooking the man's arm and pulling him down to the floor. A crack like a shot from a small-caliber pistol meant Saeedi had just broken the twin's arm.

Pistachio grabbed Saeedi and pulled him up. "We're out of here."

Saeedi started to resist and whipped his pistol out. "We'll finish them."

The rage in Khan dissipated and he realized the danger they'd just fallen into. "He's right. We have to go now!" Khan barked.

Saeedi holstered his pistol.

They hurried out of the restaurant and into the night.

When they were far enough away Khan led them into an alley. When he was sure no one had followed them he rounded on Saeedi.

"You will not derail this mission."

Saeedi opened and closed his mouth a few times. "Me? I was just defending myself. What about you? You hit that waiter like you were trying to kill him. What the hell was that about? The only one that'll screw this up will be you."

Khan saw Pistachio start to open his mouth to speak. Before he could say anything, Khan pulled his own pistol out of its holster and pushed the barrel into Saeedi's chest. "Say that again," he said quietly. Saeedi looked at Pistachio. Pistachio shook his head. Saeedi lowered his head like a wounded puppy dog.

Khan lowered his pistol. "Let's go back to the hotel. Tomorrow will be a big day."

22

Alex awoke just after 0630 to the sound of Cat's and Leila's voices. After dressing, he stepped out of his room and saw them sitting on the couch talking. Alex rubbed his eyes and asked, "Were you two talking the whole night?"

They glanced at him then giggled. At least they seemed happy.

An hour later, Pancho and John arrived with the team's weapons, ammo, and other goodies. All five armed themselves with concealed Zoaf 9mm pistols.

For breakfast, they sucked on cold energy gel tubes.

Cat called for a taxi, then she went downstairs with Alex to wait for it in the parking lot. "You and Leila seemed to have a lot to talk about," Alex said.

"Does that bother you?" she asked.

"No," he said. "Just curious."

"Girl stuff," she said, dismissing his curiosity.

Alex was still curious, but he let it go.

The taxi arrived and they both sat in the back while the cabbie took them down snowy streets past unfinished buildings, charred and bullet-riddled walls, and a partially destroyed house. They continued to a spot a block away from their rendezvous place at the Café Paris. Alex and Cat put on their sunglasses and zipped up their jackets while they walked around the perimeter checking for surveillance, or worse, a sniper. When they were sure the area was clean, they moved in closer and checked again: buildings, vehicles, and pedestrians.

Inside the café they briefly studied the people, mostly women, except for a man with a briefcase. Alex and Cat removed their sunglasses. Alex chose a table away from the windows, so any outside explosion wouldn't hit them with fragments through the glass. They sat down with their backs to the wall and a view of the front entrance and kitchen exit—Alex noted the entrance and exit as escape routes. If he needed an additional route, he could throw a chair through the window and jump through it.

They were nearly an hour early for the 1030 rendezvous with their agent. This made it more challenging for their contact if he was planning to set up an ambush. While waiting, they ordered Lebanese coffee. Their waitress brought two empty demitasses and poured the coffee at their table from a long-handled coffeepot. Alex took a sip. The coffee was thick and had a strong, bitter taste.

At 1030, there was no sign of their contact—he was late. Maybe he wouldn't show. A few minutes later, Omar Bisharia arrived, a handsome young Lebanese man wearing a tight black T-shirt and blue jeans. His eyes were piercing—something the intel pictures hadn't conveyed. He was a leader in the Arab Spring against Syrian domination of Lebanon. He recruited for his militia from a poor area of Tripoli called Bab-al-Tabbaneh. With Omar came a heavyweight who had massive biceps and forearms, a thick neck, and a small head with a little cap on top of it. His scraggly beard made him look like Brutus in the Popeye comic.

Alex and Omar exchanged bona fides and chitchatted in English before Omar switched to Arabic. Cat translated.

"I mean no offense, but our strongest supporters, the ones who will bear arms in this battle, don't like Americans," Omar said.

"I understand," Alex said. "Two Palestinians are being held hostage in the Sheikh Abdallah Barracks in Baalbek. There is another man being held there, an Iranian named Hassan Khamenei."

"The Farsi instructor. Who are the Palestinians?"

Alex showed them pictures of two men. "The Palestinians are Youssef Rahbanni and Dalal Haddad."

Omar's and Brutus's eyes widened. Brutus became tense like he was about to eat the table. "Youssef," he mumbled.

Omar leaned forward. "Where did you get this information?"

The waitress came to their table, and they became quiet. Alex ordered drinks for Omar and Brutus. The waitress left with their order.

"I can't say," Alex said.

Cat resumed translating.

"You can't say, or you won't say?" Omar asked.

"Both," Alex replied.

"And what do you get out of rescuing this man?"

"Khamenei's wife wants him rescued. If we help her, she'll help us in a separate matter with Iran," Alex whispered.

When Alex said "Iran," the edges of Omar's lips rose. *The enemy of my enemy is my friend.* "What do you need from us?" Omar asked.

"I need your help assaulting Hezbollah so we can rescue the hostages."

"Why don't you do it yourself?"

"I don't have enough men."

"Why not?"

The waitress brought their drinks. They became quiet again. After the waitress left, Alex and Omar continued talking while Cat translated.

"My guess is that if anyone finds out the United States is supporting you, it might lead us to war," Alex said.

Omar took a leisurely sip of his drink. "War is nothing new to us."

"Americans don't know war at home like you. They don't want to."

"Maybe they should. Then they wouldn't be so quick to send their soldiers to kill and be killed."

"I haven't experienced war in my own country, but I have experienced war."

"Then why risk it for your people?"

"If we don't stop Iran, we face a destruction as great as, or greater than, war. We need to rescue Khamenei as soon as possible."

"Some people say I have a gift for seeing the true nature of people." Omar examined Alex's face.

"I wish I had that gift."

"Is there anything you're not telling me that I should know? I'm not fond of surprises."

"Hezbollah might be expecting us."

Omar smiled. "They're always expecting us. They just don't know when. How many men do you need?"

"How many men do you have?"

"Forty-two. That's including us." He looked at Brutus.

"That'll have to do. If you have a bank account, I'll wire twenty-five thousand U.S. dollars to help pay for weapons and ammunition."

"We don't do this for money."

"I would've brought weapons and ammo, but the best I can do now is cash."

Omar shook his head.

"It's not for you. It's for your men. I imagine many of them will be using personal weapons."

"Yes."

"If the mission is a success, I'll wire twenty-five thousand more. For your men."

"Okay."

Alex and Omar made plans for attacking Hezbollah and rescuing

Hassan Khamenei and the two Palestinians. When the two finished, they shook hands. Omar and Brutus left.

Before Alex paid the bill, Cat pointed to the counter display next to the cash register. "These Lebanese pickles look so good."

"What?"

"Pickles."

"Can we do takeout?" Alex asked.

"I'll ask." She spoke with the woman behind the counter.

Alex was nervous. They'd already spent enough time in this café, but it would be good not to be seen leaving with Omar. The cashier put Cat's pickles in a plastic box and wrapped a rubber band around it. Cat paid the bill and asked the cashier to call a taxi. A scattering of light snowflakes drifted to the ground as the cab pulled up to the curb. Alex and Cat walked out of the Café Paris and hopped into the cab.

Cat sat in the backseat and spoke Arabic to the cabbie. Alex forgot about the mission as he flashed back to an evening with Cat in the backseat of a limousine in Paris. The chauffeur drove through Paris while he and Cat made love. Now Alex sat close to her in the taxi. Cat scooted away from him. Alex scooted closer. She moved away until there was no more space left. Her back pressed against the taxi. Alex closed the gap between them. She had nowhere to go except out, and the taxi had already picked up speed. The snowflakes became bigger and came down en masse.

"Do you remember Paris?" he asked.

"I'm trying to forget," Cat answered.

"I can't forget."

His face moved closer to hers.

"You can't do that here," Cat said.

Alex noticed that she didn't pull away.

"I can kiss you here."

"It's illegal."

"Not in Lebanon."

"It's illegal."

"You already said that. It's not true."

"They'll arrest you."

"I can kiss you in Tripoli." His eyes feasted slowly from her eyes to her lips and down to her hips. "I can kiss you in Beirut."

"Oh, no, you can't kiss me in Beirut!" she said, breathing heavily. "Not in a taxicab in broad daylight." She ran out of breath and had to inhale.

His gaze returned to her lips. "Then I'll kiss you in Tripoli."

Cat hurriedly opened her plastic box, put a Lebanese pickle in her mouth, and closed the box. The Lebanese pickle was smaller and smoother than American pickles. Alex took the pickle out of her mouth. She grabbed the pickle and put it back in her mouth. Alex pulled it out again.

"If you kiss me, I'll scream." She put the pickle in her mouth.

"You can scream easier without this in your mouth." He took the pickle and kissed her. Soon she closed her eyes and he closed his. Cat wrapped her arms around him. Alex felt the world disappear as he immersed himself in rediscovering her lips. The breath through her nose raced in and out, blowing warm against his face. Alex pulled away from Cat for a moment and opened his eyes. The rear windows were fogging.

She opened her eyes. "I can't breathe."

"Stop breathing." The rate of her breathing picked up speed, faster than the beating of the windshield wipers. She sounded like she was about to hyperventilate. He kissed her and closed his eyes. He couldn't hear her breathing, so he started to pull away, but she pulled him back in.

Alex stopped kissing her and took a bite of the Lebanese pickle in his hand. It had a mellow taste. Cat breathed calmly, and he gave her a bite. He finished chewing and swallowed. After she swallowed, she kissed him. He tasted vinegar, salt, and sugar on her lips and tongue.

"It's so hot in here, I'm burning up," Cat whispered.

Alex put the last piece of pickle in his mouth and transferred it to hers. He unzipped Cat's jacket and helped her out of it. Starting to feel hot himself, Alex took off his own jacket.

The driver stopped the cab. Alex looked around. They had reached the destination near the apartment. *Bad timing.* "Can you drive in a circle around town?" Alex asked the driver.

"Circle town?" the driver asked.

Alex finished chewing the pickle, swallowed, leaned forward, and gestured in a circle with his hand. "Can you drive in a circle around town?"

"Go Beirut?" the driver asked.

"If you say so," Alex answered.

"What?"

"Yes. Go to Beirut. Please."

"Beirut," the driver confirmed.

"Yes, Beirut." Alex placed an advance of forty thousand Lebanese pounds on the console next to the driver's seat. Then Alex moved the rearview mirror so the driver couldn't see the backseat.

The driver appeared puzzled for a moment. He took the money, shifted into gear, and drove south. The snow came down harder and heavier.

23

Alex and Cat returned to the apartment, where they found Pancho alone. Minutes later, John and Leila returned with some groceries. Although John wasn't a conversationalist, he was talking—and laughing that freakish laugh of his. Leila was laughing, too. Alex smiled. Maybe his matchmaking was working.

"What kind of wheels you get?" Pancho asked.

"A black Hummer H2 with seven seats and a white van," John replied. "I took out the dome lights so we can slip in and out of the vehicles without getting lit up."

"Sweet."

John approached Alex and quietly asked, "Can I talk to you for a minute?"

"Sure," Alex answered.

John led Alex into his bedroom and closed the door. John rarely beat around the bush and this time was no different. "So you and Leila . . ."

"The road is clear, my friend," Alex said.

"That's what she said, but I wanted to hear it from you." John smiled and walked out the door.

"You're welcome," Alex said aloud in the empty room.

Later, the Outcasts ate a late lunch and cleaned up. Next, Alex spread a map out on the floor, briefed them, and discussed the mission. After their discussion, they took the white van an hour and a half east to the Al Assi River, near the city of Hermel. There they checked out the river and its location. The Outcasts drove south of Hermel and examined the cold blue river near its source. The river was wide, deep, and fast enough to use rubber rafts.

Cat drove farther south and passed posters of Hezbollah's leader, Hassan Nasrallah, displayed on walls and in windows. Mounted to houses and shops, green and yellow Hezbollah flags flapped in the wind. There were posters of people Alex didn't recognize. "Who are the pictures on the posters?" Alex asked.

"Hezbollah martyrs," Cat answered.

The Outcasts continued to Baalbek to do some filming so if later someone became curious, they would have something to show for their visit. During the Roman period, part of the Roman Empire included the city of Baalbek, which was called Heliopolis. In 1984, the city's ruins became a World Heritage Site. Now it was home to thousands of Hezbollah supporters.

Cat parked near the temple complex ruins. The Outcasts passed two Hezbollah militia in their green uniforms. The militiamen gabbed with each other while smoking cigarettes.

A street vendor carrying his goods in bags on his shoulders approached the Outcasts waving his green and yellow flags. "You like Hezbollah flag, sir? Many people buy Hezbollah flag."

"I don't think so," Alex said in German and waved him off.

"I don't understand." The vendor turned to Cat and Leila and pushed forward a green and yellow magnet. "You like Hezbollah refrigerator magnet?"

Leila pushed it away and Cat said something in Arabic.

The man frowned. Next he showed John a yellow T-shirt designed with green Arabic writing and a green AK-47 over a green globe. "One-size-fits-all Hezbollah T-shirt."

John ignored him.

The vendor turned to Pancho and pulled out a baseball cap with a picture of two smiling men: Hezbollah's leader, Hassan Nasrallah, and the previous Iranian president, Mahmoud Ahmadinejad. "Would you like Lebanese baseball hat?"

Pancho smiled. "Would you like to *besa mi juevos*?"

The vendor responded with a puzzled grin. Alex smiled. He'd heard the Spanish version of "kiss my nuts" more than once.

John punched Pancho in the shoulder.

The Outcasts passed the vendor and proceeded to the site of the temples and their ruins. At the entrance, a man collected admission. "How much?" Alex asked.

"Twelve thousand Lebanese pounds each," the man said in broken English.

Alex started to pay the man, but Cat stopped Alex. "Don't pay that," she said. "Twelve thousand is too much." She haggled with the man in Arabic until he agreed to two thousand Lebanese pounds each.

Alex paid.

Inside the site, John and Leila filmed the remains of the Temple of Jupiter, with its six seventy-five-foot-high Corinthian pillars standing atop twenty-seven enormous limestone blocks.

Next they examined the Temple of Bacchus. Although the Temple of Jupiter was taller, much of the Temple of Bacchus remained intact, and Alex still felt like he was the size of an ant as they hiked up thirty stairs to the entrance of a hundred-foot-high building. Nineteen unfluted Corinthian columns supported an entablature carved with bulls and lions. Inside, nature reclaimed the floor—weeds poked up through uneven ground covered with broken columns and scattered rubble. On the ceiling were scenes of a god with a cornucopia, a god with a hammer, and one with arrows. The Outcasts passed smaller columns and hiked up another flight of stairs to the dark worship room.

After filming the temple complex, they packed up, then drove along a road southeast until they reached a private hospital. "This is the hospital here," Alex said. "Leila, you'll park here tomorrow night."

"Yes."

Cat pulled into the hospital parking lot and circled it before returning to the road southeast. Finally, she slowed down in front of a rock quarry located on the same hill as the Sheikh Abdallah Barracks. John pretended to film the rock quarry, but he was actually filming the Sheikh Abdallah Barracks. His fellow Outcasts stood around him like they were viewing the quarry, but they were obstructing onlookers from seeing John while he filmed.

They finished their recon and had just loaded into the van when a vehicle came speeding into the parking lot and stopped in front of them. Two Hezbollah men in green uniforms approached the driver side and motioned for Cat to roll the window down.

She rolled down the window with her left hand and started the ignition with her right.

One of the men tilted his head in a way that made it look as if it were on crooked. He spoke Arabic to Cat.

"He's asking what we're doing here," Cat said. With her foot on the brake, she shifted into low gear, ready to plow through the Hezbollah vehicle before shifting into drive and speeding away.

"We're a movie production crew," Alex said.

Cat translated.

"Who are your stars?" Crooked Head asked.

"This is our main star." Alex pointed to Pancho.

"Hi," Pancho said, waving with a smile.

"Who is he?" Crooked Head asked.

"Pancho Bardem," Alex said. "He was nominated for an Oscar two years ago."

Crooked Head poked his head inside Cat's window and surveyed the interior before resting his eyes on Pancho. "Never heard of him."

Pancho frowned and turned up his nose.

"He's well-known in Spain and Mexico," Alex explained.

Pancho smiled, flashing what he thought was a killer grin.

"I've watched behind the scenes and this isn't enough people to make a movie," Crooked Head said.

Alex allowed irritation to creep into his voice: "This is a documentary."

"Where is your film equipment?"

Alex turned to John and Leila. "Show him."

They reached down and unzipped their duffel bags.

Crooked Head watched intently.

John pulled out a camera and tripod, and Leila also took out a camera and tripod.

"What are your jobs?" Crooked Head asked.

Alex pointed to himself. "I'm the producer-director." Then he pointed to Cat. "This is my assistant. Pancho is our host-narrator, and in the back are our two camera people."

"You don't need two cameras for a documentary."

"We don't do multiple takes," Alex said impatiently. "That's why we shoot with two cameras. Our movie is honest—what you see is what it is. And I don't appreciate you insulting Pancho. You don't even know who Pancho Bardem is, and you try to act like you know how to make a documentary. Have you been living under a rock?!"

Cat's translation was only about half as long as what Alex said.

Alex's eyes burned into Cat. "Don't edit me. Tell him everything I said."

The other Hezbollah guy pulled Crooked Head aside and spoke broken English: "You make movie here?"

"We filmed the temple ruins," Alex said. "We heard the rock quarry is a good place to film so we came here, but there's nothing to film here."

"Can I see?" the Hezbollah man asked politely. He was older and seemed to be the senior of the two.

"The film? Sure." Alex turned to John. "Show him what we took of the temple ruins."

John stepped out of the van and played back the recording on the camera's swing-out monitor. Crooked Head looked over Senior's shoulder.

Senior finished viewing the monitor and focused on Alex. "What you know about Hezbollah?"

"Just what I hear on the news," Alex replied.

"The news is wrong. I tell you truth. Take my picture."

Alex took a few moments, as if he were seriously thinking about it. He looked the soldier up and down before answering. "You have the hips of a younger George Clooney. Okay. Everybody, let's film what he has to say."

The Outcasts unloaded from the van. John and Leila set up their cameras on the tripods with the sun to their backs and Senior, Crooked Head, and Pancho in front. Senior patted his hair.

"Are we filming?" Alex asked.

"Yeah, boss," John said.

Leila nodded.

"Pancho," Alex said.

Pancho, Senior, and Crooked Head exchanged greetings before Pancho asked Senior about Hezbollah.

Senior said something to Crooked Head in Arabic and he took a step back. Senior didn't want Crooked Head crowding him in the picture frame. "Hezbollah is political party in Lebanese government. We built hospital, radio station, television station, university, schools for children, and housing for poor people. Hezbollah is doctors, lawyers, teachers, students, farmers, and common people. . . ." He conveniently left out any mention of *terrorists* and went on to complain about Israel, the United States, and Europe. Eventually, he became tired of talking.

"Great," Alex said. "Let's call it a day."

Pancho shook Senior's hand, thanking him. John and Leila

packed up their cameras. Alex thanked Senior and gave him a business card for a dummy movie production company, phone number, and email address where a real secretary stood by to answer inquiries in order to maintain the cover. The Outcasts loaded into the van and waved to the Hezbollah pair before driving away. Senior and Crooked Head smiled and waved back.

24

I n the Sheikh Abdallah Barracks, Major Khan and his Hezbollah interpreter entered the building where the hostages were kept. Major Khan had heard that one of the three prisoners was a young man named Youssef Rahbanni. Having already received clearance to interrogate the young man, Major Khan and his interpreter checked in with the guard at the desk, then proceeded through the doorway and to the right. At the end of the hall, Major Khan found a guard seated in a chair. Major Khan kicked the chair. Startled, the guard stood and unlocked the door. Major Khan told the interpreter to wait in the hall. He didn't need an eyewitness. He entered the interrogation room, where Youssef was already sitting with his hands tied and a black hood over his head. It had been too long since Major Khan's last interrogation, and he ached inside with anticipation. The boy couldn't speak Farsi, so Major Khan skipped the talking and cut straight to the monster.

After his session with the young man, Major Khan left the interrogation room and he and his interpreter left the building. The interrogation session relieved Major Khan's monster for the time being, but disgusted the piece of humanity that he still clung to. Rather than dwell on it, he looked around the building and noticed the nearby stone wall. "If I were the enemy on land, I'd come over this wall," Major Khan said. He and his interpreter scaled the wall and lowered themselves outside the barracks. He scanned the area. There were numerous possible approaches, but each would probably converge at the wall near the prison building. Major Khan needed to set up a sniper hide with eyes on that spot of the wall. He didn't believe the Americans had the guts to do a helicopter insertion, but if they did, he'd have a good shot at the helo, too. To the north, a cluster of upper-class houses faced the barracks. He pointed to one that looked like the perfect location. "That one."

Major Khan and the interpreter returned to the barracks and found Pistachio, Lieutenant Saeedi, and their gear. They loaded into a gray Range Rover. Pistachio drove them to the house north of the barracks, where they met the owner, an average-looking middle-aged woman.

Pistachio had a way with women, so he gave the pitch and the interpreter translated for Major Khan. "We'd like to rent a room in your house to conduct some surveillance on the barracks."

"I don't know," she said. "My late husband left me with a sufficient inheritance, and I really don't need the money."

"I understand. We have to give you the money, it's only the fair thing to do, but this isn't about the money. This is about the security of your neighborhood and supporting Hezbollah."

Lieutenant Saeedi stared at the woman. Major Khan tried to give him the evil eye, but Saeedi didn't notice.

"How long will you need to be here?" she asked.

"A day or two," Pistachio said. Even though the mission could last weeks or months, it was easier to ask her for a couple of days. "You'll be safer with us here. Your neighborhood will be safer, too."

Lieutenant Saeedi seemed to be raping her with his eyes.

"This house is more than I need anyway," she said. "I guess it would be okay." She showed them the house without asking how much money they were offering.

Major Khan paid little attention to the first floor, and Lieutenant

Saeedi paid more attention to the owner than anything else. When they reached the bedroom on the second floor with a view of the barracks, Major Khan became fully alert. "This room is perfect," he said.

"Okay," the owner said.

"Can we be alone for a few minutes to discuss our surveillance?" Major Khan asked.

The owner nodded and left the room.

Major Khan sent the interpreter to fetch his bag.

When the three of them were alone, Lieutenant Saeedi said, "I really want to have sex with her."

"Why don't you try to get to know her first?" Pistachio said.

"Because that never works," Lieutenant Saeedi said. "Once a woman gets to know me, it's over."

"You just have to find the right woman," Pistachio said.

"That's easy for you to say. Women are always hanging all over you. Every woman is the right woman for you, but no woman is the right one for me."

Pistachio looked to Major Khan for support.

"I don't care about the woman," Major Khan said. "And I don't care about your need for sex. What I care about is the mission. After we kill Alex Brandenburg and his men, you can rape every woman in Lebanon."

Lieutenant Saeedi's face sagged. He found a chair in the corner and sat. Major Khan understood what it was like when the monster needed to be fed, and he couldn't feed it. Even so, Khan would kill Saeedi without hesitation. There was no room for negotiation.

The major pulled a table in front of the window. Then the interpreter returned with Major Khan's bag and handed it to him. He dismissed the interpreter then opened the bag. Inside was a Nakhjir, a Russian Dragunov sniper rifle licensed for manufacture in Iran. The Nakhjir's magazine held ten rounds of 7.62x54mmR ammunition, similar to the American .308. At the end of the rifle was a flash suppressor so the enemy would have more difficulty spotting him. Major Khan attached a PSO-1 optical sight and looked through it. The sight magnified everything four times its normal size.

Next, Major Khan pulled out a pair of binoculars. "We'll take turns in six-hour shifts watching the barracks with these binoculars. If anyone spots something suspicious, he'll tell me, and I'll do the rest."

25

The next day Alex and Cat met again with Omar and Brutus. Now the Sunnis were on America's side, but Alex knew that someday Islamic fanaticism might rear its ugly head, and they'd be enemies. It saddened Alex, but he didn't dwell on it.

At 2300 hours, Alex, Pancho, John, and Leila left the apartment wearing civvies and hiking boots and carrying large black duffel bags. Under the light of a partial moon, the SEALs loaded into the back of the black Hummer and Leila drove. Minutes later, Cat would head out in the van to link up at the final rendezvous point with Brutus. Alex worried about leaving her alone with Brutus, but Alex needed Pancho and John with him on the assault—and Cat wanted no special favors.

The SEALs put cammies and dark inflatable life vests on over their civvies. In Alex's pockets he carried a map, an energy gel tube, Swiss Army knife, first-aid kit (blowout kit), survival kit, PRC-112 survival radio, and gloves. From his duffel bag he pulled out his holstered Zoaf pistol and put it on. Then he took out his AKMS assault rifle and loaded it. Next, Alex donned his combat vest loaded with rifle and pistol ammo, grenades, GPS, and radio. From his radio he could transmit to and receive from each of the Outcasts and Omar. Last was his small backpack with the rest of his gear.

Alex applied olive drab green and loam paint to his skin, making sure to keep the high areas like his nose and cheekbones dark and the low areas, like around his eyes, light. Where light shone, his skin became dark, and where shadows fell, his skin became light, so he looked other than human. The SEALs checked each other's war faces to make sure no natural skin color was exposed.

A little more than an hour later, they arrived in Baalbek, where they'd seen the Hezbollah posters around town and met the Hezbollah vendor before entering the temple ruins.

Two men in green uniforms armed with AK-47s stood in the road and waved for the Outcasts to stop—Hezbollah. *Damn, we haven't even reached the objective!* "Leila, stop and see what they want."

Leila stopped in front of them. The guards approached her and gestured for her to roll down the window—they couldn't see through the Hummer's tinted windows in the dark as well as the Outcasts could see out. John quietly opened the rear door on the passenger's side and slipped out. Alex followed, drawing his sound-suppressed pistol. They crept around the back of the Hummer. Leila was speaking in Farsi, confusing the two Hezbollah men.

John turned the corner followed by Alex, both looking down the sights of their pistols. Now Alex could see the two Hezbollah men talking to Leila. John walked close to the vehicle, giving Alex space to walk on his left and an open field of fire. The Hezbollah man on the left appeared in Alex's sights, and Alex squeezed the trigger three times. The first two rounds struck the Hezbollah man in the upper torso, and the last struck him in the head just as John shot him in the head, too. Alex aimed at John's man on the right, but he was already down. Alex was smooth, but John was smoother. *Smooth is fast.* They moved forward and gave each of the Hezbollah another shot in the skull to make sure.

Alex and John dragged the bodies off the road and into the bushes. They returned to the Hummer and sat inside. Pancho was eating a bag of Keebler peanut butter cookies.

"Thanks for the help," Alex said.

"No *problemo*," Pancho said with his mouth full.

Alex wasn't happy. "Leila, take us to the insertion point."

Leila took her foot off the brake and stepped on the gas. Pancho gave her a cookie.

John held his hand out to Pancho. "How about it?"

Pancho handed John some cookies.

"Sam," John said.

"Huh?" Pancho asked.

"The nineteenth elf."

"Oh, yeah. The peanut butter baker." Pancho gestured with a cookie to Alex. "Uncommonly good cookies for uncommonly good shooters."

Alex shook his head and took it. After eating the cookie, he wanted another. Pancho must have read his mind, because Pancho gave him two more.

Leila drove a few minutes before parking behind a deserted building on a hill. The guys put on their NVGs.

Alex keyed his radio once, breaking squelch to signal everyone that he was in place. Leila broke squelch twice, Cat three times, and Omar four—they were in place, too. *So far, so good.* Pancho slipped out on Leila's side, followed by Alex and then John. Alex didn't like leaving Leila by herself, but he was short on assaulters as it was. She would have to fend for herself.

Alex could see his breath in the moonlight, but his adrenaline was pumping so hard that he didn't feel cold. Pancho led them behind the hospital southwest through a grove of cedar trees powdered with snow. The SEALs crossed a street and entered another grove of cedar trees behind another hospital. Pancho skirted around the hospital to the right and passed between two buildings before taking them across another street. Heading west, they crept behind a group of buildings laid out in an L-shape. A dog barked. *I wish that dog would shut up.*

Rather than walk across an open field, at the second house from the end of the L-shape, Pancho cut between houses. They crossed another road and walked through snow above their ankles until they reached the next road. As the SEALs rounded a large three-story building, Alex could see the Sheikh Abdallah Barracks less than two hundred yards away. They crawled between the three-story building and a farmer's field. In spite of all the snow, there were rows of bushy green plants growing in the field. Pancho low-crawled through the field, followed by Alex and John. The ground was frozen hard, and Alex was thankful for his knee pads and arm pads. Pancho stopped and slowly looked around in front of them. Alex examined the area left and right. He glanced back to see John checking behind them. When John turned back around and made eye contact with Alex, John made no indication that there was a problem. Alex returned his eyes to the front.

To the SEALs' right was a larger field. In it lay Omar and his men. They kept still. *Good.* Although Alex could see some of them with his NVGs, he wondered how well the enemy might be able to spot them. Pancho resumed crawling through the rows of bushy plants.

The SEALs exited the farmer's field and quickly crawled over a stone wall. Inside the wall of Hezbollah's barracks, they lay still for several minutes before entering a clump of cedar trees next to their target building. Pancho moved forward as far as he could without exiting the clump of trees and stopped. *This is it.* Alex's senses were so heightened that a breeze through the trees sounded like someone stomping toward him. His breathing seemed loud enough to wake up the whole Hezbollah barracks. He could even hear the quickening beat of his heart. *Breathe.* He took slow, deep breaths. His heart and breathing rates slowed.

John crept past Alex and Pancho and turned the target building corner to pick the lock on the door with a customized silent steel pick made with a polymer core inside and polymer lamination on the outside. Pancho stood with his pistol drawn and headed for the door. Alex, also with pistol drawn, crouched behind Pancho. *Who or what will be waiting for us when we step through the door? A booby trap? Ambush? Will the hostages be there? Breathe.*

John opened the door and Pancho rushed inside and to the left. Alex was second through the door and peeled right. Both were careful to get inside the door and to his position so the train wouldn't get stuck in the doorway. If the train stopped in the doorway, everyone behind the first man would become useless because they couldn't engage bad guys. They were also careful not to advance too quickly through the room—thus missing something and getting shot by a terrorist or their own Teammate. Alex scanned his area—nobody. They were in an office room. John entered the center of the room to fill in if someone was shot or had a weapon jam, but no shots were fired and there were no bad guys. Because there were only three of them assaulting, John also took the job of making sure no one sneaked up on them from behind.

Pancho led them through the doorway and turned right. Alex kept close behind. There was a wall to the left. He turned right, entering a hall after Pancho, who kept to one side so Alex had space on the other—better to have both weapons aimed down the hall than just one. At the end of the hall, outside the door leading to the hostage cell, a man in a uniform sat sleeping in a chair. He woke up and when he saw Pancho and Alex coming at him, he jerked toward an AK-47 propped against the wall. Alex and Pancho popped him. The SEALs proceeded down the hall, passing a closed door with a poster of the Hezbollah leader on it, then past another closed door.

At the end of the hall was the room where the hostages were supposedly being held. John removed the bar barricading the door and checked the lock. As expected, it was locked. Rather than search through the guard's pockets for the keys and try to figure out which was the key to the cell or find out the guard didn't have the key, John picked the lock. Pancho aimed at the hostage's door—there could be a guard inside, or worse, a trap. Alex covered the area behind them. Alex heard a sound come from behind the closed door with the Hezbollah poster. He was sure his senses weren't overreacting. Someone else was in the building.

John finished picking the lock. He looked at Pancho, who nodded. John opened the door and Pancho smoothly moved inside. Next came Alex, looking for threats—the room was empty except for a bucket, three men, and their blankets. Two hostages were lying asleep on the floor. They appeared much thinner than they did in their pictures. The smallest hostage sat in the corner, his whole body shaking and his eyes moving in slow motion. Saliva dripped from his mouth like a dog. He'd obviously been tortured severely. Each man's hands and feet were tied. The room smelled like a locker room, outhouse, and slaughterhouse combined. The stench was so thick it made Alex gag.

Pancho stayed with the hostages while Alex and John searched the room next door. It was empty except for a table and two chairs. It stank, but not as bad as the prisoners' cell. Maybe it was an interrogation room. The ceiling, walls, and floor were stained worse than the prison cell. Alex didn't take the time to imagine what horrors took place in the interrogation room, but he knew he would never be taken alive. No SEAL had ever been held prisoner of war, and Alex would rather die fighting.

Alex and John returned to the hall and Alex pointed to his ear, then the door, signaling that he heard someone inside. John tried the door—it was locked. He picked the lock. After opening the door, the SEALs entered the room to find a couple in bed. On a chair beside the man hung a pistol in a holster on a belt. The man awoke to find Alex restraining him with zip-ties on his wrists and ankles. Meanwhile, John tied up the man's significant other. Then the SEALs put hoods over the couple. Alex and John didn't need to search them because they were naked except for their hoods. Alex put the pistol belt over his shoulder.

Alex and John left the Hezbollah couple and went back to the hostages. Pancho had already searched their bodies for weapons— unlikely, but the SEALs didn't take any chances. The hostages were awake now. Pancho gestured for them to keep quiet. "Be quiet," he said. "We're friends of Dr. Khamenei and Omar Bisharia. They sent us to rescue you."

The two Palestinians didn't seem to understand.

"Omar Bisharia," Pancho said slowly. "He sent us to rescue you."

Youssef was lost in a different world, but a spark seemed to flash in Dalal's dim eyes.

Using his pocketknife, Pancho cut off the cord tied around their ankles so they could move faster, then the cord on their wrists so they could climb over the wall.

The SEALs escorted the precious cargos (PCs) into the hallway. Alex signaled for Pancho to stop, and he came to a halt. Alex broke off from them, went into the Hezbollah couple's room, grabbed them, put them in the hostages' cell, and lowered the barricade on the door. He heard them gagging on the stench inside as he returned to his men and the hostages. Alex took the ammo out of the pistol in the belt slung over his shoulder and put the bullets in his pocket. Then he threw the belt into the bedroom. Alex signaled Pancho to move out.

The SEALs sneaked out of the building and around to the back with their PCs. The Hezbollah barracks was still quiet. So far, the mission was proceeding better than expected.

Pancho scaled the barracks' stone wall and dropped over the other side. Alex helped the hostages up. They were moving too slowly, leaving the whole team vulnerable. Alex quickly followed the hostages over. When Alex landed on the other side, a shot came from the north, but he didn't see the muzzle flash. Pancho took a step back before his legs buckled and he fell on his knees. He stood up and took two steps before falling on his face.

"Sniper, front!" Alex yelled. He didn't bother to see where Pancho was hit; they needed to get out of the sniper zone—fast! Alex tossed a stun grenade north, hoping to throw off the sniper with the bright flash and loud bang. Hezbollah would be arriving any moment.

Alex hoisted Pancho in a fireman's carry and waddled east. Pancho was so heavy, and the ground so frozen and uneven, that a waddle was as quick as he could move.

"Go, go, go!" John yelled from behind. Alex didn't know if John was yelling at the PCs or him.

Alex ran faster than his feet could keep up, and he stumbled and fell. Before he hit the ground, a bullet snapped the air above, just missing him. He landed on the ground hard. Alex could barely breathe underneath Pancho's weight.

John fired in the sniper's direction, but they were so far away and the sniper was so well hidden that the best he could hope for was to keep the sniper's head down long enough for the SEALs and their hostages to get out of his sights.

Omar's men took John's cue and fired in the sniper's direction, too. Alex was happy they put the pressure on the sniper.

Alex picked himself and Pancho up and continued east, putting a building between them and the sniper, blocking his view—and bullets. Pancho was so heavy—*why did he have to eat all those cookies?*

John hustled to the front and ran point. Three armed Hezbollah men appeared from the barracks to their right. John stopped, planted his feet, and fired from the standing position: *pop-pop-pop-pop-pop-pop.* One of the three Hezbollah fired off some rounds on full auto before John's shots took him and his buddies down to the frozen dirt.

"Pancho, you okay, buddy?" Alex asked.

Pancho gasped for air.

At least he was conscious, but gasping for air wasn't a good sign. "We're going to get you out of here, just hang on."

Pancho continued to gasp.

They still had nearly a klick to go before reaching Leila. Alex passed John and headed northeast. Meanwhile, John stayed between them and Hezbollah. Alex heard a vehicle roar out of the barracks and head for them. He suddenly realized he was running on the right shoulder of the road. The even surface helped him put more distance between them and the Hezbollah, but being in the open made it easier for the bad guys to find them. Alex turned right on a road.

Taking out the driver was the most effective way of stopping any vehicle. John fired again: *pop-pop-pop*—until the sound of the vehicle behind Alex and the PCs stopped.

Alex reached a dead end. Now he was lost. He backed up against a cypress tree and balanced Pancho and checked his compass. Somehow, he had gotten turned around and headed southwest. He needed to go northeast. Alex corrected his direction and cut through residences and crossed another road. He entered a grove of trees and still didn't know where he was.

"You okay, Pancho?" Alex asked.

There was no reply.

"Just hang on, buddy."

Alex looked behind him. The PCs were still there, Hassan and Dalal helping Youssef, but he'd lost John. From the direction of the Hezbollah barracks, the air popped off like the Fourth of July. Instead of one John shooting against many, it sounded like many firing against many. Omar's men were shooting it out with Hezbollah.

Alex passed trees, bushes, and buildings before he crossed a road. Ahead was one of the hospitals. He turned around to make sure the others had stayed with him. They had. *Now I know where we are, but where's John?* Pain shot through his neck, shoulder, and back from carrying Pancho, but he knew if he could gut it out a little more, the pain would become numbness, and he wouldn't feel it anymore.

Alex hobbled clockwise around the hospital until he reached a cluster of cypress trees. Using them for cover, he picked up speed, stumbling over tree roots. Up ahead he spotted the Humvee in the parking lot. On the driver's side sat Leila. He crossed the parking lot and Leila turned the engine on. Alex struggled to open the door, then one of the PCs came up from behind and opened it. The three PCs packed into the back row of the Hummer. Because there were only two seats in the back, Youssef sat on Hassan's lap. Alex laid Pancho across the second row of seats, knelt beside him, and closed the door.

"Where is John?" Leila asked.

Alex didn't know, but he assumed John would arrive any minute. "He's coming. Just wait."

Alex called on his radio, "John, where are you, buddy?"

No answer. Maybe he was busy. Or dead.

Someone keyed the mike once. *John.*

"Is Pancho okay?" Leila asked.

"He will be." Alex didn't want to look, but he knew he had to. The veins on Pancho's neck bulged out, and he was still gasping for breath. One side of his chest looked bigger than the other and the small side was wet and making a sucking sound. Alex used his pocketknife to cut away Pancho's clothes so he could find the wound. Thick, dark liquid frothed from Pancho's chest.

Suddenly the side door flew open, and someone rushed in and closed the door. It was John. He knelt on the floor next to Alex. "How's Pancho?"

"Leila, take us out," Alex said. He pulled the blowout kit from Pancho's pocket. "He's got a collapsed lung," Alex said. The outside air was competing to get into the wound while his lung was fighting to push air out of it.

Leila drove them from the parking lot.

"We need to get Pancho to the ship ASAP," John said. "He needs a surgeon."

"I know," Alex said. He pulled an Asherman chest seal out of Pancho's first-aid pack and opened it. Alex used the enclosed four-by-four-inch gauze to wipe Pancho's blood and sweat from the wound, and he taped the Asherman chest seal on the wound. The one-way valve in the seal allowed air out without letting it back in.

Suddenly, one of the hostages screamed so loudly it startled Alex. "What the hell?" he asked.

"It's Youssef," John said. "The kid is having flashbacks or something."

The PCs tried to calm Youssef down.

"A car is coming behind us," Leila said.

Alex looked to the rear, but the approaching vehicle's high beams were ruining his vision through his night goggles, so he took them off. John did the same. Alex's vision struggled to make the transition from NVGs to unaided night vision.

"Get down," John said to the PCs. Dalal lay down on the floor, Hassan lay down on the seat, and Youssef lay down on top of Hassan.

Alex readied his weapon and flipped off his safety switch. As the vehicle came closer, Alex recognized the outline of a Land Rover. Leila was close to maxing out the Humvee's acceleration, but the Land Rover pulled up beside them. *Whatever they want, this isn't going to be good.* Leila managed to momentarily pull ahead of them, but within seconds they pulled up beside her. There were three men in the Land Rover: Lieutenant Saeedi was behind the wheel, with Major Khan beside him, and Pistachio was in the back.

"Smoke 'em!" Alex shouted. Because the Land Rover's and Humvee's accelerations were out of sync and Alex's vision wasn't a hundred percent, he flicked the selector switch on his AKMS to full auto, pressed the muzzle against the side window, and sprayed. John squeezed in beside Alex and joined him in firing through the window, too: *pop-pop-pop-pop.*

The evil trio ducked as their windows imploded, and the Land Rover's brakes squealed, decelerating the SUV. Its ass end fishtailed.

"I think I got a piece of Captain Fat'hi," John reported.

The Land Rover's headlights behind them became smaller and smaller. Then they stopped shrinking. The lights grew bigger and bigger.

"They're coming back for more," John said. The PCs seemed to have already gotten the message because now they were huddled down low. Alex was too cramped for space and moved up to the passenger seat in front. John stayed kneeling on the floor next to Pancho. Alex fired through the left side of the rear window. John shot through the middle of the rear window.

Alex hoped the hostages had enough sense to keep their heads down, because he and John were shooting right over them. In spite of the heat that Alex and John delivered, the evil trio kept their heads down and the Range Rover came at them like a rocket. It struck the back of the Hummer with a bang, and Leila lost control. The Hummer swerved into the left lane and back across to the right as Leila struggled to regain control.

John ran out of bullets in his magazine. "Changing ammo!" He ejected the spent magazine and loaded a fresh one filled with thirty rounds. Meanwhile, Alex continued shooting at Major Khan and his men. When Alex had to change ammo, John fired.

The Range Rover came in to ram the Outcasts again. Without warning, Youssef popped up screaming and waving his arms. Alex and John stopped shooting so they wouldn't hit him. "Get down!" they yelled at Youssef. "Keep him down!"

Leila translated for Hassan while speeding northwest. Pancho groaned.

Major Khan and his men didn't waste the opportunity of a lull in the shooting. They unloaded their rage on the Outcasts. Rounds punched through the rear windshield and popped the air. Instinctively, Alex ducked. Bullets ripped into seats. The Range Rover rammed into the Hummer: *bang!* Leila lost control again and swerved. Rounds stopped cracking overhead, so Alex rose from cover and took aim. John did, too. Either Hassan and Dalal pulled Youssef down or Major Khan and his men had shot him, because Youssef wasn't sitting up waving and screaming like a maniac anymore. Alex adjusted his aim to compensate for the weaving of the Hummer and scored direct hits on the Range Rover—so did John—causing Major Khan and his men to back off.

The Hummer slowed down and ran off the road.

"Leila?" Alex called.

No answer.

Alex turned to see Leila slumped over the steering wheel. "Leila?!" Alex shouted. He reached out and grabbed her arm, but there was still no response.

The Hummer ran through the front of someone's yard and into a field. They headed on a collision course with trees bordering the edge of the field.

"What's going on?" John asked, continuing to shoot at Major Khan and his men.

"Just keep 'em off our ass!" Alex yelled. The back of Leila's head was gooey wet. He pulled her off the steering wheel and took it, turning the Hummer away from the trees. Then he took her foot off the gas pedal and parked the vehicle so they'd stop rolling. Alex grabbed gauze from his blowout kit and secured it to the back of her bloody head before moving her into the passenger seat. "Leila, stay awake."

Leila opened her eyes and said something, but her voice was so faint, he couldn't hear it. He put his ear to her lips, and her voice came out in a breathy whisper. "Alex." When he looked at her eyes again, they were closed.

"Wake up, Leila. We're going home."

Alex climbed into the driver's seat. He knew that if he didn't get them out of this mess quickly, they'd all die. He stepped on the gas and wheeled them around in the direction of the road. Major Khan's Range Rover drove off the road and headed straight for the Outcasts. They appeared to be aimed at each other for a head-on collision. Alex took both hands off the wheel, picked up his AKMS, leaned forward, pressed the muzzle against the windshield, and rapidly fired at Lieutenant Saeedi in the driver's seat. Saeedi ducked, so Alex pivoted to Major Khan and unloaded, but he ducked, too. He couldn't see Pistachio in the back, but he fired into the seats anyway. The Hummer and Range Rover passed so closely that their side mirrors broke off. In the rear of the Hummer, John's AKMS sounded possessed as it blasted hell at Major Khan and his men.

Steering the Hummer with one hand and holding his AKMS in the other, Alex tore onto the main road and stomped the gas pedal to the floor. As he sped northwest, wind howled through the holes in the windshield and windows. The wind must have been cold, but Alex didn't feel it. He checked the rearview mirror—Major Khan was still more than a hundred yards behind them. "Leila, you're going to be okay. Just hang in there."

"Pancho, wake up, buddy," John said. "Come on, Pancho, wake up!"

Omar's men better be at the rendezvous site, or there'll be hell to pay. Alex raced into the city of Laboue and slammed on the brakes before turning left toward the Assi River. Soon he was off-road, blazing a trail through the woods. Major Khan couldn't catch Alex, but Alex couldn't lose him, either. Alex wanted to drive faster, but if he wrecked, they'd be in worse shape. *Smooth is fast.* His frustration level threatened to max out, but he couldn't let it. He pushed the Hummer as hard as he dared, dodging in and out of trees until he slid to a halt next to the water's edge. Fortunately, Omar's men stood by ready with rubber boats.

"We need to hurry," Alex said. "Bad guys coming." Alex wasn't sure if they understood him, but Omar's men helped unload Leila,

Pancho, Hassan, Dalal, and Youssef from the car and into their rubber boats.

"John, drop smoke," Alex said.

"Dropped smoke and a Bouncing Betty," John said. John often carried U.S. military smoke and explosives, but on this mission, he went sterile, carrying Iranian goodies to hide the Outcasts' country of origin.

Good.

Omar's men and the SEALs pushed off the rubber boats and paddled into the river until a swift current carried them away. Behind them, white smoke expanded up and outward from the ground.

26

With a blown-out front tire, the Range Rover skidded to a stop in front of a wall of white smoke. One side-view mirror dangled and the other was missing. Most of the front windshield was blown out, and the vehicle looked as if a flock of giant steel-beaked woodpeckers had attacked it. Lieutenant Saeedi's shirt was torn where a bullet had ripped it. Flying glass had cut into the side of Major Khan's face, bloodying it. Pistachio had taken a round in the left shoulder, which he had already bandaged.

The three jumped out of their vehicle and Lieutenant Saeedi sprinted ahead into the smoke. Major Khan and Pistachio followed close behind. They lost sight of Lieutenant Saeedi, but they could hear him. Major Khan heard a dreaded sound: *click*. Lieutenant Saeedi had triggered a booby trap. As Major Khan's adrenaline sped up, time seemed to slow down. *This is the end*. Instead of the boom of an explosion, there was a distinctive delay of a Bouncing Betty. *I still have time*. "Hit the dirt!" He dropped and heard a *whoosh* of air as the body of the mine hopped about three feet high into the air. The resulting explosion was deafening. With his face in the dirt, Major Khan couldn't see the explosion, but he knew its shrapnel would shred everything in a thirty-meter radius from about the waist up. Consistent with its design, everything on the ground was safe.

Major Khan stood and carefully walked out of the smoke. Lieutenant Saeedi was in the water. "What happened to you?" Major Khan asked.

"I slipped and fell in the freezing water! What the hell does it look like?!"

Major Khan had been so focused on getting under the Bouncing Betty's explosion, he hadn't heard the splash. Major Khan gave Lieutenant Saeedi a hand out of the water. "Did you see Alex and his men?"

"No, they got away. That explosion wasn't what I thought it was, was it?" Lieutenant Saeedi asked.

"You're lucky you fell in the water."

"Where's Pistachio?"

They walked through the smoke toward their vehicle. When they exited the smoke, they spotted Pistachio on the ground. The explosion had left his legs intact, but his upper body from his groin to his face was a bloody, mangled mess. "I can't move my body," Pistachio said almost unintelligibly.

"Aww, shit," Lieutenant Saeedi swore.

Part of Pistachio's jaw seemed broken. "Hospital," he pleaded.

"Hang on, Pistachio," Lieutenant Saeedi said. "We're going to fix you up and get the bastards who did this to you!"

"Hospital," Pistachio said weakly.

Major Khan brought his rifle up to his shoulder.

"Aww, no," Lieutenant Saeedi said. "We have to get him to a hospital."

Pistachio groaned.

Major Khan pulled the trigger.

"No!" Lieutenant Saeedi cried. Tears ran down his face. "You killed Pistachio!"

"That's what friends are for." Major Khan walked to the Range Rover.

"You coldhearted bastard! You're just going to walk away from Pistachio?!"

Major Khan stopped and turned around. "You think I'm happy about losing him?"

"Say his name: Pistachio."

"Get in the car."

"Say Pistachio!"

"Let it go."

"You can't say Pistachio's name because you just killed him!"

"There's nothing we can do about it here."

"There's something we can do about it!"

Major Khan stared hard through Lieutenant Saeedi, waiting for a suggestion.

"We can say something in honor of him," Lieutenant Saeedi reasoned.

"You do that." Major Khan returned to the truck, sat inside, and slammed the door.

Lieutenant Saeedi stood alone shivering, wet and bawling like a baby over Pistachio's corpse.

PART THREE

I want you to remember that no bastard ever won a war by dying for his country. He won it by making the other poor, dumb bastard die for his country.

—GEORGE S. PATTON, ARMY GENERAL

27

f Alex and his crew didn't get Pancho and Leila to the operating room on the USS *Kearsarge* soon, they'd both be dead. Alex, John, Hassan, Dalal, and three of Omar's men paddled in a large, civilian, blue and white inflatable raft carrying Pancho, Leila, and Youssef. Omar's men in the boat weren't militia types, but they were experienced white-water rafters. Everyone wore red life jackets except for the SEALs, who already wore gray life vests that they could inflate if needed. John inflated Pancho's life vest—just in case.

The river flowed so swiftly that they didn't need to paddle for forward movement. They paddled only to keep the boat from turning sideways or backward. Rocks poked up out of the water and the paddlers maneuvered the boat around them like they were moving through an obstacle course. Farther downstream, more and more rocks appeared, creating white water and small waves. The raft rode over a ledge that dropped two feet—*no problem*. As they proceeded, the river became deadlier with more white water and larger waves. Alex and the others worked harder to avoid the larger rocks. At the next ledge they dropped five feet at a 45-degree angle and hit the water below hard enough to make Alex worry that they might lose someone over the side.

As the number of rocks increased, it became more difficult to avoid them, so they ran over them, picking up speed on the down-stream side. The water rolled back on itself, creating a white, foaming hole. Alex, John, and Omar's men paddled hard through the white water so they wouldn't get stuck in the hole. Hassan and Dalal worked hard, paddling as fast as they could, but their strokes were short and shallow, having less effect. Alex and the others muscled their way through the water. The Assi River was tougher than he'd anticipated. Now Alex wished they had Pancho's brawn to help them.

The Assi calmed down, and although Alex wanted to catch his breath, they still had to get Pancho and Leila to a surgeon as quickly as possible. Alex and John continued to dig their paddles into the water and pull long strokes. The others followed their example.

After their boat rounded a bend, the river was all white water for as far as Alex could see. Then he saw a drop ahead—it looked like a big one. John stowed his paddle and grabbed hold of Pancho and Leila. Hassan and Dalal held on to John. Omar's two men on the starboard and port sides paddled diligently to keep them straight while the man in the back steered.

Youssef stood up screaming and waving his hands. Alex tried to pull him down so he wouldn't fall out of the boat. Alex didn't want to lose a hostage, and he didn't want to perform a rescue swim in icy water. Hypothermia worried him more than drowning. Youssef broke out of Alex's grip. The ledge appeared up ahead. The other side angled down at 45 degrees—a ten-foot waterfall. Alex grabbed a handful of Youssef's shirt and jerked him down to the deck just as they edged over the top of the waterfall and began to drop. When they hit bottom, the front of the boat folded upward. Still holding Youssef by the shirt with one hand, Alex landed with such force that his other hand lost its grip on the boat, but he clung to the boat with his legs. When the water calmed, Alex was happy that he and Youssef hadn't taken a swim.

They reached their rendezvous point and paddled out of the river's main current and landed onshore. After exiting the boat, Alex and the others pulled it farther inland, where Cat and Brutus were there to greet them. Brutus's two drivers each sat behind the wheel of an idling vehicle.

"Youssef!" Brutus hugged Youssef and kissed him on the left cheek, right cheek, then left—a common Lebanese greeting between friends and family.

Youssef cried tears of joy.

Brutus kissed Alex: left cheek, right, left.

Alex didn't think he'd be happy to be kissed by a man, but he was. "I'm sorry I can't stay, but we've got a medical emergency."

Alex needed Cat to translate for him, but she stood staring at Pancho and Leila.

"Cat, I need you to translate for me."

She remained in a daze.

He put his hand on her shoulder. "Tell Brutus that we have a medical emergency and need to go."

Cat translated, her voice trembling.

Brutus helped the Outcasts load Pancho and Leila into their van. Alex gave a hurried wave before sitting in the passenger seat. Cat peeled out, then sped along small roads before she reached the main road.

As she barreled along the highway, Alex radioed JSOC and told them about Pancho's and Leila's critical conditions. Alex requested a helo medevac but was told to follow the original extraction plan and that two surgeons on the *Kearsarge* would be standing by with their staff and operating rooms prepped.

Cat raced through Tripoli. Alex noticed a tear in her eye. Even though Pancho and Leila meant more to Alex than most people, his eyes were dry. *Maybe I do need to learn how to love. Maybe I do live in a lonely little dysfunctional world. But in situations where most people would've shit themselves, I kept my cool. I made the impossible become possible. And because of that, Pancho and Leila are going to survive.*

The average time to drive from Tripoli south forty-four klicks to

Byblos was about fifty minutes, but Cat reached Byblos in twenty-five. Near the end of the trip, they passed through the town of Amsheet, where Alex, Pancho, John, and Cat had cheated death before. *We'll cheat death again.*

On the Lebanese amphibious base, Alex linked up with the Lebanese marine commandos. Even though the commandos knew it was a training exercise, they treated the situation as if it were real. They loaded up their boats with the Outcasts and Hassan and took them to the USS *Kearsarge*.

Both Pancho's and Leila's eyes were closed. Alex tried to wake them up, but neither responded.

"We need to go faster!" Alex told the coxswain. Cat translated.

"Yes, sir," the coxswain replied.

But the boat didn't go any faster—it was going as fast as it could. The five-minute ride to the ship felt like five hours. On board the *Kearsarge*, only a select number of people knew that the medical emergency was real and were told to keep it a secret.

Pancho and Leila were immediately whisked off to the operating room, and Hassan was ushered off for a medical check. Alex, John, and Cat waited outside the operating room. "This will probably take a while," a Navy commander said. "Is there anything I can do for you?"

"Some water would be nice," Alex replied.

"Will do."

An hour later, the first surgeon came out. "Pancho is a tough one. He's still in rough condition, but he's better off than he was, and now his situation is stable."

Alex, John, and Cat smiled.

"He needs some rest now. I recommend you three get cleaned up, grab some chow, and then get some rest, too," the surgeon said.

"We're waiting for Leila," Alex said.

"Sure," the surgeon said with a poker face that left Alex with less hope than the little he'd had before.

Minutes later, the second surgeon came out. "We did everything we could. I'm sorry. Leila is brain-dead. I don't know how she survived as long as she did."

Pain strained John's face, and tears filled Cat's eyes.

Alex remembered being in the hospital with his sister Sarah. Now the world's colors faded and everything was turning white again. Even though his strength faded, he knew what he needed to do. "I need to see her," Alex said.

The surgeon nodded. He escorted Alex to her room, then left him alone with her.

"I'll always remember you, Leila. *Mamnoon.*" He put his hand on hers and kissed her on the lips. He knew what he needed to say, and he didn't hesitate. "Goodbye, Leila. It's okay to say *goodbye.*"

Minutes later, her EKG went flat. Alex walked out of her room and returned to John and Cat. "She's gone," Alex said.

Cat cried.

John pulled Alex aside.

Alex didn't want to talk to him. Alex didn't want to talk to anyone. He just wanted to be alone.

"In the Hummer, Leila told you something," John said. "What did she say?"

Alex looked into John's eyes and saw so much hurt. Maybe it was just a reflection of Alex's hurt. He wanted John to feel better, so Alex said what he thought John wanted to hear. "John."

"The last thing she said was my name?"

Alex nodded, then walked away. He walked down the narrow passages, not knowing where he was headed until he found himself at the forward hold. The steel door was unlocked, so Alex opened it and walked in. Rope, shrouds, turnbuckles, and other gear for deck operations and cargo transfers were stored inside. He closed the door and sat on a pile of rope in the dark. Alex felt lightheaded, as if he were going to pass out. He tried to keep a stiff upper lip, but his lips quivered. Tears ran down his face and they wouldn't stop. He tried to stop them, but he couldn't. His body shook and his throat ached like it was going to sob, but no sound came out. The tears continued to pour.

THE USS *KEARSARGE* SAILED a little over two days, until it arrived at the Naval Air Station Sigonella in Sicily. Alex, Pancho, John, Cat, and Hassan rode a helo to the air station. "I wish I was going with you all," Pancho said.

"I do, too," Alex said.

They exited the helo to find two pretty female hospital corpsmen with a stretcher. Pancho lay down on the stretcher. "Aah, Sicily," he said with a peaceful smile.

Alex and Cat smiled, too. John just shook his head.

A gray van was parked nearby with the words U.S. NAVY written on the side. The doors opened and a commander stepped out with Dr. Sheema Khamenei. Hassan rushed toward his wife, tripped on his own feet, and fell. Dr. Khamenei ran to assist him. Hassan picked himself up before his wife reached him. Between hugs and kisses, they babbled in Farsi, but Alex didn't need to understand Farsi to know they were happy. Alex was glad that Leila's sacrifice hadn't been in vain. He walked over to greet Dr. Khamenei, but she was still busy with her husband, so he waited patiently. As Alex watched, he felt a calmness come over him, and he wanted what they had. He looked at Cat, but she was too focused on them to notice Alex looking at her. *Maybe Cat is thinking the same thing.*

Dr. Khamenei turned and spoke to Alex in English. "Thank you so much. The MBD21 lab is in the jungle ten kilometers west of La Paragua, Venezuela. . . ."

28

"**W**hat is General Tehrani waiting for?" Lieutenant Saeedi asked while driving their bullet-riddled Range Rover south through Monday morning traffic toward Beirut. He wore a suit and tie, assuming the cover of an Iranian diplomat. Next to him in a diplomatic bag on the seat rested his pistol and ammunition.

General Khan was also dressed as a diplomat and hid his weapon and ammo in a dip bag on his lap. "He says he needs five more days before he has enough rat fleas and MBD21 for the attack." Three groups were scheduled to infiltrate the United States via ship. They would proceed to the domestic airport terminals in Dallas, Los Angeles, and New York, where they would unleash the fleas on passengers and the terminals. By the time airport officials figured out what had happened, the fleas would already have traveled throughout the country, spreading Black Death and reproducing while Americans helped spread the disease with their coughing and sneezing. Because MBD21 was resistant to antibiotics, no one infected could be saved. The general's goal was to wipe out half the U.S. population before a cure could be found.

"Dr. Khamenei must've already told this Alex bastard about the lab in Venezuela. General Tehrani should stop being so greedy and just launch what he has before we lose another lab."

"It's our job to see that he doesn't succeed in destroying the lab."

"Let's just get one thing straight. I don't give a damn about the lab. I don't give a damn about General Tehrani. The only thing I give a damn about is slaughtering the pigs who killed Pistachio."

"This green-face killed my mentor, and my protégé."

"You never told me that," Saeedi said.

"I just did."

"Damn."

"You lost a friend. I lost more. I've never hated anyone as much as I hate Alex Brandenburg."

Lieutenant Saeedi parked in the lot at Beirut International Airport, and the two strolled inside and boarded an Alitalia flight to Rome. In Rome, they transferred planes and flew Alitalia to Simon Bolivar International Airport, near Caracas, Venezuela. Next, they flew thirty-nine minutes to Ciudad Bolivar. From there it was a three-hour charter flight to La Paragua. In La Paragua, Lieutenant Saeedi hired a driver who drove them in his jeep ten kilometers west through a maze of dirt roads until they reached the outer gate of the MBD21 lab. No outsiders were allowed past the gate, so Major Khan paid the driver and stepped out of the jeep. Major Khan and Lieutenant Saeedi walked sluggishly from the gate to the main building. Although they'd slept and eaten as often as they could during their trip from Beirut to La Paragua, both of them were exhausted.

29

Wednesday, at Naval Air Station Sigonella in Sicily, after contacting JSOC with the location of the biological weapons lab, Alex, John, Cat, Dr. Khamenei, and Hassan Khamenei boarded a C-130 and took flight.

Cat fell asleep in her seat, but the Khameneis seemed nervous about the flight.

"You think they'll be waiting for us in Venezuela?" John asked.

"Yeah," Alex replied. "Whoever survived that Bouncing Betty you left for them will be waiting for us, and they won't be happy."

"I know our mission is to destroy the lab and capture or kill the general, but I want to take out those three creeps."

"They certainly earned it—in more ways than one."

"I agree with the priority for taking out the lab, but is the general more important than those other three men?"

"That's what JSOC thinks. General Tehrani is the ringleader, and I think JSOC called this one right."

John lowered his head.

"You ever hear of a Team Two guy called Jabberwocky?" Alex asked.

"Of course."

"He was my mentor in Iraq. Later, I found out who killed him. It was Major Khan."

"No way. Are you serious?"

"After we take care of the lab and take out the general, I want Major Khan. I don't care about Lieutenant Saeedi or his buddy, Captain Fat'hi—I want Major Gholam Khan."

When the C-130 reached a safe altitude, Alex took off his seat belt and lay on the cold deck.

Ten hours later, it was early morning when they touched down at Naval Air Station Oceana in Virginia Beach, Virginia. A lieutenant and a petty officer greeted Alex's crew on the tarmac. The petty officer took Hassan to help him find temporary married quarters. Meanwhile, the lieutenant drove Alex and the others to a secure intel building in the Dam Neck annex.

Alex thought about asking Cat to sit out the rest of this mission. She was physically fit but not as fit as Alex and John. Cat shot better than most people but not as smoothly as Alex and John. Overall, she was a great operator but not at the level of SEAL Team Six standards. Most of all, Alex didn't want to bring her home in a body bag—he didn't know how he could live with himself if he did.

On the other hand, Cat had more fire in the gut than some SEALs he knew. She wouldn't take kindly to being sidelined. The last time he left her behind, he felt he'd been unfair. That decision had pissed off not only Cat; it had pissed off the skipper, too. Also, even though she wasn't up to the insane standards of Team Six, she always managed to be part of the solution rather than part of the problem. With Pancho out of the picture, Alex could use another shooter. Keeping her on the mission seemed the only right thing to do.

Another thing that occurred to Alex was that *he* might not survive the mission. It wasn't something he dwelled on, but it was a reality he constantly lived with. He loved Cat, but he hadn't told her that yet. Alex didn't fear death, but he feared dying before telling her. But this wasn't the time or the place to tell her that he loved her.

Inside a secure conference room, Alex, John, and Cat discussed details about the lab with Dr. Khamenei. "You could destroy the fleas with a natural chemical like pyrethrin, attacking their nervous systems," she said. "Or you could attack their neural membranes with the synthetic chemical permethrin. Pyrethrin and permethrin will not stop the eggs from hatching, but methoprene will—"

Cat interrupted. "Can't we just toss in a Raid fogger? They probably have something that kills the adults and the eggs."

"Our priority is to destroy the MBD21," John said. "How do we do that?"

"Raid will kill the fleas and their eggs, but it won't kill the MBD21 bacteria. MBD21 resists streptomycin, tetracycline, and all antibiotics, too," Dr. Khamenei reminded them.

The Lut Desert was so hot that not even bacteria could survive. "Can we burn the MBD21?" Alex asked.

"I guess so," Dr. Khamenei answered.

"You're not planning to nuke it, are you?" John asked.

"No, too many civilians nearby, and our friends south of the border wouldn't be too happy with us for nuking South America," Alex said. "I was thinking of thermate." Thermate was an upgraded version of thermite.

"And burn down the Amazon rain forest?" Cat asked.

"Thermate could work," Dr. Khamenei added. "But formaldehyde would be more effective."

"Formaldehyde?" John asked.

"We use it for sterilization," Dr. Khamenei explained. "Formaldehyde kills MBD21."

Alex and Dr. Khamenei continued to discuss the lab compound, including its layout. Cat and John bugged out early, and returned to the Team Six compound. Cat would visit the head shed to gather the latest intel: satellite photos, maps, local population, terrain, weather, enemy, the target area, and infiltration and exfiltration routes. Before coming to Team Six, she had experience as an intelligence specialist, so Alex could depend on her without having to tell her what to do. John dropped in on the Explosive Ordnance Disposal guys to request Raid foggers, formaldehyde bombs, claymore mines, and thermate that couldn't be traced to the United States.

After Alex finished with Dr. Khamenei, a petty officer came and escorted her to the temporary married quarters. Then Alex joined John and Cat in the Team Six compound to discuss mission planning. *Will we insert by sea, air, or land?* They planned in reverse, starting with destroying the biological weapons lab. Next, because they would have no fire support, they discussed the insertion and how they'd be picked up. Finally, they figured out what mission gear was needed—Raid foggers, formaldehyde bombs, thermate, detonating (det) cord, antitank rocket, et cetera. They also discussed other considerations such as escape and evasion. They needed an Activity guy to meet them in Venezuela and take them to the target area. Because the Outcasts were shorthanded, if the Activity guy could assist with the assault that would be even better. Even though the Outcasts worked quickly, it took them two days, day and night, to put everything together.

At 0530 on Monday, Alex, John, and Cat arrived at the naval base in Norfolk dressed in civilian clothes and walked across the gangway of the USS *Jason Dunham* (DDG-109), an *Arleigh Burke*–class destroyer named after a Marine corporal posthumously awarded the Medal of Honor for his heroism in Iraq. The *Jason Dunham* had a crew of 380 and an armament of missiles, guns, and torpedoes. She also carried two SH-60 Seahawk helicopters.

The Outcasts stood at attention and requested permission to come aboard. They showed their ID cards to the petty officer of the watch. He checked the IDs then let them come aboard.

The Outcasts went below deck and waited until their gear arrived in boxes disguised as food supplies. After Alex was sure all their gear was aboard, he checked in with the CO to let him know they were good to go.

Later that morning, Alex lay down on the couch in the enlisted quarters. He closed his eyes to rest them for a few minutes. Alex remembered attending the funeral for his sister and grandfather, and how he'd never wanted to attend another funeral again. But he'd attended Jabberwocky's funeral. A black hearse arrived at the grave site. Alex and his platoon Teammates saluted it. Their platoon chief pulled Jabberwocky's casket from the back. Alex and six other Team guys wearing their Navy dress blues and white gloves carried it, three men on each side. The United States flag was draped over the casket, with the blue field resting over Jabberwocky's left shoulder. Alex and his Teammates carried Jabberwocky feetfirst past the people standing in front of their chairs in the cemetery. Military men and women in attendance saluted. Those wearing civilian clothes placed their hands over their hearts. Alex and his Teammates placed Jabberwocky next to the rectangular hole in the lush green grass. They made sure the flag was straight and even. The Navy chaplain performed the service.

After the chaplain's words, the SEALs removed the flag and folded it twelve times, resulting in a triangle showing only the blue field and white stars. They handed the flag to the SEAL Team Two skipper.

The skipper knelt in front of Jabberwocky's wife and presented her with the flag, a flag sailors had fought for since the days of Captain John Paul Jones. "On behalf of the President of the United States, the United States Navy, and a grateful nation, I present this flag to you in recognition of Chief Lee's heroism," he said with tears creeping into the corners of his eyes.

In contrast, Jabberwocky's wife remained stoic, with her back straight and head looking forward.

"I'm so sorry," the skipper said with a quivering voice and tears streaming down his face.

Then seven honor guard sailors fired M1 rifles in a three-volley salute. The odd number of honor guards and volleys was a representation of Jabberwocky's absence in the ranks.

Alex's platoon leader called, "Chief Lee!"

"Hooyah, Chief Lee!" Alex and his platoon shouted in unison. Alex took his Trident off his uniform—the big gaudy gold pin of an eagle perched on a trident and anchor with a musket in the eagle's claw. The trident had cost Alex more pain and sweat than many could ever understand, and it cost him blood and tears to keep, but Alex proudly took his turn in line with his Teammates and, with a pounding of his fist, he stuck his trident next to the others on Jabberwocky's casket. Then he saluted his fallen comrade.

After the SEALs pounded their tridents into the casket, a bugler stood off to the side and played taps while everyone stood. Men and women in military uniforms gave their final salute, and civilians put their hands over their hearts. Jabberwocky's preschool-age daughter saluted.

As they left the grave, one sailor remained to guard the body until it was buried.

Alex woke up. He'd slept through the ship getting under way and lunch. He ate an early dinner with John and Cat on the mess decks. Alex could stay in the goat locker, where the chiefs had small rooms and ate off plates instead of plastic trays, but he preferred to be with John and Cat. Although Cat had a separate place to sleep, she ate with the enlisted men on the mess decks. After dinner, John went to the enlisted men's berthing to read his Bible, and Alex and Cat headed for the ship's fantail to breathe in some fresh air. In the ship's passageways, sailors were checking out Cat.

"How does it make you feel when they look at you like that?" Alex asked.

"They're not looking at me; they're looking at you," she replied.

"They're looking at you."

"Nobody looks at me."

"I do."

"Because you're crazy."

They ascended one of the ship's 68-degree-angled metal ladders and walked onto the fantail. A few sailors were hanging out, one of them having a smoke. No land was in sight. The ship's massive turbines kicked up a fountain of salt water behind the ship as it sailed at about thirty knots. Alex didn't mind the cold and he liked the salty taste of the air. He and Cat walked over to the starboard side and watched the sun sink into the ocean.

"What are you thinking?" Cat asked.

"That I want to hold your hand, but I better not because we're guests on this ship, and sailors don't hold hands on destroyers."

Cat smiled. "No risk, no reward."

"I love you," Alex said.

She froze.

"What's wrong?" he asked.

She was silent for a moment. "I'm trying to figure out if you really said what I thought you said."

"I'm sorry I waited so long to tell you."

"I'm thinking I should pinch myself, but maybe I shouldn't."

"I love you." Alex wrapped his arms around her.

The three sailors on the fantail seemed to take notice.

"You're going to get us in trouble," she said.

"Are you worried about getting in trouble?"

"Are you?"

Alex kissed her and daytime faded to night.

30

Twenty-four hours later, the USS *Jason Dunham* anchored in international waters fifty nautical miles north of Puerto La Cruz, Venezuela. Located on the northern coast of South America, Venezuela is surrounded by Colombia to the west, Brazil to the south, and Guyana to the east. Because Venezuela's elevation varies greatly, its weather varies from the hot, humid rain forest of the Amazon Basin to the snowcapped peaks of the Andes Mountains.

In 2002, the United States supported a failed coup to overthrow Venezuela's then president, the late Hugo Chavez. Understandably, President Chavez was pissed. He declared the United States Venezuela's public enemy and made alliances with anti-American countries such as Iran. Although Chavez supported Iran's nuclear program, he publicly disagreed with President Ahmadinejad's statements about destroying Israel. Meanwhile, Chavez supported Iran's Quds Force's presence in Venezuela. Even though Venezuela and Iran were strengthening their relationship before 2002, Alex felt the 2002 coup was wrong, and the United States shouldn't have supported any part of it. It could succeed only in pushing Chavez further into the dark side, taking his country with him.

At 0300, Alex walked to the front of the ship and entered the Combat Information Center (CIC) to obtain the latest intel dump.

The CIC remained perpetually dark except for the glow emanating from monitors and other electronics—it was like walking into an amusement arcade full of video games—except these games were for keeps. Enlisted personnel manned the monitors while listening to communication via their earphones and responding on their microphones. The CIC was the brain of the ship. On the destroyer, its main function was to coordinate guns, missiles, torpedoes, and anti-submarine warfare, but now CIC was also supporting Alex's mission. Alex approached the Evaluator. He had to be a tactically experienced officer to be an Evaluator. He sat in the rear left corner of the room.

The Evaluator spoke with a slight lisp. "Chief, there are no changes except that we just received an urgent update from NSA. They've pinpointed General Tehrani's cell phone and locked onto it. They're tracking it now. He's in the biological weapons lab west of La Paragua."

"Sir, I need you to tell JSOC that I want an electronic divining rod linked to General Tehrani's cell phone," Alex said.

"An electronic divining rod?" the Evaluator asked.

"Yes, sir. It works like a sensor that'll beep louder when I get closer to the general."

"How do you want us to send it to you?"

"I trust you'll figure out a way."

"You got it, chief. I'll tell JSOC you need an electronic divining rod linked to General Tehrani's cell phone, and I'll figure a way to get it to you."

"As soon as possible, sir. If we fail, General Tehrani may wipe out half of the U.S. population."

"Right away."

The Outcasts caught some sleep. Just before 0400 the next day, they dressed in civilian clothes and mustered on the starboard side of the ship with their gear. A boatswain's mate extended the slewing-arm of a davit holding a Rigid Hull Inflatable Boat (RHIB), a high-performance boat used frequently by SEALs. Inside the boat were a pilot and assistant wearing blue overalls without Navy insignia. They also wore orange life vests. A boatswain's mate lowered the boat into the ocean. Carrying their bags of gear, Alex, John, and Cat descended a rope ladder down the side of the ship and into the RHIB.

Once they were all aboard, the pilot's assistant disconnected the slewing-arm and cast off. The pilot fired up the dual Caterpillar diesel turbocharged engines and pulled away from the ship. Soon the RHIB picked up speed to more than forty knots, faster than the destroyer could travel. Unlike the destroyer, each time the RHIB caught a wave, it flew, and when it landed, Alex felt the impact in his bones.

With the air temperature in the seventies, the weather felt more like summer than winter, and the wind blowing in Alex's face invigorated him. The lights from high-rises on the coast illuminated the night with a beautiful orange glow. Alex remembered from the map he'd studied that the police station was on the far right. The pilot took them to the left.

Slowing down to five knots, the RHIB approached a pier where someone stood waiting. As the Outcasts neared the pier, Alex recognized the short Hispanic man, their contact from the Activity—Miguel. While the pilot's assistant put out the fenders to protect the boat from getting scratched by the dock, Alex threw the bowline to Miguel, who tied it to a cleat. Then Cat threw the stern line and Miguel fastened it to another cleat. The Outcasts disembarked with their gear.

Miguel extended his hand. "I'm Miguel."

Alex shook it. "Alex."

"Welcome to Venezuela."

"Good to be here," Alex said. The short greetings were actually bona fides to prove who they were.

John and Cat cast off the lines, and the RHIB's pilot motored away, heading back to the ship. Miguel led the Outcasts to his green

Ford Explorer SUV, where they loaded up and took off. Gradually, the sun began to brighten the sky.

"It's about seven hours from here to La Paragua, the city adjacent to your target," Miguel said. "Feel free to get some rest if you like."

They headed southwest on Route 9 through the cities of Puerto La Cruz and Barcelona. Shortly after exiting Barcelona, Miguel turned left onto Route 16 and the road veered southeast. To their left, the sun rose above the horizon. High-rise buildings and asphalt roads gave way to smaller buildings and dirt roads. Gradually, the buildings and roads became scarce, replaced by farms, until the human grasp let go of the earth and Mother Nature swallowed them up in her jungle. Alex nodded off to sleep.

Two hours later, Alex awoke as they passed through the town of El Tigre and its large pumps extracting oil from the ground. In Venezuela, gas was literally cheaper than water. The vegetation had thinned out and much of the surrounding area looked barren in comparison to the stretches of jungle to the north. The Outcasts had traveled more than a quarter of the distance to their target area. Alex pulled out a tube of energy gel and emptied it into his mouth—breakfast.

John slept soundly. Cat put her head on Alex's shoulder, and he slept in a light combat sleep, resting his body and mind but able to flip to full auto at the click of a selector switch. After two more hours, Alex woke up. They crossed the Angostura Bridge, which extended a kilometer over the Orinoco River. "What's that?" Cat asked, pointing to the river below. "Something big and white swimming in the water."

"Maybe they're *boto*—Amazon river dolphins," Miguel said.

"I've never seen white dolphins," Cat said.

"Or river dolphins," Alex added.

"Scientists say they've lived here for more than fifteen million years," Miguel explained. "Legend says the boto live in utopia, but they want the pleasures and pain that humans experience. They love music and parties, and sometimes at night they change into hand-some and beautiful men and women. The boto wear a hat to hide their blowhole. They also like to seduce humans and have sex with them, sometimes producing illegitimate children."

Alex and Cat exchanged quizzical looks.

As the bridge reached land, it crossed over jungle treetops be-fore returning to ground level. Farms and ranches appeared on both sides of them until they reached the city of Ciudad Bolivar on their left. Ciudad Bolivar was past the halfway point in the distance to their target area.

"We'll check into a hotel here, grab something to eat, and rest until it's time to launch tonight," Miguel said.

"Aren't there other cities between here and the target?"

"There are, but they're so small, you won't find any real hotels or food there. A lot of tourists come here, so you'll blend in easier and soon be forgotten."

Miguel drove into Ciudad Bolivar and stopped at a hotel called the Posada La Casita. He left the Outcasts in the Explorer while he checked in. Miguel paid in advance so they could leave immediately. He helped the Outcasts move their gear into a small bungalow, a simple building with a high thatched roof and plain interior. After the Outcasts settled in, Miguel went out, gassed up the Explorer, and brought back lunch: cold water; mango juice; chicken salad (*en-salada de pollo*); warm pastries stuffed with beef, chicken, and cheese (empanada); Venezuelan lasagna (*pasticho*); and Sicilian pastries (cannoli). Without Pancho around, the food went further, but Alex missed Pancho's company.

After lunch, Miguel took a long siesta before reviewing his indi-vidual mission responsibilities with the Outcasts. Later, the four ate dinner and did some final preparations. At 2100, the Outcasts wore their jungle cammies, inflatable life vests, face paint, and gear. Alex handed Miguel a life vest. At first, Miguel said he didn't need it, but Alex insisted.

After everyone kitted up, Miguel drove them out of Ciudad Bolivar. As they headed south in the darkness, towns became smaller and more scarce, and the Amazon jungle became bigger and fuller. Three hours later, Highway Sixteen ended at the small village of La Paragua, pressed against the Paragua River to the southwest. Miguel cut the lights and took them through a labyrinth of dirt roads, passing a few strongly built houses but mostly small leaning and sagging shacks made of old wood and corrugated tin. Although some of the vehicles parked in front of the houses were newer, most were old trucks. Miguel continued to the western edge of the village. Ideally, Miguel would slow down to five miles per hour and drop them off, but Alex needed Miguel's gun in the fight, so Miguel parked the SUV off the side of the road.

Miguel showed the Outcasts where he put a spare key in a magnetic key holder behind the bottom of the bumper.

"You'll be driving us out of here, so we won't be needing that," Alex whispered.

John walked the point, followed by Cat, then Alex. Miguel brought up the rear. They were far enough away from the lab compound that the enemy couldn't hear them. The noisy wildlife helped hide the sound of their movement through the jungle. The Outcasts avoided unnecessary chatter—they knew from experience to expect unexpected visitors.

The crickets chattered louder and more often than any other creature in the jungle. A variety of birds called. One sounded like the same low note on a flute in a pattern of one note, two notes, one note—repeated again and again. Another bird cawed like a crow. Still another bird called once and waited for its listener to call back twice. Then the calling bird called once and the listener called twice—they continued communicating back and forth. Suddenly a bird shrieked maniacally. The crickets continued to chirp for a moment, but all the birds became quiet, and a doglike cackle sounded— it sent chills up Alex's spine. Next, different birdcalls filled the night.

A loud groan emitted, then stopped. The groan came again—like the voice of a human. The foliage was so dense that it was difficult to see where all the different noises were coming from. Alex imagined vampire bats, poisonous dart frogs, snakes, black crocodiles, and jaguars, but he began to scare himself, so he stopped imagining and focused on the mission.

The biological weapons compound was located ten kilometers west, and the building housing the MBD21 and rat fleas stood on the western edge of the compound. John took them in a clockwise circle from the east and around the perimeter of the compound. After forty-five minutes of humping through the jungle, light from the direction of the compound broke between the trunks of 150-foot-tall trees. When the Outcasts and Miguel reached south of the compound, John dropped. Cat and Alex followed his example and embraced the damp ground. Alex looked back through the weeds and saw that Miguel did the same. There was too much vegetation and darkness to see much more. Alex hoped that if there were enemies in the area, they'd have just as much trouble seeing the Outcasts. He was forced to rely on his hearing. Although his heart beat loudly, someone's footsteps coming from the south were louder. The noise became louder and louder, so that Alex expected to be stepped on or shot any moment.

Alex's palms grew sweaty, and the grip of his hand on his AKMS felt loose, so he tightened his grip. To his right, a set of eyes appeared so close he could reach out and touch them. It took discipline not to shoot until he determined the extent of the threat. The eyes were too narrow for a human. The skin was green with black spots and scaly—it was a snake. Its body was thirteen feet long. *What kind of snake?* It stared at Alex, who dared not blink.

The footsteps became quieter, fading northward. After about ten minutes, John and Cat crawled forward, but Alex didn't dare crawl or signal he was having trouble for fear of being bitten. Then Miguel used the barrel of his rifle to push the snake away. "Anaconda,"

Miguel whispered in Alex's ear. "No venom—it's a constrictor." The snake slowly slithered away.

John started crawling toward the perimeter wall of the compound, but he stopped again. A Guard sat on top of the biological weapons lab. John pulled out his sound-suppressed pistol and took him out with one shot to the head.

Alex keyed his radio two times, signaling the USS *Jason Dunham* that they were about to enter the compound. The *Dunham* responded by breaking squelch twice.

John continued until he reached the wall. It was made of crumbling brick. He scaled it, but as he reached the top, the section of brick beneath him caved in. John came crashing down, wall and all. If this had been a training mission, it would have been hilarious. Alex hoped the enemy hadn't heard it. John stayed on the ground and crawled around to the side where the door to the MBD21 lab was. Cat crawled through the space where the wall had been and covered John as he worked on opening the door. Alex helped Cat cover the area. The door was locked, so John began picking it, but the lock wasn't opening. A Guard appeared to investigate and when he saw John, he started shouting in Farsi. *So much for stealth.* Cat plugged the guard with three rounds from her sound-suppressed AKMS. John put his lock-pick set away and kicked the door near the doorknob. The door flew open.

John quickly entered the building and peeled left—his rifle fired: *pop-pop-pop-pop*. Cat followed inside, peeling right: *pop, pop, pop*. Alex entered next to discover the mudroom—just as Dr. Khamenei had described. Three guards lay bleeding on the floor. One was still twitching—he appeared dead, but his nerves were still sending signals to his body. Alex conserved his bullets. He didn't have time to look back at Miguel—Alex just trusted that Miguel was right behind him covering their rear and setting a customized Chilean claymore mine with an infrared trigger for rear security. The interior of the lab was air-conditioned, keeping it cool.

Alex knew that the room to their right was the mechanical and electric room. The Outcasts didn't have time to clear every room, so they passed the mechanical-electrical room and the janitor room on their right and headed straight for the objective. An Asian man stepped out of the restroom to the right. He was unarmed—probably the North Korean scientist. Alex blasted twice into the scientist's chest, blowing him back through the doorway and onto the toilet. His biological weapons days were over. The Outcasts proceeded through a door and on the right was an eye wash and emergency shower station. The Outcasts continued straight into a large, rectangular lab area with three sinks, shelves full of chemicals, test tubes, Bunsen burners, centrifuges, various lab devices, and thousands of rat fleas in two large glass boxes.

John gunned down an unarmed Iranian scientist before turning left. The Outcasts skipped the first and second doors to their left. To their right was a storage cabinet with a flammables symbol on it. Alex gently tipped the cabinet over on its side and dragged it with him. Finally, John reached a large metal door on the left. He opened it and walked in. The others followed.

Inside was a long walk-in freezer. Shelves surrounded the Outcasts and Miguel except for one bare wall. On the shelves were stacked columns and columns of petri dishes containing MBD21. Alex dropped the flammable cabinet in the middle of the floor and opened the door.

"If this job doesn't work out, you've got a future as a pest exterminator," Cat said.

"Yep," Alex replied.

John, Cat, and Miguel cleared out of the room.

From the direction of the front of the building came a claymore explosion followed by a scream. Fourteen hundred steel balls blasted whoever opened the door—most likely Iranian Revolutionary Guards.

Alex dumped the contents of the flammables cabinet in the

middle of the floor and pushed the cabinet against the empty wall. He took off his backpack, reached inside, and pulled out two thermate bombs. Each bomb consisted of three nondescript thermate canisters bound together with their fuses connected to a timer and detonator—courtesy of Team Six's Explosives Ordnance Disposal (EOD) operators. The thermate bomb contained 68.7 percent thermite (aluminum powder and metal oxide), 29 percent barium nitrate, 2 percent sulfur, and .3 percent polybutadiene acrylonitrile (PBAN). The PBAN glued the chemicals together to keep a uniform consistency throughout the bomb. The aluminum and metal oxide would create a chemical reaction, causing a fire that burned at approximately 4,000 degrees Fahrenheit (2,200 degrees Celsius). The sulfur and barium nitrate would increase the thermal effect, making the bomb hotter than thermite alone. Alex set the timers for ten minutes and marked the time on his watch. "Ten minutes," Alex announced over the radio. He placed the two thermate bombs on the flammables in the center of the freezer. *That should thaw things out quickly.* He exited the freezer and propped the door open to let all the cold air out. Alex heard a firefight near the lab's entrance: John, Cat, and Miguel were engaging the enemy.

John and the others were supposed to have cleared the adjacent room, but Alex slid open the slide door and entered, ready to stitch up any bogeymen who might have slipped through the cracks. Two Iranian scientists lay still on the floor in puddles of blood. The majority of the scientists worked during the day, and these were the unlucky bastards who worked the night shift.

Three Class III biosafety cabinets (BSC) were connected to each other. The gas-tight BSCs protected the scientists and their environment while the scientists experimented with the MBD21 bacteria. The BSCs also protected MBD21 from outside influences that might weaken it. Scientists could put their hands through a pair of stainless-steel circular openings and into the attached gloves and manipulate the bacteria without coming into direct contact with it.

Alex pulled out three formaldehyde bombs. With his left hand, he opened an outer door on one of the BSCs, reached in, and opened the inner door. With his right hand, he triggered the bomb and it started spraying a fog of formaldehyde. Alex placed it on the dunk tank and closed the inner door. Then he closed the outer door. Finally, he triggered the dunk tank, dropping the formaldehyde bomb into the container of MBD21. Alex repeated the process for the other two BSCs. By the time the fire from the freezer crossed into this room, the bacteria would already be covered in formaldehyde. Alex finished, left the room, and glanced at his watch. "Five minutes," he called over the radio to his crew. The *Dunham* would hear his transmission, too.

31

"We can't break out the front door," Miguel said over the radio with irritation in his voice. "Too many of them."

Alex pulled two Raid Flea Killer Plus Fogger canisters out of his backpack. He pressed the button on one. Then he lifted the lid on one of the glass containers full of fleas and dropped the canister inside before closing the lid. He did the same for the other glass container of fleas. "Fall back on me," Alex said. "I'm blowing an exit through the south wall."

A swoosh followed by an explosion rocked the air: John giving the Guards a parting taste of a disposable antitank rocket for close spaces (AT-4 CS). Salt water absorbed much of the back blast, so John could fire the AT-4 CS in close quarters without melting Cat and Miguel. The Guards quieted down.

Alex reached into his bag of magic tricks and pulled out a thin plastic rope containing compressed powdered explosive (pentaerythritol tetranitrate)—det cord. He taped it in a small door shape on an empty spot on the south wall. Then he attached the blasting cap, fuse, and detonator. Alex stepped out of the blast area and detonated the cord, blasting a small, crudely shaped doorway through the wall.

John arrived with Cat and Miguel.

Alex glanced at his stopwatch. "Three minutes. Follow me out."

John hung back and secured the door to the rectangular room with glass cases full of rat fleas. *Probably leaving an explosive surprise for the Guards, too.*

Alex led Cat and Miguel through the crude doorway and out into the compound, where he felt the jungle humidity again. Alex arrived next to the compound's generator. Alex couldn't see power lines to cut, and he didn't have time to search for an off switch, which would only be temporary until somebody turned the generator back on. He placed a single-canister thermate grenade on it, pulled the pin, and backed away. The thermate grenade had no timer. "Thermate out!" Alex called. No more than two seconds after he pulled the pin, the thermate grenade burned white hot, spewing thick smoke up in the air.

John appeared from the crude doorway in the wall. The lights in the lab behind him went out. The generator had died, and more important, the walk-in freezer full of MBD21 in petri dishes was dead. Alex heard Guards rushing into the lab and breaking down the door, triggering another claymore explosion followed by a screech.

From inside the lab building, an angry platoon of Guards' voices shouted. One of the Guards poked his head through the crude doorway. Alex brought his AKMS up to shoot him in the head but fired too soon and shot him in the base of his neck. The Guard stood in shock in the crude doorway, blocking the others from exiting.

Alex glanced at his watch. The thermate bombs in the freezer were already burning. With flammables in the freezer, flammable formaldehyde in the room next door, and flammable fog in the flea cases, Alex didn't want to stick around and become more fuel for the fire. Neither did John.

They sprinted for the south wall. "Alex and John coming up on your rear," Alex called so someone wouldn't mistake them for the enemy, but Cat and Miguel were nowhere in sight.

As they sprinted, out of the corner of Alex's eyes, ten yards to the left, a pair of dead Guards lay on the ground. If Alex heard the shots, his mind hadn't registered it. More Guards appeared to the left, but these were alive. They shot at the SEALs. Alex and John ran faster. They hit the wall at full speed, jumped, grabbed the top, and pulled themselves over.

On the other side, Cat and Miguel were waiting.

"John, take us out," Alex said.

John assumed the point and led them south at a fast walk. Behind him patrolled Cat, followed by Alex, with Miguel acting as rear security. Soon they'd need to go east, in order to return to their vehicle, but loud thrashing noises came from that direction—the Guards were cutting off their escape route. The Outcasts couldn't return to the hornet's nest they stirred up in the lab compound to the north, and heading west would take them only deeper into the Amazon rain forest. If the Outcasts stopped where they were, the Guards could outflank them and cut off the south, too, leaving them with nowhere to go.

John seemed to understand the situation because he continued leading them south. It was a difficult balance to patrol quietly enough not to be discovered, but quickly enough to escape the Guards.

Alex spotted a fallen tree to John's left, perfect for the four of them to take cover behind. The thrashing became louder and louder. Birds and other wildlife became silent. Contact was inevitable. Surprise, speed, and violence were the keys to winning a firefight. If the Outcasts didn't set up a hasty ambush now, they'd end up in a firefight anyway—minus the element of surprise and the tree for cover. It sounded like the Guards outnumbered the Outcasts four-to-one. *Those are good frogman odds.* When Cat turned around to look at Alex, he held his right arm out at a 90-degree angle with a closed-fist signal: *halt*. She stopped walking and passed the signal up to John, who also stopped. Alex signaled for everyone to get down behind the fallen tree. Then he pumped his fist in the direction of the enemy, like he was punching them—*hasty ambush*. When Alex passed the signals back to Miguel, Alex saw flames rise from the direction of the biological weapons lab—knowing they'd destroyed the lab left a good taste in Alex's mouth, but he didn't have time to savor the victory.

Alex laid out two ammo magazines on the ground so he could grab them more quickly than having to pull them out of the pouch on his combat vest. Similarly, he laid a fragmentation grenade on the damp ground. John, Cat, and Miguel did the same. John had one more AT-4 CS.

Alex waited for the majority of the enemy to enter the kill zone. His crew waited for him or an immediate threat to initiate the ambush. Alex looked for Major Khan or his comrades, but he didn't see them. He searched for a leader to shoot, but Alex couldn't tell who was in charge—probably someone out of sight in the rear. Not all the Guards had entered the kill zone, but most of them had, and a few of the Guards were moving in too close to the Outcasts for comfort. Alex chose the closest man in his field of fire and slowly squeezed the trigger. Alex didn't anticipate and rush the shot. He knew his AKMS would fire somewhere between his finger touching the trigger and squeezing it all the way to the rear. The best shots were the ones where the timing surprised him, as this one did, dotting the Guard neatly between the eyes. John, Cat, and Miguel opened fire, too. Four more Guards went down without a fight—John was dropping them two at a time. More Guards began to return fire, but five more fell. Some Guards smartened up and hugged the ground or found cover behind trees. Enemy shots whizzed over Alex's head, but they weren't close enough to make mini sonic booms. One by one, the Outcasts picked them off until the jungle became still. All that remained were the scared, the critically wounded, and the dead. Alex ejected his empty magazine, loaded a fresh one, and smiled. But his smile didn't last long.

For an instant, he saw Major Khan. A whistle, like a coach's whistle, pierced the air. Suddenly the whole jungle in front of the

Outcasts moved. It seemed like there were a hundred new Guards behind those who'd fallen. Alex and his team shot five of the new Guards, but there were ninety-five more to take their place. Lieutenant Saeedi appeared, screaming in Farsi and cursing the Outcasts, the land they stood on, and the air they breathed. His MGA3 machine gun spewed 7.62x51mm rounds like a flamethrower.

The air around the Outcasts lit up. Pieces of bark sprang up from the fallen tree in front of Alex and the air above him popped like popcorn. John fought like a fireteam of four SEALs.

Major Khan was yelling commands in Farsi. Lieutenant Saeedi's machine-gun barrel glowed white hot, and the heavy volume of fire focused on John's position. Alex thought he had it bad, but now John had it worse. John ducked behind the tree. Splinters flew off the tree in front of John as Lieutenant Saeedi and the Guards made toothpicks out of it.

"Sierra One, this is *Dunham*, over," the ship called. "NSA reports that General Tehrani has departed the biological weapons compound and is bugging out. JSOC wants to know if you're pursuing."

JSOC can kiss my ass. "Now is not a good time." Alex left the mike on without speaking for two seconds so the *Dunham* could hear the Outcasts getting their asses pummeled. "Out."

"Now is not a good time, roger. Uh, *Dunham* out."

Alex picked up his fragmentation grenade, pulled the pin, let the spoon fly, cooked off a couple of seconds, and threw the grenade like a baseball from center field to home plate—right in front of Lieutenant Saeedi. "Frag out!" Alex, Cat, and Miguel took cover. The grenade exploded, but Lieutenant Saeedi continued to curse like a madman—his MGA3 machine gun unrelenting. *Is this guy human?*

Alex popped up and fired at Lieutenant Saeedi. Cat and Miguel tossed their grenades and shouted, "Frag out!" The stereo duet of *frag out* reached Alex's ears like sweet music. *Swoosh* went John's

AT-4 CS. Alex and his crew ducked behind the tree. The explosions took the fight out of the Guards for the moment, but the moment wouldn't last forever. The Outcasts weren't going to have a better chance of hoofing it out of Dodge than now. "John and Cat, leapfrog back!" Alex called.

32

Lieutenant Saeedi lay on the ground with the bottom half of his right leg blown off and his intestines spilling out onto the ground. As his right leg spurted blood, he picked his intestines off the ground and tried to put them back in his body, but they slipped through his bloody fingers. "Help me, Khan!" he cried.

Major Khan advanced to Lieutenant Saeedi's position and looked down on him. "I've been helping you since I first commanded you." Major Khan blew his whistle. "But I can't help you now." Major Khan advanced with his Revolutionary Guards.

"Help me, please!" Lieutenant Saeedi sobbed.

33

"John and Cat back!" John and Cat yelled as they turned and ran to the rear.

A whistle blew, and Major Khan and his Guards advanced on the Outcasts' position.

Alex and Miguel fired at the Guards, but they continued to advance. Miguel was an experienced operator and Alex probably didn't have to tell him, but Alex told him anyway: "Miguel, stand by to leapfrog back!"

"Standing by to leapfrog back!" Miguel said.

John and Cat began shooting. That was Miguel and Alex's cue.

"Miguel and Alex back!" Alex yelled. The two stood up and raced to the rear. In the corner of Alex's eyes, he saw John and Cat ahead ten yards to his left.

Major Khan was shouting commands at the Guards again. The Guards' shooting picked up, especially in Alex and Miguel's direction.

Alex ran harder—so did Miguel. They passed John and Cat's position and kept going ten yards before dropping down and firing at the Guards. The Outcasts continued leapfrogging in pairs to the rear, but the Guards regained their confidence and pursued, increasing their firepower. The next time Alex and Miguel ran to the rear, the air around Alex burned: dirt chunks hopped out of the ground, tree wood sprayed his face, the air sounded like the inside of a popcorn popper, and branches fell on his head. Alex wanted to crawl under a rock and hide, but he had to lead. Alex and Miguel dropped down behind John and Cat's position and returned fire, but their firepower had the mere effect of pissing at an angry herd of charging buffalo. Alex and his crew needed to put more distance between them and Major Khan—fast.

John and Cat leaped to their feet and sprinted. Before they passed Alex's position, Alex yelled, "Don't stop running—just keep going!" He faced Miguel. "Miguel, let's get the hell outta here!" They stood up and beat feet.

The four Outcasts ran at the same time without stopping. Alex jumped over bushes and logs. He dodged trees left and right, running for his life. The others did the same. A bullet grazed the inside of Alex's right thigh, tearing his trousers and cutting his flesh. John ran with a limp and slowly fell behind. Seconds later, Miguel went down. *Shit!*

Alex stopped to help Miguel up, but he didn't respond, so Alex hoisted him in a fireman's carry and ran with him. Now Alex was behind his team. He raced to catch up. A bullet struck Alex from the back, almost knocking him to the ground, but Miguel's body absorbed the bullet. Alex pumped his legs until they burned, then he pumped them harder. His lungs ignited, and he ran until he literally puked.

John ran with a limp twenty yards ahead of Alex. Cat continued twenty yards ahead of John. They were too spread out, but Alex didn't want to tell them to slow down.

Fortunately, the Outcasts put so many trees between them and Major Khan's men that the Outcasts couldn't see any more Guards. The Guards probably figured that shooting trees was a waste of ammunition, so they stopped. Unfortunately, now they were probably running full speed after Alex and his crew.

The Outcasts couldn't keep running west—deeper and deeper into the rain forest. They needed to get back to the ship. About five klicks south was the Paragua River. When a SEAL is in trouble, he heads for his home, the water. Alex radioed John and Cat. "Rally at Papa," he said. *Papa* was their code for the Paragua River.

Alex saw John and Cat shift direction south before he lost eye contact with Cat. Even though John was running with a limp, he was still ahead of Alex. After about a kilometer, Alex lost sight of John, too. Alex tried to run faster but slipped and fell. Before he could pick himself and Miguel up, he noticed someone standing there watching. He startled Alex. The someone was a something—a monkey. The monkey bared its teeth and shrieked. As Alex stood up, the monkey charged him, but Alex jammed his rifle muzzle into the monkey's chest. This time the monkey let out a scared scream and ran away. The monkey stopped and turned around to watch Alex, but he poked his rifle in the monkey's direction, and it ran away for good. Alex picked up Miguel and ran south.

Eventually, Alex reached the river. The waters were dark and stretched three kilometers wide; he couldn't see John or Cat. He called them on the radio. Cat gave Alex their GPS coordinates. He hurried downriver, where he found the two on the shore. John lay on the ground with his leg and arm patched with blood-soaked bandages. Cat sat next to him. "He lost a lot of blood," Cat whispered. "Just passed out again."

Alex felt the pulse in Miguel's neck—nothing. Then Alex put his cheek next to Miguel's mouth, but Alex felt no breath. Then he noticed a bullet had penetrated Miguel's chest where his heart was. "Miguel is dead."

"Oh, no."

Alex glanced inland. "Major Khan and his friends will be showing up any moment. We need to get to the ship."

"Time to get wet?"

Alex nodded. He blew air into Miguel's life vest, inflating it.

Likewise, Cat inflated John's. Then Alex and Cat inflated their own vests. Miguel wouldn't be needing his AKMS magazines of ammo anymore. Alex opened Miguel's pouches, found four magazines, and divided them between himself and Cat. "Ready?" Alex asked.

Cat nodded. She and Alex pulled John and Miguel into the water with them and floated northeast holding on to each other. "John, wake up, buddy."

John didn't respond.

"Come on, John, wake up."

Nothing.

"John, wake up."

"Amen," John said groggily.

Alex was happy to hear John's voice. The river felt warm as they drifted down it.

"Cat, you okay?" Alex asked quietly.

"Just some scratches," she replied. "Nothing serious. How about you?"

"Just some scratches."

After five kilometers, they floated around a bend. Even if Major Khan tracked them to the water, now he couldn't see them. Alex's concern of Major Khan following them was replaced with a new concern. Something large and low to the ground waddled from shore toward them and disappeared with a splash—a thirteen-foot-long crocodile. With all the blood on Alex's crew, he was sure they smelled like a delicious meal. He hoped the four of them together were too big for the crocodile and that its prey was something else. Not seeing the croc made Alex nervous, and he wished he had a bigger blade than his Swiss Army knife.

After Alex and Cat had floated fifteen more kilometers, Alex stopped worrying about the croc and started worrying about John. "Hey, John, buddy, wake up."

John didn't move.

"John, wake up." Alex shook him, but there was no response. Alex tried some more. John still had a pulse and was breathing, but he wouldn't wake up.

Soon, up ahead appeared the village—La Paragua. A school of fish swam through Alex's legs.

"Ah!" John yelled.

Alex was happy to hear his voice but concerned about what the problem was. "What is it?"

"My leg! Something bit me."

Something sank its teeth into Alex's leg where a shot had grazed the inside of his thigh. The teeth were sharp as steak knives. Alex yelled.

"Piranhas!" Cat gasped in a whisper. "Swim to the shore!"

Alex kicked as hard as he could, worried the piranhas' next target would be his crotch. Cat and John kicked, too. A piranha nipped at Alex's trouser leg, so he kicked faster. *Better to be a target that's moving than one that's stationary.* One bit into his left calf and hung on. The pain was excruciating. Alex kicked so fast that his lungs ached. He turned in the water to swim on his side, which was the easiest position in which to hold Miguel and swim a one-handed sidestroke. Then Alex turned onto his back, where he could only kick. Alex kicked and turned until he flipped the piranha off, but all the movement seemed to stir the blood in the water and whip the piranhas into a feeding frenzy.

"Ow!" Cat yelled.

More piranhas gathered. Miguel received the worst of it because Alex, Cat, and John were too busy protecting their lives to protect his corpse. The piranhas feasted on Miguel.

Alex, Cat, and John reached the shore. Alex pulled Miguel out of the water, laid him down, and kicked the vicious little bastards off his body. Cat helped. John collapsed. After Alex and Cat had knocked all the piranhas off Miguel's body, Alex stomped a piranha's head into the mud.

Alex hoisted Miguel onto his back, and Cat carried John using the same fireman's carry. They headed northwest through La Para-gua. The village was quiet except for some dogs. After hiking the first klick, Alex was winded, but Cat seemed fine. Alex didn't want to be beaten by a woman, and he didn't want to show weakness. He didn't like carrying Miguel through the village, but Miguel had given his life for the mission, and it was the least Alex could do. It was like many experiences in the Teams: *You don't have to like it; you just have to do it.*

While walking the next klick, Alex wondered if the SUV would still be where they parked it. *Did one of the locals steal it? Did the Guards find it?* He wanted to prepare himself for the kick in the crotch when he found out it wasn't there, but thinking about it now only made the hike more difficult. *Live in the moment and just take things one step at a time.* As was often the case, he'd just have to let himself be surprised by the kick in the nuts. *The only easy day was yesterday.*

One more kilometer later, Alex and Cat reached the green Ford Explorer, right where they'd left it. Alex and Cat laid Miguel and John on the ground. Cat covered the area with her AKMS rifle while Alex checked around the vehicle for signs of tampering or booby traps. There were none, so he retrieved the key from Miguel's pocket and opened the door. Alex loaded Miguel into the third row of seats and Cat laid John across the second row. She elevated John's wounded leg, placing it on his backpack, to slow the bleeding. Cat put his wounded arm on his chest to give it more elevation. Alex was too tired to drive, but Cat looked like she still had energy, so he gave the keys to her. She looked at him for a moment. Alex wanted to ask her what the look was for, but this wasn't the time or place for a conversation, so he kept quiet and hopped into the passenger side of the SUV. Cat quickly sat in the driver's seat and drove away with the lights off. Alex kept watch for anyone following. Cat drove through La Paragua, reached Highway 16, and traveled three kilo-meters north. "I'm going to turn on the lights so I don't crash into something," she said.

"Sure. No one is following us."

Cat turned on the lights. There were no other cars on the road in front of them, and she gunned the engine.

Alex grabbed a water bladder from Miguel's backpack and a blowout kit from Miguel's pocket. Alex examined John's breathing and pulse—he was still alive, but his skin was cold. He woke John.

"Let me rest," John said.

"Just drink some water," Alex said. "Then you can rest." He tilted John's head, placed Miguel's water bladder tube to John's lips, and squeezed it, wetting John's lips. John drank for nearly a minute until the water stopped in his mouth and spilled out onto the seat. Alex decided not to push it, worried that John might vomit, resulting in more dehydration.

John passed out again. Blood had soaked through his bandages. Removing John's bloody bandages would only cause more bleeding, so Alex put fresh bandages from Miguel's blowout kit on John's old bandages. Then Alex cleaned a particularly nasty bite from the piranha on John's leg and bandaged it, too.

Alex radioed the USS *Jason Dunham* and gave them John's medical status. They said they were ready to give an IV, blood transfusion, and whatever else he needed.

The jungle hid the horizon to the east, but the sky above was brightening. Alex offered Cat some water.

"That's Miguel's water, isn't it?" she asked.

"Yes."

"That's pretty sick."

"I'd expect him to do the same. Wouldn't you?"

"You guys can use my water when I'm dead, but I'm not going to drink Miguel's."

"And if you run out of water, whose water are you going to drink? John's? Mine?"

"Just let me dehydrate."

"Have you been dehydrated? I don't mean thirsty, I mean—"

"I said I'd rather die than drink Miguel's water!" Cat cut him off.

Alex put the water down. He waited several minutes before speaking again. "You gave me a look when I gave you the keys to the SUV."

"I was going to tell you that you look like how I feel."

"I was pretty exhausted."

"Is that why you asked me to drive?"

"Yes."

"It's awfully brave of you to admit that."

Alex shrugged.

The sun shone brighter, and Cat would need to blend in as a civilian. She unbuttoned her cammie top and removed it with one hand while driving with the other. Beneath, she wore civilian clothes. "How are you feeling now?"

"I've got the feeling back in my legs and shoulders," Alex said.

"That's a start."

Alex opened a packet of alcohol wipes. "If you need a break, just tell me, and I'll drive."

"Are you saying that because it's your job, or are you saying that because you care about me?"

Alex used a wipe to take the camouflage paint off her face. "Both. Jabberwocky told me that if you take care of your SEALs, they'll take care of you."

"Who's Jabberwocky?"

"He was my sea-daddy. At SEAL Team Two." *Sea-daddy* meant *mentor*.

A rusty truck drove slowly in front of them, and Cat passed it. "I've heard of him. Didn't he die in Iraq?"

"Major Khan killed him."

Cat became quiet.

Alex wiped the camouflage off her neck. Then he cleaned her hands. "You're quiet all of a sudden."

More vehicles drove on the highway, and Cat passed another. "Does that bother you?"

"I'm just wondering," he said.

"I just don't want to tell you."

"Now I'm really wondering."

"You said you'd be finished after this mission."

"It's true."

"After you kill General Tehrani, you're going after Major Khan."

Alex took off his cammie top, revealing his civilian shirt underneath. "Yes."

"That's not part of the mission."

"It's part of my mission."

"Why?"

"For Jabberwocky."

"Just Jabberwocky?"

Now Alex knew where this was heading, and Cat was no fool. "Leila, too," he said.

"Jabberwocky and Leila are dead. They don't need you to kill Major Khan."

Alex didn't say anything.

"They kill one of yours, then you kill one of theirs, then they kill one of yours," Cat said. "The cycle never ends."

"You're still mad about Leila. That's what this is about, isn't it?"

Cat passed a car—then another. "Yes, I'm still mad. I don't want to lose you—not to Leila, not to Major Khan—not to anybody. I've loved you since Indonesia, and I've tried to fight it, but I still love you." A tear ran down her cheek. "I still love you."

34

Alex put his cheek next to John's mouth—he was breathing. Then Alex felt the artery in John's neck—his pulse raced. The racing heart was a sign that John was running out of time.

Cat finished driving north, 487 kilometers in under seven hours, arriving at Puerto La Cruz. Sailors wearing civilian clothes and piloting an unmarked RHIB picked up her, Alex, John, and Miguel at the pier and motored away. Fortunately, the winds were calm and the ocean smooth as glass, shining under the afternoon sun—peaceful. Lying on his back, John looked peaceful, too—for all the wrong reasons. Alex had cleaned the camouflage paint off John's skin, and John's face looked gray. Alex put his cheek down to John's lips— he wasn't breathing. Alex checked John's pulse—it galloped like the lead horse in a Kentucky Derby. Alex used his left hand under John's chin to tilt his head back until John's chin pointed up, making John's air passageway straight. Alex placed his cheek to John's mouth—still no breathing. Alex put his ear to John's mouth—no sound. With Alex's right hand, he pinched John's nostrils closed. Then he sealed his lips over John's and blew air until John's chest rose. After John's chest contracted, Alex blew again—long and slow.

"John stopped breathing," Cat told the RHIB pilot. "We have to hurry!"

"We're going full out, ma'am," the pilot said. "This is as fast as she'll go."

Every five seconds, Alex breathed into John. After three minutes, Alex stopped to see if John would breathe on his own. "Breathe, John. Come on, John. Breathe, damnit!" John still wasn't breathing. Alex resumed giving him mouth-to-mouth resuscitation.

The USS *Jason Dunham* had moved closer to shore while remaining in international waters—every little bit helped. A chief hospital corpsman met the Outcasts when they arrived, quickly ushering John to sick bay, where he gave him an IV and blood.

Alex and Cat waited outside sick bay to find out John's condition. When the doorknob to sick bay turned, Alex's anxiety level rose.

The chief hospital corpsman smiled.

Alex's anxiety level suddenly dropped. He felt like he was on a roller coaster.

"How is John?" Cat asked.

"Better," the chief hospital corpsman said. "He had injuries caused by the shock effect of the bullets, and he lost well over forty percent of his blood. If he wasn't in such excellent physical and cardiovascular shape, even if he could have survived the trauma, his cardiovascular would have collapsed. John is lucky to be alive."

"Can we see him?" Alex asked.

"I guess," the chief hospital corpsman said.

Alex and Cat thanked him and walked inside. John lay hooked up to an IV. His eyes were open.

"John," Alex greeted him.

"Hi, John," Cat said.

John turned and looked at them and didn't say anything—he was quiet that way. Alex's sister was quiet, too, and Alex was comfortable with that.

"Anything we can do for you, buddy?" Alex asked.

"Take me with you," John pleaded.

"You know I can't do that. Not while you're in this condition."

"I know," John said sadly.

They were silent for more than a minute. "Anything else?" Alex asked.

Alex had never seen John cry, but now moisture glistened in the corners of his eyes. "You know what I want," John said.

Alex knew. "With extreme prejudice."

Cat lowered her head.

Alex and Cat left the operating room.

"The captain would like a word with you in his stateroom," the chief hospital corpsman said.

Alex and Cat walked to the nearest ladder and climbed to the third floor (0-3 level) amidships, then found the captain's door and knocked.

"Enter," a voice said.

They walked in to find the ship's captain, seated with two naval officers Alex didn't recognize and the Evaluator officer who spoke with a lisp. In the center of the navy blue carpet was the U.S. Navy's blue and gold seal—an eagle gripping an anchor and a ship sailing in the background.

"Please, sit down," the captain said.

Alex and Cat sat.

"We just finished talking with JSOC, and they said they'll give you the divining rod at your final destination. JSOC traced General Tehrani's location to an Iranian Aframax-category oil tanker."

"Where is the tanker now, sir?" Cat asked.

"After the tanker left Venezuela, JSOC lost it, but the tanker's manifest reads that it's sailing for St. Petersburg, Russia, to deliver crude oil. The tanker should arrive in St. Petersburg in about thirteen days. Right now we're returning to Virginia. When we're within helicopter range, our Seahawk will fly both of you to NAS Oceana, and you'll be shuttled to the Dam Neck annex, where you'll debrief from this mission and brief for the General Tehrani mission. After taking a couple of days to prepare, you'll fly a civilian flight the rest of the way: Norfolk to Washington, Washington to Frankfurt, and Frankfurt to St. Petersburg. You both should arrive a week before the oil tanker."

35

Killing General Tehrani would be the easy part. Throughout history, prominent people have been killed by focused madmen: John Wilkes Booth and Lee Harvey Oswald numbering among them. The hard part would be escaping—requiring a rational mind and sense of calm that men like Booth and Oswald didn't possess.

It was Thursday morning when Alex and Cat's Lufthansa plane landed on a black runway surrounded by snow on the tarmac at Pulkovo Airport in St. Petersburg, Russia. It was Alex's first visit to Russia, and as the passengers disembarked the plane, his nerves kicked in. If he didn't control his feelings, he'd become his own worst enemy. Both he and Cat could end up in a Russian jail or dead. Alex thought to himself: *You've done this in countries around the world—Russia is just another country.*

The interior of the Pulkovo-2 terminal appeared more modern than Alex expected. Skylights brightened the terminal with natural sunshine, and artistic geometric shapes and lines adorned the ceiling. Alex and Cat stood in line for fifteen minutes before their turn came to pass through immigration and customs.

The immigration officer greeted them and asked for their passports.

Alex and Cat handed him their passports. Alex's was German, and Cat's was Lebanese.

The officer's lips pressed tightly together. He slowly eyed the passports before checking the pictures with Alex's and Cat's faces. "What is the purpose of your visit?" he asked in unaccented English.

It bothered Alex that this officer might be a cut above the rest, but Alex didn't show his concern. "Travel."

"You two are married?"

"Yes," they said emphatically.

The officer's gaze focused on Cat. "But you're from Lebanon?"

"Yes, we met while skiing in Germany."

"Where in Germany?"

"The Black Forest," she said.

"How's the skiing there?"

Cat grinned mischievously. "I'm a better skier than he is."

"How long have you been married?" the officer asked.

"Just a little over a year," Cat said.

"Why did you come to St. Petersburg for travel? Most people choose Moscow."

"We didn't want to go where most people go," Cat explained. "We wanted someplace unique—for us."

The officer smiled. "Welcome to St. Petersburg, Mr. and Mrs. Lehmann. Enjoy your visit."

Alex felt relief, but he tried not to show it. They proceeded to the baggage carousels and retrieved their luggage. Then they entered another line to pass through customs. Alex and Cat carried separate bags. Together they approached the customs officer. He pointed to Alex's bag and gestured for him to put it on the metal counter and open it. Alex did.

"Do you have anything to declare?" the customs officer asked with a thick Russian accent.

"No," Alex and Cat replied.

The customs officer rifled through Alex's clothing, leaving a wrinkled heap. Then the officer dumped the toiletries out of Alex's toiletry bag on top of the heap of clothing. He flipped the pages of Alex's German paperback novel then tossed it on the heap. Next, he opened Alex's notebook computer and turned it on. He opened the DVD drive and saw it was empty. After tapping his finger on the keyboard, he closed the cover, returned it to Alex, and waved him through. Cat volunteered to show the customs officer the contents of her luggage, but the officer waved her through, too. Alex wasn't pleased about the mess the customs officer left him with.

Cat snickered.

Alex glared sideways at her. People passed through customs around him as he repacked his suitcase.

Cat laughed. It was contagious because Alex laughed, too. His anxieties about passing through Russian customs and immigration and his irritation about repacking flowed out with his laughter. Nothing else seemed to matter more than her. Rather than fold the rest of his clothes, he just stuffed them in the suitcase and closed it. Alex lowered his suitcase to the floor and rolled it over to where Cat was standing.

"You think that was funny?" Alex asked, pretending to be angry.

"Sidesplitting."

"You know what I think?"

"What?"

"Your smile is irresistible." He kissed her in front of customs and all the people passing by. Instead of keeping a low profile and moving on, he'd just committed one of the dumbest moves of his tactical career, but Alex didn't care. They continued to kiss as arriving passengers bumped into them on their way out of the customs area. Finally, the Russian officer who'd rifled through Alex's suitcase yelled at them in Russian, gesturing for them to get out. Alex and Cat stopped kissing.

"You smell funky," Cat said.

Alex aimed his nose at his right armpit and took a whiff. "I need a shower."

"I do, too," Cat admitted.

They grabbed their suitcases and walked through the sliding glass door. Alex and Cat navigated their way through the airport until they found the exit. Outside the wind blew and the weather was below freezing, so they put on their jackets, gloves, and knit caps. Alex and Cat located the Avis rental car agency and rented a Mercedes-Benz E-class—*capitalism*.

Alex drove them out of the airport area and on a road that cut through white-powdered evergreens and leafless trees before turning left. Snow blanketed the countryside. Because most everything was written in Russian, Alex couldn't read it, but he could read "Coca-Cola" written on the factory they passed on the right side of the road. Then Alex drove under two levels of highway before reaching an oval-shaped intersection in St. Petersburg.

Formerly known as Leningrad, St. Petersburg was originally founded by Tsar Peter the Great at the beginning of the eighteenth century and had served as the capital of Russia until 1918, when the capital shifted to Moscow. On the western edge of Russia, St. Petersburg also had the distinction of being the northernmost city in the world with a population of more than a million.

In spite of being in the city, trees seemed to grow everywhere. Deeper in the city, bus stops appeared more frequently, and there was what looked like the entrance to a subway. Soon they crossed a hundred yards over a canal. Above the city rose two skyscrapers: a broadcasting tower and the golden dome of St. Isaac's Cathedral.

Although the main streets were clear of snow, side streets were untouched by snowplows or crews with snow shovels. A prosperous city like St. Petersburg with more than five million inhabitants should have generated enough money to clean snow off the streets— instead, the money probably went to corrupt officials or organized crime.

Finally, Alex stopped in front of the Grand Hotel Europe. The five-story building covered half the block and was more than a hundred years old, but its baroque façade retained its elegance. Alex and Cat removed their bags, and Alex handed the valet the car keys. The valet parked the car, returned, and gave Alex a laminated ticket to use later when he needed to pick up his car. "You will love hotel," the valet said. "Tchaikovsky, Pavarotti, and Elton John stay here. Many famous people stay here."

A porter greeted them and carried their luggage as they checked in. Marble and gilt decorated the interior, friezes were carved in the ceilings, and antique furniture added class to the five-star hotel.

After they checked in, the porter pushed their baggage on a cart to room 112, the Fabergé Suite, inspired by the Russian jeweler, Carl Fabergé. Alex tipped the porter, and he departed. Standing inside the suite's vestibule, Alex surveyed the living room. Nineteenth-century gold-colored patterns covered the walls like the designs on Fabergé Easter eggs. Also, the bases of the dark-colored table lamps were patterned like Fabergé eggs. A picture of the jeweler hung on the wall next to the window. Aged copper and precious stones encrusted the antique-style furniture. A painting of a young nineteenth-century woman hung over the couch. There was a closed wooden cabinet for the TV, and the ceiling was more than twelve feet high. Walking farther into the room, Alex saw a king-sized bed in the bedroom. The bed looked soft and luxurious.

"Do you want to shower first, or shall I?" Cat asked.

"Go ahead." Alex walked over to the window and looked out. It was snowing, but he could see the Russian Museum, Arts Square, and the statue of poet Alexander Pushkin—Alex read Pushkin's "The Gypsies" while studying at Harvard: "In the deserts you were not saved from misfortune, / And fateful passions are found everywhere. / And there is no defense against fate." Alex sat and checked his computer for a secure email from JSOC, hoping for an update on General Tehrani's location, but there was no message.

When Cat finished showering, Alex took his turn in the spacious bathroom made of Italian marble. After they both had cleaned up, Alex and Cat ate lunch in the hotel restaurant. Then they went for a ride to do a reconnaissance of the pier where General Tehrani's oil tanker was scheduled to arrive. Although it was bitterly cold outside, Alex and Cat stayed warm inside the Mercedes. She snuggled up against him as he drove.

After their reconnaissance, they returned to the hotel and stopped at the Caviar Bar and Restaurant. Even though the restaurant wasn't open on Mondays or Tuesdays, Alex and Cat were in luck because the restaurant opened on the other days. They were also fortunate because the menus were in English. In the center of the white tablecloth at their table was a lit white candle sitting in a silver candleholder.

The waiter pushed a cart over to their table. Cat hungrily eyed the wide selection of caviar on display.

"Would you like some, Mrs. Lehmann?" Alex asked.

"Yes, I'd love that, Mr. Lehmann."

Alex ordered the caviar bar cocktail: beluga, osetra, and salmon roe.

Using a small spoon, Cat put chilled caviar on small blini and added a touch of sour cream, chopped egg, and a sprinkle of chives.

"The way you eat caviar makes it look so delicious," Alex said.

"You want to try one?"

"No, thanks. My parents tried to initiate me, but it didn't stick. Sarah and Grandpa didn't care for caviar, either."

Alex put his hand on hers. She looked in his eyes as she pulled her hand away. His eyes locked on hers. She put her hand on his.

"I'm thirsty," Cat said.

"Russian Standard Premium Vodka?"

They continued gazing into each other's eyes until their drinks arrived. Alex and Cat took a sip. "I didn't know you liked vodka," she said.

"You know what I like?"

"What's that?"

"Your eyes. The way the candlelight flickers in them."

The waiter arrived and served their soup. Alex ate meat *solyanka*. It was thick and tasted spicy and sour. Cat had clear Russian mushroom soup made with barley and vegetables. They shared a taste of their soups with each other.

Alex enjoyed the soup. It was masterfully made, but also just being with Cat had elevated Alex's sensations. On the downside, he felt as if he were softening as an operator. "You ruined me," he said.

"What? When did I do that?"

"As an operator. You ruined me in Switzerland."

"You kissed me first."

"It wasn't part of the mission."

"You make me feel alive," she said.

"You make me forget things."

"That doesn't sound so good."

"Things that don't matter."

"You know we could walk away from this mission, if we wanted to."

"This mission still matters."

"We could." She slid her finger around the rim of her glass.

"Don't say that, please. Don't push me away tonight."

Cat let it go.

For the main course, Alex enjoyed beef Stroganoff. Cat tried the steamed Kamchatka crab Romanov-style with champagne sauce and salmon caviar. Although it didn't sound good to Alex, she fed him a bite with her fork, and he liked it. From his fork, Cat sampled the Stroganoff.

For dessert, Cat ordered the Composition of Russian delights: Russian mille-feuille, baklava, berry *kissel*, and lemon vodka sorbet. Alex ate Pavlova cake with berries—meringue cloud with Chantilly cream and berries. They ate more of each other's dessert than they ate of their own.

Alex paid the check. "What would you like to do tonight?"

"You know what I like?" Cat asked.

"What's that?"

"Your eyes."

He took her hand in his and didn't let go. Even when they returned to their room, turned the lights on, and gazed into each other's eyes, he didn't let go. Alex took her other hand. She kissed him.

He pulled away so he could stare into her eyes.

"I wish . . ." she said.

"You wish?"

"You're easy on the eyes."

"That's not what you were going to say."

She let it go and kissed him again.

Alex stopped kissing her and kicked off a shoe. Giggling, Cat kicked hers off, and the shoe hit the far wall. Laughing, they kicked off their remaining shoes together, hitting the far wall. He led her to the bed, and they stood next to it. Snow continued to float down from the sky outside their window. They kissed. He finally released her hands to unbutton her blouse. She stripped him down to his silk shorts, and he stripped her down to her bra and panties.

Cat giggled.

"What's so funny?" Alex asked.

"You still have your socks on."

He smiled. "So do you."

"Does it matter?"

"No."

Alex stripped off her bra and panties, and Cat removed his silk shorts. They kept their socks on and lay in bed embracing each other. At some point during the heat of passion, they lost their socks. Afterward, they showered together and made love under the hot water spray. When they returned to bed, they made love once more. Morning came quickly, and Alex ordered breakfast in bed. Shortly after Alex put the empty dishes in the hall, he and Cat made love again. Finally, they fell asleep in each other's arms.

When Alex awoke, it was Friday evening. Cat's side of the bed was empty, and he heard the shower running. After she finished in the bathroom, Alex showered, too. Then they left their room to eat dinner in the hotel at L'Europe. The spacious hall featured high illuminated arches above balconies that filled the length of the hall. An enormous stained-glass window, Apollo riding in his chariot, covered the end of the hall. On a stage below the window, two musicians played Tchaikovsky, one on harp and the other on a baby grand piano. More stained-glass windows served as skylights that ran the length of the ceiling. Potted plants added color to the restaurant. Alex and Cat ate the gourmet menu for two: truffle-flavored scrambled egg inside an egg topped with salmon caviar, American prime beef tenderloin, and cake layered with milk chocolate and berries. In spite of the exquisite surroundings and delicious meal, it was merely foreplay. Alex and Cat hurried back to their room and made love again.

Sunday, the weather warmed above freezing, and since Alex and Cat needed pictures and souvenirs to strengthen their identities as tourists, they ventured out and took a walk through the Winter Palace Square before touring churches under onion-shaped domes. In one of the churches, Alex and Cat sat on a pew. He closed his eyes and said a silent prayer. *I'm sorry I was angry at You for all these years.* After he said *amen*, a burden seemed to lift from his shoulders, and he felt lighter.

Later, they took a boat ride on one of the city's canals. In the evening, they attended a ballet in the Bolshoi Zia, the main hall of the St. Petersburg Philharmonic, where Tchaikovsky had conducted.

Monday, the temperature dropped to its lowest point and snow fell constantly. Alex and Cat kept warm inside the Hermitage Museum, created by Catherine the Great. Currently her museum held more paintings than any other museum in the world.

Although Alex and Cat took more than enough tourist pictures and purchased enough souvenirs, they needed weapons. Tuesday morning, Alex and Cat woke up at 0500 and before 0700 entered a nearby hotel. The lobby was crowded with people checking out and departing for the day. Alex carried a newspaper under his left arm as part of his identification and rolled his black Samsonite suitcase with his right hand. From inside the hotel, Alex spotted a man outside who was rolling an identical black Samsonite suitcase with his left hand and squeezing a gray raincoat under his right arm. The man entered through the front lobby door and walked toward Alex and Cat. Likewise, Alex and Cat walked toward him. Alex and the man bumped into each other.

"I'm sorry," the contact apologized. Alex knew he worked for the U.S. government, but Alex didn't know which of its alphabet soup agencies.

"It's okay," Alex said. It seemed like an innocent exchange, but they were exchanging bona fides.

"Are you sure?"

"Yeah."

The contact reached down with his right hand and grabbed Alex's suitcase handle before he shifted his jacket to his left hand. Alex reached down with his left hand, grabbed the contact's suitcase handle, then shifted his newspaper to his right hand. They walked past each other as if nothing happened, and nobody seemed the wiser. Now Alex had weapons, ammo, grenades, flash-bangs, the divining rod, and the rest of their mission equipment.

"You've got that look again," Cat whispered.

"What look is that?" Alex asked.

"That scary look—like you're about to kill someone."

"Day after tomorrow—Thursday."

36

Wednesday afternoon, Major Khan stood with General Tehrani outside on the oil tanker as it sailed at full speed—sixteen knots an hour—for St. Petersburg. The general appeared about to puke as the tanker pitched and rolled in the sea. General Tehrani tightened his jacket to protect himself from the stinging cold as he spoke on his cell phone to his superior in Tehran. "I contacted the Ground Forces of the Russian Federation, but they won't send anyone to meet us tomorrow in St. Petersburg—not one person. It's an outrage, sir!"

General Tehrani listened. His face looked green, and he belched.

"I know we've had some tense times with Russia," General Tehrani said, "but I looked the other way when they persecuted our brothers in Georgia. After the fall of the USSR, I established better relations with Russia—even purchased weapons from them. I agreed with their opposition to Turkey's regional influence, and I sided with Russia and China to oppose U.S. influence in Central Asia. And this is how the communists repay me? America is the devil, not me!"

General Tehrani shook his head as he listened to his superior on the phone. He burped again and swallowed hard.

"I was hoping you might be more successful than me in reminding Russia that they owe me," General Tehrani said.

General Tehrani listened, but something was wrong.

"Hello?" General Tehrani said. "Come in. Hello?!" He frantically fidgeted with his phone. "Damnit—I lost them! Damn!" He staggered to the side of the ship and vomited over the side.

37

Before sunrise on Thursday morning, the snow fell as if a giant dump truck had unloaded its bed on St. Petersburg. Alex and Cat parked their Mercedes near the docks. As they walked to the ships it looked to Alex like a scene out of World War II. A large warehouse had obviously burned down within the last few weeks and those adjacent to it had been severely damaged. Steel girders leaned at extreme angles and piles of charred rubble took on the appearance of white pyramids. It looked like a war zone.

They surreptitiously boarded an oil tanker tied to the pier. The crew had unloaded the vessel days ago; now it was empty. Unlike other ships, where the bridge was located near the bow, the oil tanker's bridge was located at the stern. Alex and Cat broke into the bridge and closed the door on the freezing weather behind them. Inside the ship, the bridge was still cold, but not as cold as outside in the wind. Windows spanned the 180 degrees in front of the bridge, giving Alex and Cat a panoramic view of ship's lights on Neva Bay in the Gulf of Finland, leading out to the Baltic Sea.

The sun that leaked through the clouds and snow warmed up the bridge, but it didn't warm up the cold tubes of energy gel Alex and Cat ate for lunch. A ship neared the pier, but it wasn't General Tehrani's. Again and again, Alex and Cat became anxious at a ship's arrival, only to find out it wasn't the general's oil tanker. Although General Tehrani's ship was supposed to arrive at noon, it was late.

As the sky became darker, another ship approached the pier and stopped in the bay while a tugboat brought it the rest of the distance to the pier. Cat handed Alex the binoculars. *Finally!* The vessel was the Iranian oil tanker, General Tehrani's ship. A dockworker helped tie the ship to the pier, and the ship's deckhands lowered the gangway from the stern. Soon the Venezuelan crew scurried off the ship—they wouldn't be offloading oil tonight. Alex worried that one of the crew might be General Tehrani in disguise, but with the divining rod attached to Alex's combat vest, he picked up the first *beep* in his earphone. "General Tehrani is on board," Alex said.

Alex and Cat put on their black balaclavas and readied their sound-suppressed AKMS assault rifles. "There's a guard standing just outside the bridge," Cat said. "He's got an AK."

Alex slipped out of the bridge on the side away from the Guard. He rested his rifle on a metal lip protruding from the ship and took aim through his scope at the upper torso of the man. Alex exhaled, and in the natural pause before he inhaled, he pulled the trigger slowly until he heard the shot and felt the recoil. The Guard fell, but he stood up again, and Alex shot him in the upper body again. This time, the Guard didn't stand up.

Another Guard stood inside a passageway near the gangway. Alex moved to a different location to enable a clearer shot. This time, Alex aimed higher, and after the shot, the Guard went down.

Alex motioned to Cat, *Let's go.* She exited the bridge behind him, and they descended the stairs to the main deck, where they surveyed the general's ship once more. There seemed to be no more shooters outside waiting for them, so Alex and Cat jogged across the gangway of their ship, hurried onto the pier, and ran across the general's gangway and onto his ship. The divining rod beeped more frequently. They were nearing the general.

Alex took the point position and Cat covered his six. Alex put a bullet through the head of the fallen Guard in the passageway. The head wobbled, but the rest of the man's body remained still. Better safe than sorry. Alex stepped over his body and into the ship's interior. To Alex's right was a metal bulkhead, and in front was the passageway that led to the port side of the ship. Alex turned left, pulled on a metal bar, and opened the hatch before he proceeded aft through its passageway. To his left was the starboard bulkhead, and to his right was an open door leading to the living spaces for the crew—it looked empty. Alex didn't have enough shooters to clear each room, so he just passed the open door—following the beeps on his divining rod. The beeps sounded in staccato as if Alex were right on top of the general, but he was nowhere in sight. To Alex's right was a closed door leading to the crew spaces. Alex expected General Tehrani to be on the deck above, where the ship's officers berthed, but he had learned to expect the unexpected. He quietly turned the doorknob and opened the door. Creeping inside, he searched the berthing area with its racks standing three high, like bunk beds. The deeper Alex and Cat searched into the crew's quarters, the less frequently the divining rod beeped. General Tehrani must have been directly above or below them.

Alex took Cat out of the berthing and moved aft. At the ladder, Alex went up. As he reached the top of the ladder, he heard shots below. Cat was shooting it out with someone. Alex looked down and saw someone near the ladder below the crew's deck, but he couldn't see if the person was armed. Alex was now near the galley and mess on the officers' deck. From inside the galley on Alex's deck someone fired shots, missing. Alex fired back, missing the shooter. Shots rang out from the man near the ladder below the crew's deck, and when the rounds hit the ladder next to Alex, they sparked. Alex ducked into the galley to avoid the man in the ladderway and waited for the man in the galley to poke his head out again. Meanwhile, he was cut off from Cat on the deck below him.

When the man in the galley poked his head up, Alex didn't miss.

He snapped off two shots and saw that at least one tore through the top of the man's head. Blood spurted high in the air as the man fell. Alex realized that the beeps had become less frequent. The general wasn't above the crew's deck; he was below. Alex returned to the stairwell as the man below the crew's deck was climbing up. Alex wanted to shoot him—if Cat stuck her head out a little, Alex's shot would miss her; if she stuck her head out a lot, he'd hit her. If he didn't take the shot, the man climbing the ladder might take her down with a shot from behind while she was shooting it out with someone else. "Shooting down!" Alex called before firing. Alex's round cracked the man through the top of his head. The man in the ladderway made a clanging sound as he and his weapon crashed to the deck below.

No more shooting sounds came from Cat's position. Either she'd popped the bad guys or they'd popped her. "Alex coming down!" Alex shouted before he descended the ladder to the crew's deck. Cat appeared. Behind her a bullet-riddled man in a green uniform with an AK lay motionless.

"You okay?" Cat asked.

"Yeah. You good?"

Cat nodded. "Take us to the general."

She sounded positive and Alex hoped she could remain upbeat—their situation would probably become worse before it got better. Although Alex was stationary, the general's beeping became even less frequent. "The general is escaping." Alex returned to the stairs and smoothly descended them until he stepped on the man with a bullet hole through his skull, lying next to a large storage compartment. General Tehrani's signal beeped faster. Alex glided down another flight of steps, landing on the engine room deck. He paid attention to his earpiece to find out if he was heading in the correct direction. The beeping rate increased. Alex could hear that Cat was above him, engaged in a firefight with Guards on an upper deck.

From the engine room, a Revolutionary Guard peeked around the side of a post covered with gauges, pipes, and control panels. He shot at Alex. Alex returned fire. Alex's shot hit the post but missed the Guard. None of the Guard's body showed to the left of the post, but he overcompensated by allowing his leg to stick out on the right side of the post. Alex drilled the Guard's leg near the kneecap. The soldier yelped and fell to the deck, exposing himself from his leg to his gut. Alex tattooed him in the gut with three shots. The Guard grunted.

From behind a labyrinth of pipes in the engine room flashed three AKs, their shots striking all around Alex—deck, bulkhead, and overhead. Alex took cover behind a bulkhead and waited for a lull. He needed to fight through the Guards in order to advance to the general's position. Alex switched to full auto, lay on the deck to vary his location, and when the three Guards' shooting slowed, Alex looked around the corner and sprayed about ten rounds at the maze of pipes they had fired from. Water sprayed from bullet holes in pipes.

In spite of Alex having delivered what he thought was an effective counterattack, three Guards answered Alex with a hurricane of lead. Alex hid behind the metal bulkhead, but the onslaught was so furious, he wanted to hide under the ship. When the firing eased up, Alex leaped to his feet, turned around the corner, and unleashed ten more rounds on full auto, emptying his magazine. More water sprayed, and the Guards stopped firing. Once again Alex took cover behind the bulkhead. "Changing mags," Alex informed Cat, then reloaded.

"Cat coming down." Her footsteps on the metal steps echoed from the ladderway above.

Before Alex could enter the engine room, another storm of lead punched the bulkhead and surrounding area. *What the hell? Did I miss all of them? Are these reinforcements?* Meanwhile, the beeps in his earpiece slowed. "General Tehrani is getting away." Alex grabbed a grenade from his vest, pulled the pin, and let the spoon fly. "Frag out!" He cooked three seconds off the five-second fuse before giving it an underhand toss into the engine room. *Boom!* "Moving forward," Alex said.

"Moving forward," Cat repeated.

Alex shuffled forward into the engine room as efficiently as possible. If he went too fast and missed a shooter, he could die. Efficiency trumped speed. *Smooth is fast.*

He searched behind the labyrinth of pipes and found three Guards lying on the deck. Two more writhed on the ground. Alex shot each of the writhing Guards in the head. A bloody Guard sat with his back against the wall and his AK rifle on his lap. He raised his hands in surrender, but Alex didn't have time for prisoners—or tricks. Alex shot him in the forehead.

Alex scanned for threats as he proceeded through the engine room looking for the general. He wasn't anywhere in sight. *He must have fled up the ladder on the port side.* Alex climbed the ladder on the port side, aiming his AKMS up the passageway. The higher Alex climbed, the higher the rate of beeps sounded. Alex reached the storage deck and continued up the metal ladder to the crew's deck. The metal hatch leading to the ship's passageway was open—someone had left in a hurry. Alex entered the passageway where the dead Guard from earlier lay, hopped over him, and hurried outside. Alex ran across the gangway. Before he reached the end of it, he spotted a lone man running from the pier. Alex stopped, planted his feet, and aimed. "General Tehrani!" Alex yelled.

The man turned and looked in the direction of Alex's voice. *It's him.* General Tehrani rushed away, just before Alex took the shot, missing him. Before Alex could take a second shot, the general ran past the heavily burned warehouse and disappeared.

A shot zipped past Alex's ear. He ducked and spun around, but couldn't see the shooter.

"Sniper!" Alex shouted into his mouthpiece. "On the deck."

Alex debated dealing with the shooter, but realized Tehrani had to be stopped. He spotted a length of coiled rope near the railing.

He took a smoke grenade from his vest, pulled the pin, and threw it toward the shooter. As soon as the smoke billowed up ten feet Alex got up and ran to the gangway, charging down it onto the dock after Tehrani.

Snow and concrete kicked up by his foot as the sniper got off another shot at him. Alex didn't bother to return fire, but ran after Tehrani, following his tracks in the snow.

38

The run winded General Tehrani, and he knew he couldn't go much farther. He jogged between a line of railroad tank cars on his left and the long, shattered hulk of the burned warehouse on his right. After the building ended, there was a gap between it and a small two-room building. Frantically looking for a good place to hide, he spotted a huge mound of snow on a triangular patch of land surrounded by piles of twisted girders and smashed concrete cinder blocks. Off to the left it looked like children had hollowed out the snow in the rubble and created a small snow cave. Adjacent to the snow cave sat a giant snowball, possibly the base for a large snowman. In front of it lay a smaller-sized snowball cracked into three chunks. General Tehrani picked up one of the three chunks of snow and put it in the cave. Next, he pushed the giant snowball, but it wouldn't budge. The base seemed frozen to the ground. He put his shoulder into it and pushed harder until the snowball broke loose from the ground and rolled forward. Then General Tehrani knelt between the snowball and the snow cave and pulled the snowball toward him until it closed off much of the cave. Freezing wind blew snow through the upper right portion of the cave, where it remained open. General Tehrani's hunters might see him inside the cave, so he used the chunk of snow he'd deposited in the cave and plugged the biggest opening of the hole, protecting himself from most of the frigid wind and the hunters' eyes.

39

Alex chased after Tehrani, tracking his movement through the snow. He came up to the rail line and stopped. The tracks were lost in a mess of slush.

Suddenly, something hit Alex from behind, like a hot baseball bat striking his left shoulder. It hit him with such force that his left hand lost its grip on his AKMS, and he almost fell onto the tracks. His vision blurred and his ears rang and he fell to his knees. The ringing in his ears took away his equilibrium. "Sniper," Alex reported weakly. He didn't recall the sound of a rifle, but he sensed he'd been shot by Major Khan.

"Alex!" Cat yelled. "Get up and run, Alex! Run!"

"I can't see," Alex cried.

"You have to try!" Cat shouted.

Alex scurried on his knees toward the railcars, knowing he'd buy himself a few more seconds. His vision remained blurry. Everything was a swirl of white and black. His hearing still ringing, Alex felt unbalanced, afraid to move because he might fall and he wasn't sure he could pick himself back up again. The shot had pierced his shoulder, and he knew it wouldn't be long before Major Khan took his second shot. In that moment, Alex regretted not being able to see Cat's smile again, but he imagined it.

He heard two more shots, but he could tell they weren't aimed at him. His left hand went numb and he looked down. Cat was holding his hand, helping him to his feet.

"I've got your hand. Just run with me, baby. Run."

Alex stumbled with her across the railway tracks and into the warehouse. His feet tangled up in some wire and he stumbled and fell, dragging Cat down with him. A shot zipped past them. Cat returned fire, then helped him up, and they ran. He couldn't hear if Major Khan took more shots. Maybe he was still working Alex into his crosshairs. Alex ran for Cat, and he ran for himself—he wanted to live. As he ran, the ringing continued in one ear.

They weaved through the rubble, up and over crumpled metal siding and a pile of huge gears. Cat led him to a heap of rebar and then stopped when they got around to the far side.

Alex's vision began to clear. He noticed a black object in her hand. "What's that?"

"I think it's General Tehrani's cell phone. It probably fell out of his pocket. I found it on the gangway."

"That's why my ear keeps ringing." He took out the earpiece that monitored the divining rod. The ringing in his ear stopped.

"Your shoulder is bleeding."

Alex looked around the debris and snow for any signs of General Tehrani. "I lost him. I know he's close, but where?"

Cat grabbed his shoulder and Alex winced. "We need to get you bandaged up."

"Khan will be coming, and we're too out in the open to stay here," Alex said, looking around them. "There, see that ducting. It must have fallen from the ceiling when the building burned down, but a lot of it is still intact."

Cat peered around the rebar and swept the area. "Okay, we'll get in there and I'll patch you up. Go."

40

General Tehrani's body heat warmed the inside of his snow cave, and the temperature became almost comfortable. The general smiled. *An officer fights to become a general, and when he succeeds, he spends the rest of his career protecting his rank.* In 1979, Iran executed eighty-five senior generals and expelled the majority of its junior generals. Officers like Tehrani who were loyal to the regime were promoted to general. In 1980, Saddam Hussein invaded Iran, but during the Iran-Iraq War, General Tehrani repelled Saddam Hussein's army from Iran and commanded human-wave attacks through barbed wire, machine-gun fire, and chemical weapons attacks—taking over land in Iraq. Finally, a truce was called between the two countries, and Iran told General Tehrani to give the Iraqis back their land. He beat the Iraqis, and now in his ice cave, General Tehrani was beating the Americans. *I cannot be defeated.*

He heard two people outside his cave speaking English, a man and a woman. The woman said, "General Tehrani." *They're looking for me.* Although he wanted to put snow in the cracks of the entrance to his snow cave to better conceal himself, he dared not move for fear of alerting the Americans to his location. Also, his body heat quickly warmed the snow inside his cave to water, which froze into ice, so it was becoming more difficult to scrape together a handful of snow anyway. Fortunately the wind drove the heavy falling snow into the cracks of his cave, cloaking the general in darkness. *Now they'll never find me. If I stay here until morning, they'll be gone. When I hear the Russians come to unload the crude oil, I can ask for help.*

General Tehrani's knees weren't as strong as they used to be and the soft snow beneath him had become ice. He shifted his body from a kneeling position to sitting. Because he couldn't sit up straight in the cave, his neck ached from bending over. The aching slowly traveled from his neck down his spine, but he'd rather have an aching spine than be dead. *I can recover from an aching spine.* Soon his ass ached from sitting on the ice.

The air inside his cave became stale, and he loosened the top button on his collar so he could breathe more easily. After a while, he lost track of time, and the air became more uncomfortable to breathe. It occurred to General Tehrani that he might not have enough oxygen, and if he didn't let some oxygen in soon, he might suffocate. He used his finger to try to poke a hole where the snow had filled the cracks at the top of his cave's entrance. If the hole was small enough, he could let air in without being seen from the outside. In spite of his effort, his finger couldn't poke through. He tried other locations, but the snow had frozen solid.

I could be trapped in here. General Tehrani pressed his hands on the cave's entrance, searching for a soft spot to break through, but he found none. He searched the rest of the cave—ice. Now he feared suffocating in the ice cave more than he feared the Americans.

General Tehrani hoped the Americans had left the area. He pounded on the cave's entrance, hoping to beat a hole through to the outside, but the harder he pounded it, the harder he packed the ice. The pounding made his hands and fists sore, and he expended more of his precious oxygen, making it more difficult to breathe. He pressed his shoulder against the entrance, but the ice didn't budge. He kicked at the entrance until his feet became too sore and weak to kick anymore.

He reached for his cell phone, but it was missing. He'd dropped it somewhere. "Help! Somebody help me! Can anyone hear me?! I'm suffocating!" General Tehrani remembered his metal belt buckle and took it off. Then he used it to scrape the ice, but he expended too much oxygen for a small amount of progress that would take days to complete. *"Help! Please help me from this tomb!"*

After screaming for help for as long and as loud as he could, he ran out of energy and breath. "Help! Please, help!" He curled into a fetal position, and his voice became faint: "Help. Please, some-body . . ." General Tehrani could no longer speak. Dizziness gripped him and the edges of his vision began to gray and then darkness overcame him.

41

"You're lucky, it was a clean through-and-through," Cat said, wrapping the bandage tight around his shoulder.

"Don't feel lucky," Alex said, grimacing as Cat finished her work.

"Poor you," Cat said, picking up her rifle and peering out from the ducting.

"Thanks," he said, reaching out and patting her leg with his right hand.

"Wait until you get my bill," Cat said.

Alex crawled a few feet away from Cat and looked out through a tear in the ducting. He knew that if Major Khan wanted to stop him before reaching downtown, Khan would have to pass between the narrow length of land stretching between the piers and the city. Alex and Cat couldn't keep all of the piers under surveillance, but they could monitor that narrow stretch of land. Alex looked for a good sniper position. Rows of oil tanks stood ten stories tall—taller than anything in the area. A ladder led to the top of each tank, but since the ladder was the only entrance and exit to the top, it would be easy for a sniper perched on top to become trapped. Also, the tanks were too far away from the narrow stretch of land. A three-story building had a great view of the narrow stretch of land and was well within range of Alex's rifle. The three-story building had the added bonus of a raised roof that sheltered it from view from the ten-story-tall oil tanks. It seemed like the best place for a sniper. Major Khan would think the same. Alex quickly looked for where Major Khan might set up a countersniper position. There was a smaller two-story building that didn't have a commanding view of the narrow stretch of land, but it had a view of the three-story sniper position. Alex felt strongly that Major Khan would set up a countersniper position in the smaller two-story building, so Alex looked for a counter-countersniper position, and he found it in a pile of girders and rubble. If Major Khan set up in the sniper position, Alex wouldn't be able to see him. Worse, if Major Khan set up a counter-counter-countersniper position, Alex was screwed.

"Okay, let's move," Alex said, pointing outward.

"You sure?" Cat asked.

"One hundred percent," Alex said.

He crawled back out of the duct and slowly stood up while Cat covered him. He tested his legs and was relieved that his equilibrium was back. His shoulder was a screaming nightmare, but it could wait. He waited until Cat got out of the duct, then led her past a line of tanker cars on a train track. They crawled the last twenty feet to the pile of snow-covered debris. Alex pointed to a depression five feet away for Cat to use. He waited until she was in place, then wormed his way under a girder and to the left of a spool of steel cable. He carefully unwound several yards of the cable and heaped it up in front of him. He poked his rifle between the loops and made sure his scope had a clear view. Next, he grabbed some metal shards and placed them to his right, angling them so they were parallel with his rifle barrel. He found a section of tarp and slowly pulled it over his head to further break up his form. Satisfied, he watched the counter-sniper position and the surrounding area.

The snow continued to fall, making spotting anything difficult. Alex began to shiver and started tensing and relaxing his muscles to combat the cold. A sniper who couldn't shoot straight was useless. He began mentally cataloging shapes and distances. The mounds of rubble made it an almost impossible task, but Alex kept at it, focusing on likely areas and discarding those he knew he'd never use.

After half an hour, Alex sensed movement near the countersniper building, but he couldn't pinpoint where it was. Minutes later, he saw movement through a window on the second floor. Although Alex could see only the vague silhouette of a person sitting behind his rifle, positioned on a table, Alex knew it had to be Major Khan. The movement stopped.

As Alex inhaled, he aimed carefully, trying to empty his mind. If he emptied his mind then his target wouldn't sense Alex was thinking about him. Adjusting for distance and wind direction, Alex's sights lined up perfectly on Major Khan's upper body. During Alex's exhale, he didn't wait until he expelled all his air. Instead, he held his breath so the movement of his lungs wouldn't throw his shot. If he held it too long, his body would crave oxygen and tremble. Alex squeezed the trigger, building the tension in his finger until his AKMS fired. The recoil thumped his shoulder with a satisfying wallop. It was a perfectly placed shot. The figure of Major Khan remained sitting in his chair as if stunned. Alex shot him again in the chest. Major Khan slumped face-first onto the table in front of him.

Before Alex moved from his position to make sure Khan was dead, Alex sensed something eerie. *Somebody is watching us.* He froze.

"Cat," he whispered. "Stay perfectly still. Khan's still out there."

The countersniper wasn't Major Khan. That was one of his Guards—bait. Alex's eerie feeling changed to fear. *Where's Major Khan?*

If Major Khan knew our exact location, he'd already have taken his shot. He may know our general location, but he's waiting for us to move so he can pinpoint us. Alex remained still, waiting for Major Khan to make the first move. Behind Alex and Cat there wasn't much land between them and Neva Bay. Normally, Alex would consider the water as one of his primary retreats, but with the freezing air temperature, near-freezing water conditions, and no wet suit, the water wasn't his first choice of retreat. Whether he was winning or losing, Alex always tucked emergency exits into the back of his mind.

Between Alex and the city, a little over a hundred yards away, shots were fired at full automatic from another pile of rubble. Thirty shots sprayed Alex's rubble pile. Some of the shots were so close that snow fell down on him. The enemy knew Alex and Cat were in the debris, but he didn't know exactly where. He was trying to flush them out.

Alex spotted the muzzle flash and traced the rifle barrel to the shooter lying on the ground. He wasn't Major Khan. *Where is Major Khan? Probably waiting for me to whack this Guard and give away my exact position.* The shooter was doing something—probably changing magazines. The shooter stood up and walked toward Alex's position, aiming his AK at him and Cat. As he arrived within less than a hundred yards, Alex realized their discovery was inevitable. Snipers who froze in place too long were dead snipers. Now Alex had to get the jump on the shooter before the shooter jumped him. When the shooter reached fifty yards away, Alex pounded him twice in the chest. The shooter fell back as if he'd been struck by a sledgehammer.

"Follow me," Alex whispered. He ran across the tracks and into another of the damaged buildings. There would be more options for cover in there. Alex glanced back. Cat was right behind him. When he reached the middle of the narrow stretch of land, he headed southwest toward the city, where the land would expand and give him even more options for maneuvering. Especially after getting shot in the left shoulder, Alex wasn't going to stick around and wait for Major Khan, who had obviously upped his game since their days in Iraq.

As Alex ran southwest, he passed the fallen countersniper's building on his left and a snowy mound on his right. Fortunately, the building and mound covered Alex's left and right from anyone shooting at him. Unfortunately, he was in a kill zone where he could escape only backward or forward—with little wiggle room in between. *Shit!* After fifty yards, there was a break in the mound to the right and Alex took it. *Bang!* A shot sounded from behind. Alex glanced back to see if Cat was still with him. She was.

Alex's new location was no better than the previous one. Although he had more space to maneuver, he had no cover to protect him from Major Khan's bullets, and he had no idea how many Guards the major had brought with him. Alex nearly panicked trying to find a better place for maneuvering, but he remembered to breathe—deep and slow. His legs pumped hard and fast. He zigged and zagged southwest through the open space. *Bang-bang, bang-bang!* Alex felt one hot round pass the left side of his neck and heard another pop the sound barrier above his right ear. Alex slanted left before continuing southwest. He sprinted through a narrow stretch that opened to several buildings and a large oil tank. The terrain gave him more places to take cover, but it was still limited. Alex ran to the right, behind the tank, looking for a better place to make a stand. Finally, to the southwest, he found a maze of buildings, metal pillars and pipes, and train cars to provide him multiple sources of cover while he maneuvered—*perfect.*

Alex entered the maze, taking cover behind a tangle of metal pipes, and when he turned around to catch Major Khan and his men in less favorable terrain, Alex realized that Cat was nowhere in sight.

"Cat, where are you?" Alex called over the radio. He heard gunshots in the distance.

Meanwhile, six Guards and Major Khan came around a building corner. Alex thumped the first Guard twice in the chest. The remaining five Guards and Major Khan advanced quickly to cover behind a long storage shed. Alex fired at Major Khan, hitting the shed just as the major hid behind it.

Alex moved to a new position so he wouldn't be a predictable target, behind a large metal pole. Two Guards appeared, one on each side of the shed. The Guard on the right exposed his whole body and peppered lead in Alex's direction. Alex answered the Guard on the right with two rounds. Although Alex was aiming for the Guard's chest, Alex inadvertently leaned into the shot, pressing his muzzle down, and hit the Guard in the right side of his belly. Alex's second shot went higher, but too far right, missing the Guard. The Guard fell on his ass.

The Guard on the left emerged again and fired. Alex squeezed off two rounds, missing him. Alex ducked behind some pipes. He pushed his weapon around the side of the pipes and aimed at the left side of the shed, waiting for the Guard to show his face again. When he did, Alex busted a cap in the Guard's eye. His second round struck the Guard in the forehead.

Major Khan and his three remaining Guards had only two places to stick their heads out from: left of the shed or right of the shed. Between the shed and Alex, the Guards would be in open territory. If Alex allowed Major Khan and his men to advance to his position, they could use the multiple sources of cover and their superior numbers to shoot at him from more angles than he could protect himself from. He had to hold his ground.

Alex hustled to a position behind another tangle of pipes. All three Guards appeared from the left side of the shed, advancing toward his position while shooting. Their shots gave the pipes concealing Alex a severe spanking—oil sprayed from them. Alex flicked his selector switch to full auto and cut into the Guards, stopping their advance.

While Alex focused on halting the advance of the Guards to the left of the storage shed, Major Khan had taken aim from the right of the shed. *Bang!* An AK round struck Alex in the back of the right hand, exiting his palm and knocking his rifle out of his hand. "Damn!" Alex's rifle dangled by its sling.

Alex sidestepped and ducked to the left, avoiding Major Khan's line of fire, but Major Khan advanced while shifting his fire in Alex's direction, popping holes in pipes that gushed oil into a pool on the ground. Alex kept moving to the left while he gripped his rifle with his left hand. He rose and fired on full auto, emptying his magazine. Alex wasn't accurate enough to hit Major Khan, but he was accurate enough to cause the major to slip in his tracks and fall on his back. Alex attempted to wiggle the bloody fingers on his right hand, but they wouldn't obey. His whole hand felt like it'd been stabbed with daggers. And his rifle had run out of bullets.

Major Khan must have sensed Alex was in trouble, because the major hopped up and charged Alex, spitting hell out of his rifle barrel. Alex crouched down to avoid being shot. The noise alone terrified him, but Alex knew he couldn't let his fear take over. He wanted to reload a new magazine into his weapon, but he wasn't sure he could do that with only one hand and at the same time successfully dodge Major Khan's bullets. Although Alex's customized Zoaf sound-suppressed pistol was in the holster on his right hip, he could reach around with his left hand, draw it, and reposition it for firing. There was also the option for Alex to use his last grenade.

With his left hand, Alex jerked the pin out of the grenade, but the grenade fell out of its pouch, landed on the ground, and the spoon flew. Alex ran away from the grenade and Major Khan. He dodged pipes and took cover behind a cluster of them.

Major Khan pursued. *Boom!*

A piece of shrapnel ripped through Alex's trousers and stabbed him in his thigh. He grunted. Ignoring the pain, he sneaked around to the side to see what had happened to Major Khan. Dozens of geysers spouted black oil from pipes, permeating the air with fumes and changing the white snow to black. Slowly, Major Khan rose from the ground, his feet unsteady. The oil had transformed him into a hideous black monster.

Fire. I need fire. Alex could shoot at metal and hope a spark would ignite. He didn't have a thermite grenade or even a lighter that would stay lit as he threw it. However, he remembered he hadn't used any of his flash-bangs. Alex put a flash-bang under his right arm and held it tight while he pulled the pins, then he tossed it at Major Khan. More than a million candela flashed, 170 decibels of boom shook the air, and the oil around Major Khan combusted.

Major Khan became a human flame. He ran away from Alex, passing through the fire surrounding him, screaming in Farsi.

With his left hand, Alex reached across his stomach and drew his pistol. Then he manipulated it until he acquired the proper grip. He crouched while moving in Major Khan's direction, limping around the inferno. Fire had replaced the snow on the ground, and pipes sprayed flames like Roman candles. Alex felt the heat, especially on his face. The blaze lit up the surrounding area, helping Alex spot fresh tracks in the snow. He followed the tracks until he came to Major Khan crawling in the snow facedown. Major Khan was black from head to foot, his clothing tattered and smoldering. Maybe he sensed Alex standing there, or maybe he tired of crawling on his stomach, but Major Khan turned over on his back. He had no visible weapon. His badly burned face showed no emotion as he stared into Alex's eyes. Major Khan said something in Farsi.

"This is for Leila." Alex shot Major Khan once in the left thigh.

Major Khan gritted his teeth and hissed.

"This is for Jabberwocky." Alex shot him in the crotch.

Major Khan wailed.

"And this is for me." Alex shot him in the forehead.

Blood oozed out of Major Khan's forehead. His eyes remained open as snow fell on them. Soon a light sheet of white covered his charred body, flickering in the light of the nearby inferno.

Alex sat down exhausted. He knew the oil might explode at any moment, but he was too tired to move. *Just need a little rest.*

A minute later, out of the corner of his eye, he saw movement. He turned his head and looked up to see an Iranian Revolutionary Guard standing there aiming his rifle at Alex's face. *So this is it. This is how it ends.* The Guard grinned and squeezed his trigger. Alex closed his eyes. *Pop.* Alex felt a warm spurt of blood on his face.

Something was wrong. The shot wasn't loud enough, and Alex felt no pain. He opened his eyes. The Guard bled from the middle of his face. He swayed once before toppling over. Behind him stood Cat with her sound-suppressed AKMS aimed at where the Guard's head had been. "Sitting down on the job?" she asked.

Alex smiled weakly. "What took you so long?"

"Took the scenic route." She noticed his right hand. "What happened?!" she exclaimed.

"Let's just get to the car before we run into any more surprises."

"You need a doctor."

"Not in St. Petersburg. Not after what we did here."

"I'll charter a boat to Finland and contact our embassy. Take you to an operating room."

"Thanks." Alex stood and limped southwest.

Cat walked beside him. "What do we do about General Tehrani?"

"No idea."

"Maybe he fell in the ocean and drowned."

"I doubt it. He'll turn up one of these days, and when he does, he'll be somebody else's problem."

EPILOGUE

J ust before sunset, Alex parked his SUV in the parking lot of a AAA four-diamond steakhouse on the beachfront at Atlantic Avenue in Virginia Beach. Wearing khaki slacks, a white button-down shirt, and leather car coat, he walked inside and a cheery hostess greeted him. She noticed the bandages on his hand, then pretended she hadn't seen them. "Welcome to Salacia. I'm Jennifer. May I help you, sir?"

"Yes, I have a reservation."

The waitress waited for a moment. When Alex didn't respond, she inquired, "May I ask your name, sir?"

Alex paused. He had used so many aliases throughout his career that remembering sometimes became a burden, but he always kept his first name the same: "Alex." Then he remembered the alias for his last name. "Alex Brown."

"Right this way, sir."

Alex followed her through the restaurant. They passed patrons dressed in business casual. Alex walked behind the hostess as she went out onto the veranda. Although it was still winter, the day was unusually warm and most of the seats outside appeared full. He could see and smell the ocean—it made him feel peaceful. The hostess sat him at an intimate table for two. "Is this table okay?"

Alex sat. "Perfect."

"Your server will be with you shortly, sir."

"Thank you." For several minutes, he watched the shimmering sunlight fade on the ocean.

Alex sensed Cat before he saw her step out onto the veranda. She created her own breeze as she moved forward, air flowing through her blond hair. She took a seat.

"How's the hand?" Cat asked.

"Doc says if I continue the rehabilitation, I should regain full use of it."

Cat smiled.

"I was afraid you might not come," Alex said.

"Since when have you ever been afraid?" she teased. Her voice became serious. "I know how much this means to you." Cat looked around the veranda and inside the building. "Where are Pancho and John?"

"Um, I didn't invite them."

"What?" She looked stunned. "Did they piss you off or something?"

Alex smiled. "No."

"What about the skipper? I thought the skipper was going to swear you in?"

Alex shook his head. "Skipper isn't coming, either."

"Then who's going to swear you in?"

"I asked the skipper to let you transfer with me to Coronado, but he didn't want to let you go."

Cat sat with a numb expression on her face.

"I like the view here," Alex said. "Do you like the view?"

"So will you still go to Coronado?"

Alex shook his head. "No reason to go, if I can't be with you."

"So you're going to stay here."

Alex said nothing.

"Who's going to swear you in for your reenlistment tonight?" she asked.

"I did a lot of thinking. About the future. About the sacrifices I made for the Teams. About what Sarah would want me to do. About who I really am." Alex spoke slowly, each word weighted with the decision that would change his life forever.

"Who you really are?"

"It's something I'd like to find out," Alex said.

Cat shook her head and brushed back her hair. "I don't understand what all this has to do with your reenlistment ceremony."

Alex took a deep breath. "I'm not reenlisting."

Cat looked confused. "You can't be serious."

"I am."

"What will you do?"

"I have investments—stocks, bonds, and real estate. Money isn't a problem. I thought I'd go to graduate school for my MBA while I'm figuring out what to do next."

"Sometimes you don't make a lot of sense!" She raised her voice.

Nearby patrons turned to look at them.

Alex spoke quietly. "When Sarah died, I felt so empty. Then angry. My job was a way of protecting others from having to feel what I felt. And honoring her memory. It helped channel my anger. But this job has left me feeling so lonely. After I met you, I didn't feel angry, and I didn't feel lonely. I thought maybe I'd changed, but when I thought about my childhood, I wasn't an angry or lonely kid then. After you and I spent some time apart, I realized how much I missed you."

"You're talking in riddles. Have you gone crazy?"

"You once told me that I should think about trying something else. You gave me my life back." Alex reached into his jacket pocket and pulled out a small black square box.

Cat's hands covered her mouth, muffling a gasp.

Alex opened the box so she could see the engagement ring.

"If this is some kind of sick joke, stop it now because my heart can't—"

Alex pressed on. He had never been more certain of anything in his life. "This ring is my mother's. She wants you to have it."

"I've never even met your mother."

"I told her all about you. She wants to meet you."

A tear rolled down Cat's face. "You sure do know how to ambush a girl."

"Will you marry me?"

She didn't speak.

"I'll understand if you say no," he said.

"Don't be a dumbass," Cat said, wiping away the tears.

Alex was fairly certain he knew her answer, but he wanted to make absolutely sure. "Is that a yes?" he asked.

Cat threw up her hands. "Of course it's a yes."

A woman at the table next to them clapped her hands and others followed.

Alex gestured for Cat to give him her hand. She did, and he put the sparkling ring on her finger, but in that moment her eyes sparkled brighter than the ring.

Dinner was a blur after that. Alex couldn't remember what he ate, what he said, or even if he paid the check as they walked back outside. He put his left arm around Cat and held her close. She leaned her head against his shoulder.

"I love you," Alex said, squeezing her.

"You better, mister," Cat said, squeezing him back.

Alex fished in his pockets for his keys, not quite sure this wasn't a dream. He was quitting the Teams, and he was engaged!

He heard the *click-click* of stilettos on pavement and looked up. He recognized her immediately: it was the blonde from the supermarket.

She was walking through the parking lot toward them. She wore a shimmering blue dress that was every bit as stunning as the red dress she'd had on the first time they had met. *Talk about long odds*. It seemed ages ago when he'd first caught sight of her.

"Friend of yours?" Cat asked.

Alex shook his head. "Nope, don't even know her," he said, which was true. He didn't want to start his life with Cat with a lie.

"She's staring at you. I don't like it," Cat said.

Alex was about to say it was nothing, but when he caught the blonde's eye he paused. She wasn't smiling. This wasn't the flirty dream woman he remembered. She looked angry. His running out of Whole Foods couldn't have been that traumatic for her.

Movement off to the left drew Alex's eyes away from the blonde. Two men were stepping out of the shadows by a large hedge. Alex's mind cleared in an instance. *Shit, I'm not carrying!*

"Cat, get ready to run. Head between those two parked cars over there, then work your way back to the restaurant," Alex said.

"What?" Cat asked. She lifted her head from his shoulder. "What is—she's got a gun!"

Alex looked away from the men to the blonde. She was now thirty feet away and walking with obvious purpose. She had a pistol in her hand and was aiming it at him.

"Mohammed says hello," she said, her voice harsh, and tinged with a Middle Eastern accent now.

Alex's mind reeled. *Mohammed?* Which one? Then he remembered: the teenage son of the terrorist he'd killed on their last mission, the one terrorist who got away.

"I don't know any Mohammeds," Alex said, stepping in front of Cat to shield her with his body. "I think you have me mistaken for someone else." He knew it was useless, but every second she didn't shoot was one more second he might think of something.

"He knows exactly who you are. Allahu akbar!" she shouted,

bringing her left hand up to steady her right hand as she squeezed the trigger.

"No!" Alex shouted. Three shots rang out. Alex gritted his teeth, bracing himself as the steel tore through his flesh. The blonde crumpled to the ground, the pistol clattering from her hand. Alex didn't understand. He looked down at his chest. She'd missed. He spun to look at Cat; her eyes were wide with fear.

"Alex, are you okay?"

Alex turned and saw Pancho and John running out of the shadows of the hedge.

"How?" he asked.

John ran over to the woman and kicked the pistol away from her while keeping his own pointed at her. Pancho met John and punched his shoulder before saying to Alex, "We knew what you were up to tonight. We figured we'd wait until after you proposed and surprise you."

Alex clapped Pancho on the shoulder. "I owe you."

"You can name your first kid after me," Pancho said.

The wail of police sirens sounded in the distance. People were crowding around the entrance of the restaurant, too afraid to come any closer.

"Who was she?" John asked, coming over to stand with them. "I don't remember her being on any target list when we went after those terrorists on our last mission."

"Mohammed's been recruiting," Cat said, glaring at the body of the blonde. "Looks like the son is taking after the father."

"Not exactly the way I imagined tonight going," Alex said. A shootout *and* a marriage proposal; well, maybe he should have expected it.

"So she said yes?" John asked.

Pancho laughed. "I sure hope she said yes, because if she didn't I might just ask her myself," he said.

Over the blare of the approaching sirens, Cat held out her left hand to show Pancho and John her engagement ring. She rotated her hand, using the diamond to catch and refract the red and blue lights of the first police car pulling into the parking lot.

"I haven't had time to register for gifts yet," Cat said, "but I'm thinking Heckler and Koch."

GLOSSARY

The Activity: See ISA.

AK-47: The name is a contraction of Russian: *Avtomat Kalashnikova obraztsa 1947 goda* (Kalashnikov's automatic rifle model of year 1947). This assault rifle fires a 7.62x39mm (.308) round up to an effective range of 300 meters (330 yards) and holds thirty rounds. It was developed in the Soviet Union by Mikhail Kalashnikov in two versions: the fixed-stock AK-47 and the AKS-47 (S: *Skladnoy priklad*) variant equipped with an underfolding metal shoulder stock. The modern version is the AKM (M: *Modernizirovanniy*).

AKM: Modern version of AK-47.

AKMS: Modern version of AKS-47.

AKS-47: See AK-47.

AT-4 CS: An 84mm, one-shot, light antitank rocket designed to operate within closed spaces. Salt water absorbs much of the back blast, so it doesn't fry teammates.

Basij: Paramilitary militia in Iran who police morals and stop opposition to the government or Ayatollah. Individual members are called *basiji*. Regular members are unpaid. Active members are volunteers with additional training who are paid. Special members are paid as members of both the Basij and the IRGC army.

Blowout kit: First-aid kit.

Bouncing Betty: See M16 mine.

BUD/S: Basic Underwater Demolition/SEAL training.

Burqa: Traditional clothing worn by a number of Muslim women to cover themselves from head to toe.

Civvies: Civilian clothes.

Claymore mine: Anti-personnel mine that is sometimes used against unarmored vehicles. Can be fired by remote control or rigged as a booby trap. Mostly used for ambushes and defense of a stationary position. Fired forward like a shotgun, blasting nearly seven hundred steel balls in a sixty-degree arc out to about one hundred meters.

CO: Commanding Officer.

C-130: Lockheed C-130 Hercules. Large military plane often used to transport troops.

HAHO: High altitude, high opening. Parachutist jumps from 25,000 to 35,000 feet and deploys parachute within seconds, then glides miles to the target. Useful tactic for avoiding enemy detection such as radar.

Helo: Helicopter.

Hezbollah: Terrorists trained by Iran's Revolutionary Guard. Hezbollah's headquarters is in Lebanon, where they recruit mostly from Shiite Muslims. Hezbollah mainly serves Iranian and Syrian interests to control the region and has received recognition as a political party in Lebanon.

IRGC: See Islamic Revolutionary Guard Corps.

ISA: Intelligence Support Activity, nicknamed the Activity. Tier 1 unit that provides intelligence mainly for SEAL Team Six and Delta. Same as Team Six and Delta, ISA is commanded by JSOC.

Islamic Revolutionary Guard Corps: The Islamic Revolutionary Guard Corps (IRGC) serves as Iran's military and squashes internal opposition to the Iranian government or the Ayatollah. Their army, navy, and air force are made up of about 125,000 troops. In addition, they command approximately 90,000 Basij militia.

JSOC: Joint Special Operations Command, located at Pope Air Force Base and Fort Bragg in North Carolina. After the 1980 failed attempt to rescue fifty-three American hostages at the American Embassy in Iran, it became clear that the Army, Navy, Air Force, and Marines couldn't work together effectively on Special Operations missions. In 1987, the Department of Defense grafted all the military branches' Special Operations onto one tree—including Tier 1 units like SEAL Team Six and Delta. SEALs, Rangers, and Green Berets are truly special, but only the best make it to the top tier: Team Six and Delta. JSOC is Team Six's boss.

Kit: Team Six word meaning gear.

Klick: Military slang for kilometer.

KLS-7.62: Iranian copy of the Russian AKMS.

Knot: One knot equals roughly 1.15 miles per hour.

Maghnaeh: A scarf that conceals the hair and neck.

MBD21: Madagascar Black Death 21. An advanced strain of Black Death crossbred with pneumonic plague that can be transmitted by fleas, human coughing, or sneezing. MBD21 is immune to antibiotics.

MPT-9KPDW: The Iranian copy of the German MP5K-PDW short submachine gun.

M16 Mine: Nicknamed the Bouncing Betty. When an enemy trips the trigger, there is a delay for the enemy to step past the mine before the mine launches into the air about three feet and explodes, showering shrapnel 360 degrees. After the M16 has been tripped, troops have dived to the ground and avoided the blast of shrapnel.

Niqab: Veil to cover the face.

NOD: Night Optical Device. Used for seeing in the dark.

NSA: National Security Agency. Collects foreign communications and signals intelligence and protects U.S. government communications.

PT: Physiology technician.

Quds Force: Quds Force is the Iranian Revolutionary Guard's special operations unit. Quds Force trains and assists terrorists such as Hezbollah to influence governments abroad. Quds Force reports directly to the Ayatollah.

RHIB: Rigid Hull Inflatable Boat. A thirty-six-foot-long Naval Special Warfare boat designed primarily for inserting and extracting SEALs. The RHIB travels at speeds of over forty knots (sixty-four kilometers an hour). It is also tough enough to operate in heavy seas and high winds. Armament can include a 7.62 machine gun, .50-caliber machine gun, and 40mm grenade launcher.

RPG: Rocket-propelled grenade.

SEAL: The U.S. Navy's elite *SE*a, *A*ir, and *L*and commandos. During World War II, the first Navy frogmen were trained to recon beaches for amphibious landings. Soon they learned underwater demolitions in order to clear obstacles and became known as Underwater Demolition Teams (UDTs). In the Korean War, UDTs evolved and went farther inland, blowing up bridges and tunnels. Years later, after observing communist insurgency in Southeast Asia, President John F. Kennedy—who had served in the Navy during World War II—and others in the military understood the need for unconventional warriors. The Navy created a unit that could operate from sea, air, and land—SEALs—drawing heavily from UDTs. On January 1,

1962, SEAL Team One and SEAL Team Two were born. By the end of the war, the military decorated SEAL Teams One and Two with three Medals of Honor, two Navy Crosses, forty-two Silver Stars, 402 Bronze Stars, and numerous other awards. For every SEAL killed, they killed two hundred. Over time, because SEALS could do both UDT and SEAL jobs, the UDT Teams were absorbed by the SEALs. The SEAL Teams expanded. Currently, the odd-numbered teams—One, Three, Five, and Seven—are stationed on the West Coast at Coronado, California. (Team Nine hasn't been created, but if the Teams expanded, it would probably be next.) The even-numbered teams—Two, Four, Six, Eight, and Ten—are located on the East Coast at Little Creek, Virginia.

Shiite: Followers of one of the two main sects of Islam. Iran is predominantly Shiite, and although Syria is mostly Sunni, Shiites control the government, including the military and police.

SIG Sauer P226 Navy 9mm: SIG stands for Schweizerische Industrie Gesellschaft, which is German for "Swiss Industrial Company." The P226 pistol has phosphate corrosion-resistant finish on the internal parts, contrast sights, and an anchor engraved on the slide. Holds fifteen rounds in the magazine. Designed especially for the SEALs.

Sunni: Followers of the more popular of the two main sects of Islam. Lebanon is predominantly Sunni, and although Iraq is mostly populated with Shiites, under the rule of Saddam Hussein, Sunnis controlled the country.

XO: Executive Officer. The second in command, under the CO.

Zoaf: Iranian knockoff of the SIG Sauer 9mm pistol (see SIG Sauer P226 Navy 9mm).

ACKNOWLEDGMENTS

I would like to thank God for my success and my blessing at being born an American. As I never thought I would live past forty, I am in awe of my world being seen through fifty-year-old eyes. My first grandchild, Emma, has changed and inspired me and has made life seem even more precious.

Special thanks to Jo-Ann and Harley Grove. Without their input and editing skills there is no doubt that my part of the project would not have been as constructive.

Last, thank you to the hundreds of thousands of you who have bought and enjoyed our books. You have both humbled and inspired me.

God bless America and our troops.

Dr. Howard E. Wasdin D.C.

I'd like to thank Reiko, Kent, and Maria for their emotional support and inspiration. Also, I appreciate Carol Scarr for her excellent editing advice for earlier drafts of *Outcasts* and *Easy Day for the Dead*.

Stephen Templin